More praise for *Jenny and the Jaws of Life*

"Marvelous . . . The language is tight, the scenes are built like blocks until an unexpected end that Willett works in a kind of gothic 'Gotcha.' She's a master of modern technique. Don't expect your usual short story here."   —*Winston-Salem Journal*

"Willett is masterful at catching character in crystalline form. Her imagination is wild, her language rich with intelligence and airy wit. . . . Her sentences are so careful and insightful, they're ultimately moving. . . . It's exhilarating. Her art has passed through anxiety and come out the other side, completely honest yet purged of the confessional whine or the need to call attention to its bravery."   —*Village Voice*

"Willett's command of controlled madness is superb."
—*Virginian-Pilot*

"Willett is a versatile writer as well as a skillful one."
—*Boston Globe*

"Resonates with understanding." —*People*

"Powerful, quirky, always interesting. . . . Willett's stories are refreshingly about *ideas*, their smooth narration infused with little jolts of startling insight, reflecting the tough, poignant perceptions that lie at their core."   —*Publishers Weekly*

"*Jenny and the Jaws of Life* is first-rate comic writing about adultery and breast cancer without the whisper of a false note or indulgence; *Jenny* reminds one at moments of, say, *Mrs. Dalloway,* with its deftness and depth."   —*Kirkus Reviews*

"Clearly a writer to watch." —*Library Journal*

"Willett's stories are, by turns, funny, frightening, and poignant. She writes with both power and elegance."
—Lois Battle, author of *The Florabama Ladies' Auxiliary & Sewing Circle*

"Every story in this collection is fully achieved and carries its own full quotient of mordant observation and grieving mirth. As a whole the volume bubbles with the wittiest melancholy seen since Cheever was in his prime."   —R. V. Cassill

JENNY ▲
■ AND THE
JAWS
OF LIFE

SHORT STORIES BY
Jincy Willett

Thomas Dunne Books
St. Martin's Griffin
New York

THOMAS DUNNE BOOKS.
An imprint of St. Martin's Press.

The following stories originally appeared in other publications and are reprinted by permission:

"My Father, at the Wheel," *The Massachusetts Review,* Spring 1987; "Anticipatory Grief," *The Yale Review,* Winter 1983; "Under the Bed," *The Massachusetts Review,* Spring 1984; "Justine Laughs at Death," *Playgirl,* November 1986; "Mr. Lazenbee," *The Yale Review,* Winter 1987.

"Melinda Falling" received a *Transatlantic Review* Award in 1981 from the Henfield Foundation.

www.stmartins.com

Library of Congress Cataloging-in-Publication Data

Willett, Jincy.
 Jenny and the Jaws of Life.
 ISBN 0-312-00614-4 (hc)
 ISBN 0-312-30618-0 (pbk)
 I. Title.

 PS3573.I4455J4 1987
 813'.54   87-4373

10 9 8 7 6 5 4

For Edward T. Kornhauser

CONTENTS

JENNY ▲
■ AND THE
J A W S
——— LIFE
OF

FOREWORD

Like most of the books that have made a profound impression on me, I first discovered *Jenny and the Jaws of Life* in the New Fiction section of the Chicago Public Library. I was a voracious reader then, a student shoplifting for a voice, and there was nothing I felt I couldn't learn from. Had Pol Pot released a chapbook I doubtlessly would have taken it home, violating the margins with check marks and little notations reading "That is so true!" The publisher's name or author's pedigree made no difference whatsoever. If it had gone through a printing press or even a Xerox machine I added it to my stack and read it without discrimination.

We were told in the 1980s that this was a golden age of American short fiction, that stories were "in," much like caterpillar eyebrows and, for a brief period, lesbianism. It seemed to me that a golden age was best defined in retrospect, that, when marketed as trend, a thing was doomed to suffer accordingly. What's in today is, by its very nature, out tomorrow—scorned, the object of embarrassment and ridicule. It made sense with shoulder pads, but how could you dismiss an entire medium? What could replace the pleasures of a short story, and to what purpose? It's like replacing oral sex or chicken. I mean, why even try?

If the age was golden what made it so was the giddy wealth of material. Publishers were much more willing to take a chance, and each trip to the library yielded someone new. The great Tobias Wolff, Jean Thompson, strange Joy Williams; I'd read a collection, examine the blurbs on the back of the book, and seek out those authors as well, following a trail that would often lead me full circle. There were stories in magazines, anthologies devoted to every imaginable theme or pathology, and obscure reviews and quarterlies; a seemingly endless supply of stuff.

There are great story writers now but I doubt I'll ever read the same way I did in the 1980s. My brain is not the democracy it once was, and I've developed an attachment to traditional punctuation. The carte blanche reverence is gone as well, an unfortunate side effect of wish fulfillment. I now know what it's like to see your own book on the library shelf, to watch as a stranger frowns at your author photograph, hedges a bit, and then dumps you in the romance or self-help section. Authors are no longer omnipotent gods and goddesses, but the people you share a bathroom with at Yaddo, the people who follow a fantastic joke or after-dinner story with the words, "I'm already using it."

While the business of writing holds no particular excitement, the act of writing continues to mystify me, especially when practiced by such people as Jincy Willett. Of the umpteen story collections published over the last twenty years, hers is one of the dozen that continues to gnaw at me. Who is this person, and why don't more people know about her?

I'd hoped that *Jenny and the Jaws of Life* might be followed, immediately, by another collection, but for whatever reason, that was not the case. As it is I've had to satisfy myself with regular rereadings, hardly a disappointment as each time I come away with something new. What I loved first was her humor, which is black rather than jokey and displays an unfailing, perfect sense of timing. "This is a very old story, the one about daughters and fathers. It ends in marriage and the promise of renewal. So it must be a comedy" ("My Father at the Wheel"). "Her mother and her father's sister had each had out-of-body experiences, her sister was always talking about Velikovsky, and both her grandmothers had met Jesus Christ" ("The Haunting of the Lingards").

It's the sort of book that leads to late-night phone calls. "I know you're busy sleeping or whatever, but wait, I just want to read you this one passage—." The one then leading to another, and another. For me that first passage was always from "The Best of Betty." Written in the form of increasingly hostile letters, it documents the breakdown and eventual rebirth of a bitter, smart-mouthed advice columnist. (It's a bit long for inclusion in an introduction, but please bear with me. These paragraphs alone are reason enough to buy the book.)

Dear Betty:

You hear from so many unfortunates with serious problems that I feel a bit ashamed to take up your time this way. I am an attractive woman of 59; my thighs are perfectly smooth, my waist unthickened, I still have both my breasts and all my teeth; in fact I am two dress sizes smaller than I was at eighteen. My three grown daughters are intelligent, healthy, and independent. My husband and I are as much in love as when we were first married, despite the depth of our familiarity and the, by now, considerable conflation of our tastes, political beliefs, preferences in music and art, and, of course, memories. He still interests and pleasures me; miraculously our sex life remains joyous, inventive, and mutually fulfilling. I continue to

*adore the challenge and variety of my career as an ethnic
dance therapist. We have never had to worry about money.
Our country home is lovely, and very old, and solidly set down
in a place of incomparable, ever shifting beauty; our many
friends, old and new, are delightful people, amusing and wise,
and every one of them honorable and a source of strength to
us.*

*And yet, with all of this and more, I am frequently very sad,
and cannot rid myself of a growing, formless, yet very real
sense of devastating loss, no less hideous for its utter irrationality. Forgive me, but does this make any sense to you?*

Niobe

Dear Niobe:
Certainly. You're lying about the sex.

I learned, over time, that it was better to simply lend people
the book and let them read the letters for themselves. The story
suffers from a vocal recitation as it is, in part, about writing,
that particular type of writing that hopes to be published in the
newspaper. Read out loud the story is simply incredibly funny.
Read on the page it is sad and hopeful, the humor even bleak-
er, and more complex.

Read "Justine Laughs at Death," or the short, masterful
"Resume," and you might peg Jincy Willett as a satirist, but her
stories are slipperier than that, jumping off the board at the
very moment you try to pin them down. Yes, they're often
funny, but there's something else at work here. Read "Julie in
the Funhouse." Read "Mr. Lazenbee."

Like all the best storywriters, Jincy Willett excels in the
moment, that split second when everything changes, and
there's a discomfort to this. We like to think we'll recognize
such moments in our own lives, but when the time comes we

almost always get it wrong. Our eyes peeled for the Big Event, we point out the usual suspects—the death of a parent, the car spinning out of control—not realizing that the damage was done weeks or maybe years earlier, over dinner or while washing our hair, the moment cunning in its very resemblance to everyday life. "There's the violation," says the narrator in "Under the Bed." "There's the damage. There's the tragedy."

I once accepted a teaching job, knowing full well that I'd be very bad at it. Like any petty dictator, what attracted me was the power. Friends insist that you watch their favorite movie or read a particular book, but you don't really *have* to do anything. It's not like they'll stop talking to you. A teacher says, "You have to read this story," and your evening is pretty much shot, at least that's what I hoped. I thought of my students as younger, better-looking versions of myself, and imagined the pleasure they would doubtlessly experience while reading my favorite books. But of course it doesn't work that way.

Assignments were skimmed in the cafeteria, lost on the subway, stolen, eaten by bees. Then there was the lip. "I won't read stories threatening violence against women." "Why aren't the characters younger?" "Who are you to tell us what to read?"

"I am the teacher," I said, but already they were looking through me.

By the time I had a little authority, *Jenny and the Jaws of Life* was out of print. Now, fifteen years after its release, the book is back, and I can once again go about the business of pushing it. There's a singular joy in discovering something for yourself, a personal satisfaction that is numbed and cheapened by salesmanship. In spite of the pleasure I'm bound to diminish, I am prepared to wear a sandwich board for this book. I can't help myself. It's just too good. (That is so true!)

—David Sedaris

JULIE
IN THE
FUNHOUSE

After I moved to Illinois, my sister and I wrote to each other once a year, if that, and neither of us liked to talk long-distance. We were happier apart. I could never see Julie, or hear her voice, without becoming at some point, then or later, aware of our drab and banal defeat. I had married an ungenerous woman; Julie, a big good-looking fool. I had started out to be a surgeon and ended up a druggist; and Julie, who had too much beauty and arrogance and wit for any single ambition, never even left home. She had planned to be a world rover—an artist, if she had the talent; an adventuress, if she didn't—and in the end she never, literally never, lived anywhere but in the house where we were born.

No matter what we talked about, all we ever really said was, Here we are. This is how we turned out. And she never offered us the comfort of a shrug, the summing up and laying to rest of a sigh. She never accepted it, or even complained, which would have been at least a kind of acceptance. Seeing her always produced a delayed disturbance in me, an obscure panic.

"She depresses you," observed my wife, who thought Julie cold and critical, and chose to believe that I, not she, was jealous of Julie's money, her "business acumen." This was absurd, but so was the truth: Julie always made me feel that time had not quite run out for us, that I only had to do some simple, obvious thing and everything would be all right. I didn't know if the feeling came

3

from Julie or from me, or which of us I was supposed to save, and from what. The future, vague and sad, did not frighten me half as much as knowing that it was not carved in stone.

She didn't dote on her children, it's true. They'll make hay out of that. She was a competent mother, when I still knew her, and she often scolded me for not having kids myself, but she let Samson do the doting, the clowning. Samson was the one who made faces and talked baby talk. "He's so good at it," she said.

She treated him with an affectionate contempt that suited him well. Their marriage, begun in heat like my own, had become an antiseptic partnership, amiable, frictionless, curiously graceful. She regarded all her losses squarely, with unforced humor and a perverse delight, as if at some ragtag parade of shabby miracles. She took none of it personally, not even the early loss of her beauty. "I am going to be," she once observed, "one of those barrel-chested women with stick legs." She made it sound like a caprice.

The last time I saw her we sat in her kitchen, our old kitchen, and her children played outside in the summer grass, and Samson puttered in the basement with his electronic kits, or ham radio, or whatever it was that year. Julie said, "Here's another one for the scrapbook. There was, until recently, an Australian crocodile hunter by the name of Basil Hubbard. Leguminous by name and, as it turned out, by nature as well. His widow—this was in *Collier's*—claims that all his life he was 'obsessed' by the fear that a big croc was going to 'get him.'" Julie grinned. "You're way ahead of me. Well, that's the beauty of this story.

"One day, while hunting, he sat down on a riverbank to eat his lunch and take a nap, which proved to be his last. Basil may have cursed his destiny, but he certainly didn't fight it. I picture him as a sort of cross between Hamlet and Mortimer Snerd. Anyway, in a couple of days they found his boots ... with his feet inside, natch."

Julie had been collecting these stories since she was twelve.

To qualify, the story had to be "All Too True," the title of her scrapbook. "They caught the croc, a behemoth with no tail, and Basil the Squash inside. Here's the wonderful part: this crocodile had been stalking him for *months*." She hunched over the table and walked two fingers around the sugar bowl and pepper shaker in a figure eight. "They found the tracks of the Squash, some of them pretty old, leading up at last to his final resting place . . . and right behind him, all the way, the unmistakable trail of You-Know-Who. Hah!"

"Captain Hook," I said. I couldn't laugh.

"Don't you love it!"

Well, no, I didn't. I didn't always have the stomach for the All Too True.

But I remember it now, and the red afternoon light on the kitchen table, and her children's voices outside the window. I remember it all, in amazing detail, as my night plane whines toward Pennsylvania, and I am tempted, for one sickening minute, to give it *significance*. To *make sense* of the way my sister died.

And sure, how "wonderful," if she had been pregnant then, with the one who killed her. If, while she told about the crocodile, the Demon Baby had kicked out and bumped the table and given us a scare, so that later I could remember and add it to the list of *things that make sense now, when you think about them, you know?* But all the children she would ever have were playing outside in the yard.

Too bad for the storytellers. Too bad for the sense makers, the apologists, that nothing, then or ever, *nothing* was inevitable. It's just too bad.

▼ ▼ ▼ ▼ ▼ ▼

I learned about my sister's death from a radio news report. My cashier, like the one before her, and the one before that, tunes in eight hours a day to our local all-news and information station.

I hate what radio has become, and most of all these talk stations, with their constant hysterical updates. Why do we have to know these things? What are we supposed to do about them?

A kidnapped ambassador is heard on tape begging for his life. Forty thousand Soviet troops are put on battle alert. A fifth-grade class in Des Moines adopts an ailing zoo hippo. Record turnip unearthed in Greensboro. Bizarre double murder in Pennsylvania; children sleep through shotgun slaying of their parents. In Clarion, Pennsylvania. My home town.

I was filling Mrs. Holley's Librium prescription. Mrs. Holley is a pretty woman in her thirties, chubby like a doll. Mrs. Holley has had it. She comes in here with her full-length fox and orders refills of diet pills and tranquilizers and roams the aisles loading a wire basket with bath beads, tampons, bags of licorice and candy corn, boxes of Dots and nonpareils, tortoiseshell barrettes, panatelas, coloring books, Harlequins, and the *New York Times*. She spreads the evidence of her domestic life before me on the counter with a demure and wicked lopsided grin, and lets her coat fall open, flashing her pink flannel bathrobe. Mrs. Holley's grocer doesn't know what I know. Even her liquor dealer doesn't know her this well.

I love Mrs. Holley and would take her home with me, and punish her, and comfort her, if I were not myself so tired and old and incompetent. I was thinking of this, of poor timing and lost opportunity, of sad clues and hopeless mysteries, while Mrs. Holley, clowning sweetly, waved the empty Librium container in my face like a lacy handkerchief, telling me as always to "Fill her up," and smiling her smile, when the news came over the radio that Julie was dead.

▼ ▼ ▼ ▼ ▼ ▼

When she heard about Julie, my wife drove all the way from Urbana, and let herself into my apartment with a key I forgot she had. She was there when I got home. Coffee was brewing and my old suitcase was open on the bed and half-packed. She had already booked my flight to Pittsburgh. When I walked in she just hugged me, and her ruined hair, clipped and brittle and bottle-red, held a trace of its old clean perfume. For a while she sat beside me on the couch and massaged the muscles of my neck and shoulders while I leaned forward, elbows on knees, and my hands, long and white like my father's, dangled pointing at the floor. When my eyes filled it was not for Julie, not yet, but for my wife and our failure and the astonishing fact of her kindness at this time.

But then she said, "I don't know why, but I'm not surprised. She was a bitter woman. You refused to see it." And I said, "You're not surprised that my sister was *murdered*? You're not *surprised*?" She said she had called the Petersons, old neighbors in Clarion, and gotten "the inside story" from them. As she related the details her voice revealed, despite itself—for my wife is not a bad person, no worse than I—a mean excitement, and she drew out her tale for maximum shock effect, saving until last the horrendous and apparently well-founded suspicions of the police. As I listened, at the dead center of my horror and disbelief I felt ashamed of her and sorry for the silly woman she had become. She ran with me once, right beside me, matching stride for stride, down a clean white stretch of the Atlantic coast in early morning, and her hair was long and gold.

▼ ▼ ▼ ▼ ▼ ▼ ▼

According to the papers, Samson Willoughby died on his feet, in the doorway to his wife's room, shot twice in his chest with his own shotgun. They say Julie died in bed. "As she slept." She was shot just once, point-blank, in the back of the head.

The three children, ages twelve to sixteen, said they heard no shots, but woke up in the morning to find the living room in disarray, their father's safe open and ransacked, the clock overturned and broken at some early morning hour. They found their parents, and the daughter, Samantha, four years old when I saw her last, called the police.

Their story made no sense. Even small-town police could tell there were no intruders, no robbery. Every piece of evidence, beginning with the temperature of the bodies, argued otherwise. The bodies were too cold. I'll remember that. The rest of it— tire tracks, deadbolts, broken windows—could not possibly matter less to me. Julie's children should have been more clever. When challenged, they turned sullen and briefly silent. They swiveled their heads toward one another and blinked like owls.

"The Willoughbys were not a close family," says an anonymous neighbor; "Looking back you could see it coming"; and I honestly wonder if the papers don't invent these people. (Julie would have clipped this for the All Too True and pasted it beside that old yellow photograph from the *Clarion Call* of a horse-faced woman in a straw hat captioned PAINFULLY INJURED. She was twelve when she cut that one out.) Another Solomon reports that Julie and Samson were "workaholics," whatever the hell that means, and seldom home, and "the kids ran wild." So naturally. "Drugs." Michael and Samantha, the older two, were often "spaced out." Therefore.

Mr. Peterson is quoted in the Sunday *Tribune*, and bless his sensible old soul. "They were strangers," he says. "They came and went like strangers. There's a lot of families like that now."

But everywhere they display the same picture of Julie the Real Estate Woman, heavy, hard-eyed, thin-lipped, vulgar, her terrible professional smile framed by deep crescents of discontent; her regulation helmet of brassy hair. A face I have never seen and will never accept. A photographer's trick; falsified evidence, for

8

the storytellers. Here is a fitting subject for cheap tragedy. These are the women whom their young must turn on and devour.

▼ ▼ ▼ ▼ ▼ ▼ ▼

I'm staying at the Petersons', waiting for the funeral. I can see the old house from my bedroom window. Julie had it painted tan, or beige, or camel, one of those new colors you can't remember from one time to the next. The grounds are landscaped now. It looks like someone lifted up the house and unrolled the grass beneath it. There are flower beds and fruit trees set out on the green like furniture. Out back all that's left of the woods where Father took his long walks are a few birch trees, to mark where the next property, the next lawn, begins. I didn't know she'd sold the woods.

Yesterday a gardener came and worked on the rose garden in the backyard, a perfect square with sunburst gravel paths and a sundial and a birdbath, where once there was a smaller, shapeless plot of dirt, dug and planned and turned by children, that summer we tried to grow tomatoes and I used to pick green hornworms off the leaves and throw them onto the roof for the birds to eat.

Mrs. Peterson caught me watching the gardener, and she said, "The inside's all changed around, too. You wouldn't know it." Somehow she knew she was comforting me.

It's the Murder House now, and the neighborhood kids are going to want to believe that it's haunted. But it isn't. I can tell that from here. It really was once, haunted, by living children. I wonder if Julie exorcised our ghosts before she died; if in her lifetime she ever stopped running into the ghosts of those children whose kingdom this had been. All I know is, now the house is truly quiet, now that she is gone.

The night before the funeral I sit up with Mr. Peterson and we drink Iron City in the rumpus room, where the electric trains used to be, and stare at the black screen of his old RCA TV. He tells me all he knows. I can stand to hear this much, and only this much, and only from him. He knew us when we were children.

Samantha and Michael planned to rob the house and steal Julie's Mercedes. They were going to run away and they needed money for drugs to sell, in New York City, or Timbuktu. Samson had an old-fashioned safe in his basement office, and when they discovered the combination they set their plan in motion: a complicated, romantic thing involving sunglasses, wigs, and phases of the moon. They could have ripped their parents off in the daytime, when they were out. But this wouldn't have been as much fun.

Mr. Peterson shakes his head. "All I can tell you is what Larry told us," he repeats. Mr. Peterson's youngest son is a reporter for the *Clarion Call*. "The police kept asking the kids, 'But why take risks when you didn't need to?' They were trying to make sense out of it, you know. And you know what Samantha said? Something like, 'It made a better movie this way.' A better movie! And they asked her, 'Were you planning to make a movie? What are you talking about?' But she just laughed at them and said, 'Yes, that's right, we were going to Hollywood to make a movie!' She said the cops were stupid. She said, 'Don't worry about it. There's no way you could ever understand us.' You know, the way kids do." Mr. Peterson sips his beer. "Although, I think maybe she was right about that.

"So that night the kids snuck down to the basement and opened the safe. And don't you know, what they found in there was a whole lot of nothing. Samson was a hell of a nice fellow, but kind of dim. He always had some little project going down there, some scheme to keep himself busy. I think he only had the safe because he liked the *idea* of having one, for his 'important papers,' his 'valuables.' All the kids found were the old mortgage, which your

10

folks paid off forty years ago, and some carbon copies of letters he wrote to magazines, that never got published, and old snapshots of themselves, when they were babies, and of Julie. When she was young, you know.

"The kids were mad as anything, and Samantha thought about her mother's jewelry, in her mother's room, in a case on the bureau."

"Which room?" Mr. Peterson looks at me, surprised. "I take it they weren't sleeping together any more. Did she keep the big bedroom? Mother and Father's old room?"

"Yes. Samson slept in the guest room."

The only overnight guest we ever had was Samson himself, the night he came here, with his car broken down in the rain, and Julie in her nightgown, at the top of the stairs.

"They went up there to her bedroom, in the dark," Mr. Peterson says. "They took Samson's shotgun from the basement to keep Julie quiet, in case she woke up." He clears his throat, apologetically. "John, they're going to claim that they never meant to hurt her. They're going to say it was an accident."

"Uh-huh. And then that darn gun went off again when the old man came through the door."

"No, Samson wasn't accidental." Mr. Peterson hesitates, holding his breath. His stomach rumbles. "They're saying Samson was temporary insanity."

I laugh out loud and apologize at the same time, but Mr. Peterson is eighty-two years old now, and he smiles at me, acknowledging horror and despair with a sweet smile, the way some old people do, and some not so old people who have suffered early.

"That's all right, John," he says. "I think so, too."

"So. I knew she wasn't asleep. She saw it coming." After a while I ask for it. "What did she do? What did she say?"

11

Mr. Peterson leans toward me, with his terrible sweet smile. "They're saying she didn't do anything. She switched on the light by the bed and just looked at them standing there, with her jewelry box and the gun. They're saying she just stared at them for a long time with a funny look on her face. Like . . . 'Now I've seen it all.' No, that's not it. Isn't that awful." Mr. Peterson shades his eyes, taps his foot in frustration, disgusted with himself. "Break. Something about a break. 'Give me a break!' That's it." For a moment he is triumphant; he recollects himself. "That's the way they put it. 'She looked at us like *Give me a break.*' Then she switched the light off and pulled the covers up and turned her back on both of them.

"Made 'em mad, John. Michael or Samantha—they won't say which one, they're thick as thieves—went over to the bed and did something with the gun, to make a sound, to get her attention. Waved it around, maybe; fooled with the trigger." Mr. Peterson is quiet for a long time. "You can see how it'd go from there," he finally says.

"Yes," I say. "I can take it from there."

▼ ▼ ▼ ▼ ▼ ▼ ▼

Our parents had us when they were both in their forties and were, for different reasons, too worn out and distracted to pay us much attention. Mother was a tiny, grim lady who rarely spoke above a whisper, and I cannot picture her upright without one hand pressed into the small of her back and her lips indrawn in showy stoicism. She had migraines and backaches, and slept a good deal of the time. Father slept a lot, too, though he was large, robust, and still handsome when we knew him. I realize now he was a manic depressive. Most of the time when he was not at work he lay on the living room couch with his face to the back cushion and his white-shirted arms tucked around his head, like

12

a foxhole-soldier. Sometimes he would spend hours in the cellar banging out tarnished melodies and sour chords on our massive Mason & Hamlin upright—ragtime and barrelhouse, Mussorgsky and Liszt; or get us kids out of bed in the dead of night to go out for ice cream cones; or kneel on the back porch firing his .22 rifle at the woodpeckers who rattled on dead maples in the woods out back. His unpredictable eruptions never seemed to bother Mother. We never knew them to have a disagreement; they treated each other with faultless, vigilant courtesy. Before it became second nature for Julie and me to tiptoe, mute our songs and conversations, and work doors, windows, and drawers like professional burglars, we were continually, gently admonished to *hush*: Our father, or our mother, was sleeping.

On some occasions—holidays, times of minor crisis—we carried on like an ordinary family, and every so often one or both would turn outward from their benign self-absorption and display a depth of concern for us which it did not occur to us to doubt. But by the time Julie and I were self-sufficient—when she was seven and I was nine—we were less a family than two congenial couples living by necessity in close quarters and making the best of it. We were used to them. They did not bother us, or interest us very much.

When I was five I almost died of scarlet fever. For two months I lay alone in my attic room, visited and tended only by Mother, and my earliest memory of Julie is from the first day she was allowed to see me. She crawled up on the foot of my bed, sat down cross-legged, and welcomed me back with a gorgeous smile, so sudden and intense that it shook the bed. She was a fat, wide-nosed little kid with wispy white hair and bags under her eyes, and so beautiful in her love for me that I grabbed her under her chubby arms and pulled her against my chest, as I had seen Father do on his good days, and she lay still, heavy and warm, and I

13

squeezed her and tasted her hair, and black spots swam in front of my eyes. From exertion, of course, but it was a fine moment and I knew it. I had discovered my sister, and myself. I was the one Julie loved.

From then on she always came to me instead of Mother in the early morning, padding in and standing by the head of my bed until the sound and moist heat of her breath on my face woke me, and together we would go downstairs and turn on the kitchen light and fix our own breakfast. I taught her to work the toaster, and tie her shoes, and make letters. There wasn't much talk at first—she chattered all the time, incomprehensibly—but we played many games, mostly of her devising. She was a bossy little kid. At one stage her favorite game was "Poppa," which usually involved me curling up on cushions on the floor and asking her to bring me things. She brought me oranges, ashtrays, blocks, and damp washcloths for my forehead. "Are you comfortable?" she crooned. "Are you better now?" Throughout, I would have to keep my eyes closed, peeking only when she wasn't looking, at the burgeoning mountain of medicine, and at her, waddling around the room drawing blinds and plumping pillows, one hand dug into what would eventually be the small of her back, muttering, "Oh, his poor head." I was a little young to see the funny side of it, but I didn't spoil it. She was different from me, and crazy, and I loved her.

We fought like lovers too. When she was angry she clammed up, narrowed her eyes, and refused to look at me. She could keep this up for hours and it drove me wild. I hit her more than once, on the top of her platinum head with my fist, with all my strength, so hard that she sank to her knees, but she didn't run upstairs to tell, any more than I would have if she had set my room on fire.

We got our first taste of life on the outside when the Petersons moved next door, a loud, jovial family with five kids. We were invited there to play and found them odd. Mr. Peterson was always grabbing the kids or Mrs. Peterson in some fashion, hugging, roughhousing, slapping their bottoms; Mrs. Peterson, a terrible housekeeper, yelled, shrieked with laughter, and broke dishes on purpose; and the children, who seemed happy enough, were rude to one another and fought among themselves like wild dogs. "They're silly," was Julie's conclusion, and I had to agree, but we went back from time to time, because we enjoyed the scandal, and they had electric trains.

We were the odd ones, of course, as I discovered when I got to school and began to visit other homes. I was worried and ashamed, and kept it to myself, brooding, especially about Father; trying to understand, define, and place in some rational perspective just what was wrong with our family. This process was to go on throughout my adolescence, with great intensity and lavish melancholy, my nature being what it is. When Julie first came to school, my stomach was in a perpetual knot, from fear that the oddness I so carefully concealed would manifest itself for the whole world in my little sister. And sure enough, after one week her teacher came down the hall and called me out of class. Julie kept wandering off at recess, getting up and leaving her seat whenever she felt like it; Julie did not seem to understand that there were *rules* here; and would I please explain, since nobody else could get through to her. The teacher spoke gently, and looked amused—at us, I thought with horror, because we're so strange.

I badgered Julie all the way home. "Why don't you do what the teacher *says?* You're going to get in trouble. You have to do what they *say.*" I was practically wringing my hands.

"Mrs. Holcomb is silly," Julie said.

"You have to wait for the *bell,*" I told her, close to tears. She was playing pretend hopscotch, with a dreamy look on her face.

Hopscotch with no chalk lines. I thought, Oh God, and I grabbed her and pulled her still to face me. "You have to watch the other kids and do what they do. You have to stay until they say you can leave. This is very, very important."

She regarded me seriously. "When does it stop?"

"Never."

I saw in her eyes that she believed me, but then she looked spacey again and smiled, with one side of her mouth, and started hopping up and down on one foot. "That's silly," she said. I pushed her down, viciously, into a pile of dirty leaves, and she did not speak to me for two days. But the teacher never complained to me again. Julie had decided to humor them.

Not long after this she brought three little girls home with her. I watched from the living room window as they filed down the street, Julie in the lead. She briefed them when they got to the front porch. "You must take off your shoes. You must not make any loud noise, because our Mother is sleeping. Loud noises go through her like a knife. There's cookies in the kitchen, and a big piano in the basement, but you can't play it. We're going in now. Just remember what I said." I shut my eyes and slumped down on the couch, in a fever of embarrassment, while the silent troupe crept through the first floor and basement of our sad, sunless house. After a long while they came back upstairs. "This is my father's rifle," I heard her say. "You'll have to leave when he comes home." They entered the living room, where Julie disengaged herself and sat down beside me. "This is my brother, John," she said. The three little girls, one fat and two skinny, blinked, smiled shyly at us, and waited, I could see, for some further dispensation. Finally one of them spoke up. "Julie said maybe you'd show us the chest of treasures." And we did, Julie and I.

We had toys of our own, but the chest of treasures was our prize, and the focus of our best games. It was a steamer trunk

16

crammed with old things of Father's, and Mother's, and maybe our grandparents' too: a cracked leather holster, a lavender veil, a tiny pair of lady's boots, with silver eyelets, peacock feathers, pewter candlesticks, a horseshoe and a partial set of rusty iron quoits, the disembodied arm of an old Victrola. As Julie gravely removed each item and passed it around, with a brief description ("This is our pirate flag and pieces of eight", "This is our magic lamp"), I saw them for the first time as they were, stripped of all those qualities we had imposed upon them between us. Our private world, the source of all our pleasure, would suffer humiliating and utter collapse in the light of ridicule, or a mere lack of enthusiasm. These people had seen horseshoes and old clothes before. So I watched, with amazement and pride, as the ceremony continued unchecked by a single giggle or skeptical yawn. They looked at an old candlestick and *saw* the magic lamp, and rubbed it, and could not have done otherwise in the face of my sister's splendid, majestic self-possession.

From then on she brought kids home with her whenever she felt like it. I was neither excluded nor expected to play with them. We were never jealous of each other's friends. She played the queen with them but not with me, and we saw them off together and cleaned up their messes while we rehashed the events of the day. Company days usually went smoothly, although once in a great while someone would go away mad or crying. Julie was naturally generous, and by training considerate, but on those rare occasions when a visitor proved intransigent or dull, she would walk away without comment and disappear into the upper rooms until the offender left. Mother took the time once to scold her for this—I think the parent of a distraught child had called to complain—and Julie seemed genuinely sorry. But she didn't change her ways, and she never lacked for friends

Just as it had taken a trio of outsiders to show me the shape

17

and force of her personality, I didn't realize she was pretty until my own friends started acting up around her. There was one, Charlie Metz, an awfully nice kid, beefy and easygoing, with a bad complexion, who would tense up and nod his head a lot, instead of talking, whenever she was with us. I thought for a long time he didn't like her. Once she asked him to get something for her out of a high shelf in the kitchen. In his alacrity he ripped the cupboard door off its hinges. Julie fell down laughing. Another one, George Limberacus, my chess partner, I caught peering into her empty room when we walked by, with the keen and foolish look of a souvenir hunter.

She was almost as tall as I, and big-boned, like Father. A big healthy girl, narrow-hipped, full-breasted, with broad, straight shoulders. Her face was wide and bold, with pale green eyes, large and set in deep above high, sharp cheekbones, and a long, fine-drawn, ironic mouth. At fourteen she had already the proud carriage and aggressive, slightly mannish good looks of the movie stars of our day. She experimented with clothes, wearing bulky, boxy schoolgirl outfits one week, stockings and tailored dresses the next, but I never got the impression that anything important rode on the experiment. Even in puberty she seemed at perfect ease.

"Do you know about sex yet?" I asked her once, with some trepidation, but no embarrassment.

"Pop gave me the lowdown. What do you want to know? Ask me anything."

"Watch your mouth."

She grinned and handed me a dish to dry. She tucked in her chin and deepened her voice in a wicked, unsentimental parody of Father's oracular style. "I am, though I am not aware of it, a strikingly lovely young woman. While I innocently play with my dolls and whatnots, and dream my childish dreams, I stand, all

18

unknowing, at the very brink of a strange and wonderful—ouch! You goon."

"Julie, I'm serious."

She clasped my hands in her soapy ones and fixed me with a solemn, hypnotic stare. "I should be informed that young men—and older ones too—have certain *urges*, terribly powerful *imperatives of the blood*, and they are going to want to, well, *hug* me, and—"

"The point is—"

"The point is . . . ," she sighed and turned back to the dishes. "The point is that you're both ridiculous. The whole thing is ridiculous."

"There's a girl at school, Hermione Felcher. She lets everybody."

She turned her head toward me but did not look up. "You?" she asked, in a small voice, and then blushed.

It was so satisfying to see her off balance that I stopped worrying, and somehow forgot to start up again. There was so much else to worry about: college, and the war, which was winding down but still lethal; and the future, in general; and whether or not I had the right to have a family of my own. I was still obsessed with my tainted origins.

When she was sixteen, the year before our parents died, she took lovers. Other girls her age petted, gave in, did things they shouldn't. Julie took lovers. Two, that I know of: Charlie Metz, humble and likable as ever, still crazy about her, and who never knew I knew; and a married algebra teacher named LaMott. He gave her a bad time, I think.

When Father didn't have the living room, which was much of the time—he spent most evenings upstairs now—we often read together after supper sharing the rosy light of a single hand-painted globe lamp, and one night there, and for the first time, I saw her cry. I looked up at the flat sound of a tear falling on a page—no outsider can imagine the quiet in our house—and she suffered, wet-faced, while her eyes scanned the page, across and down, across and down, as though the tears were no concern of theirs. It frightened me badly, and pleased me, too: I myself had, by then, made a woman cry. And in the unnerving confusion of my emotions, and at the sight of her, I knew that we were separable, not just in theory but in fact, and that the process of farewell was implacable and smooth and well underway. Though I had for as long as I could remember been planning and fretting on this very assumption, this was thrilling, terrible news to me, and a moment as brilliantly lit as the one she had brought with her to my lonely bed so many years before. Though not as fine.

She looked up and saw me watching, and returned to her book again, with a cool, languid blink that sent new tears down both her cheeks, but she had stopped reading. Silence stretched between us like a thick rope. "Men are bastards sometimes," I said, and felt immediately like a colossal fool. She looked up again, slowly, and smiled at me, the old sudden, reckless smile, for me alone. "You dirty dog," she said.

Many times that last summer, long after nightfall, we slipped outside together, to our similar, separate destinations. I drove her, usually, and let her out at the places she designated. A large white house, unlighted, flanked by tidy rows of azaleas and lilacs; the motor hotel in the center of town; an empty dirt road in the county park. And much later, I would come back, at the time agreed upon, and wait for her. We had always made our own law. And sometimes we went out on foot, and met again without a word of greeting, and drifted through the heavy, fragrant darkness and the precious time, and past monuments and deep ravines, and one time she took my arm like a bride, not mine, but mine, to give away. And we walked together toward the proud old house where our parents slept.

20

▼ ▼ ▼ ▼ ▼ ▼ ▼

Father died that winter of a massive stroke, on the day after Christmas. Mother found him in the woods, where he took his afternoon walks. He had not been gone long, and we never knew what made Mother come downstairs that day and go search for him. She put on Julie's old rabbit fur coat, gently shut the door behind her, and walked out to him, straight-backed, on slippered feet, across the crusty snow. She died of cancer seven months later. When she was dying, Julie and I kept scrupulous vigil in her hospital room, spelling each other like sentries. We did this without talking about it. I don't know to this day if we were moved by duty, love, or pity. She was kind to us, and uncomplaining, and one morning early she tricked us, sending me out to the nurses' station for a glass of milk; she died while I was gone. "Sometimes they prefer it that way," the doctor said. "It doesn't mean anything."

▼ ▼ ▼ ▼ ▼ ▼ ▼

Our parents' room was small and stark under the dim overhead light. We could not remember having ever seen it so well exposed, for on those few occasions we had been invited in, or had reason to intrude, or happened to look past the briefly open door, the light there had been murky even at noon, the shadows thick and blue. There was a single long window, with a northern exposure, draped in faded brown velvet; the walls were closely patterned with crimson flowers against a gray background, like the inside of an old sewing case; the floors bare, of unvarnished oak. There were only three pieces of furniture, all mahogany: an armoire and matching bureau, and the great four-poster, sagging badly beneath a spread of snowy chenille. A ghost ship, wide and pale, in dark harbor.

We had had six weeks since the funeral to come here, to go through our parents' possessions. Tomorrow I would head north to Tufts, leaving Julie behind to see about selling the house before sailing for Europe in October. Because it really couldn't be put off another day, we had tried to make an occasion out of it. We had drunk too much wine at dinner, and banged on the piano, and acted hilarious and sophisticated and false. For the first time in our lives we were self-conscious together, and painfully young.

And we had miscalculated, waiting too long to come up here. A late summer storm, which had encouraged our suppertime theatrics with thunder and flickering lights, had moved north, stranding us under a windless spout of loud, depressing rain. The room was formidable, claustrophobic. Our heads were pounding. "Why are we afraid?" she asked.

"Because we have no business here."

"That's not it," she said. She opened the armoire and handed me a stack of business shirts. "It's not as though they would mind. We're not snooping."

This was an unfortunate, unguarded choice of words, and we worked stealthily, folding and sorting with careless speed until the wardrobe and the largest bureau drawers were empty and their contents in two shapeless mounds on the floor, one for discard, one for Goodwill. We recognized most of Father's clothes, but Mother's were a small shock. She had so many beautiful old dresses, spring-colored and delicate, trimmed with satin and ivory lace. Julie held against herself a tea gown of pale lemon silk and sighed mournfully. "God, she was tiny." She crumpled the gown and let it fall. There was a brief, still moment, at once poignant and stagy, while we thought about our mother as she must have been at one time, and the pathetic waste of their two lives. Then Julie slid open the narrow drawer in the top middle of the bureau, and found the photograph.

It was sandwiched in a stack of white linen handkerchiefs and silk scarves, in a drawer that was obviously, inarguably, for Mother's use alone. Father stood on what looked like a dock, in front of what appeared to be some sort of bathhouse, a small outhouse-sized enclosure fitted with an abbreviated swinging door. He stood with his feet well apart, hands on hips, facing, smiling, into the camera and the sun beyond, which bleached his face and the length of his body. He was naked. We stared at the picture, and then at each other, with identical expressions of amazed stupidity. "This isn't possible," I said.

"It was taken recently," she said. "It's not old. Look, even with the overexposure, his hair is definitely white—" I snatched the photograph from her in a sudden access of prudery. "Don't be an ass," she said, giggling nervously. "Give it back."

"It's grotesque," I said.

"It's wonderful," she said.

"Wonderful? Who took this picture? Where is this place? I don't recognize any of it. It looks like some kind of summer camp. He couldn't even swim! Don't you remember, those times he took us to the lake and paced back and forth on the shore, shouting at us when we went out too far?" I was furious, a trial attorney rendered foolish by an inappropriate confession.

Julie flopped on the bed and clasped her hands behind her head. "He used to give her back rubs," she said. "I saw them sometimes in the afternoons. She would lie here in her nightgown, untied in the back, and he would bend over her. He had such big hands. And her hands reaching out, gripping the bedstead. I always thought she was in pain, you know? I felt so sorry for her." Julie laughed. "The wonderful part is, they were as happy as we were, all these years."

I stretched out beside her. "Did she leave it for us to find?"

"Don't be silly." Without looking at me she caressed my cheek with cool fingers. "Let it go," she said.

"I will."

23

"No you won't. You'll let it get to you, the way you always have."

"We never knew them," I said, after a long while.

She raised up on one elbow and watched me cry. She was ageless, and thought herself wise, and I used to believe she was. I don't know. "We were lucky," she said.

▼ ▼ ▼ ▼ ▼ ▼ ▼

The front bell rang some hours later, revising and resolving my nightmare, so that I sprang awake, in my parents' bedroom where she had left me, convinced of disaster in progress. The house was burning and we were trapped outside. I was shaky going down the stairs, stumbling and grasping the rail like an old man, and opened the door with the full expectation that no one was there.

His name was Willoughby, Samson Willoughby, and he was sorry as hell, but his car broke down in the storm, and could he please use the phone. He was a little older than I, and taller, broad-shouldered, husky, with coarse, handsome features. An apparition absurd and fitting, dripping rainwater on our faded oriental carpet. Sorry as hell, he said, and I liked him. He smiled the way honest salesmen do, irresistibly. And his eyes widened and he hushed, respectfully, at the sight of Julie, standing at the top of the stairs in her long blue nightdress, rubbing the sleep from her eyes.

▼ ▼ ▼ ▼ ▼ ▼ ▼

She is buried under a hot white sky, in a small graveyard at the top of a hill not far from the old house. There's a large crowd: news people, officials, a few mourners. Julie's children stand on the other side of the grave from me, within a cluster of uniforms. I wouldn't know them otherwise. The expressions of the older

24

two are identically bored and wary; only the young one seems to have any real sense of the occasion. He looks confused The girl, Samantha, catches sight of me and nudges Michael with her elbow. They stare together, talking, standing a little apart and not looking at each other, like movie spies. She decides something, and after a short, animated discussion with two uniformed matrons, walks toward me by herself, her fists jammed into the pockets of her gray jacket. The suit is dowdy She wears it like a joke. "You must be my Uncle John," she says. She smiles like a little girl, or the closest approximation she can manage. "You look just like her."

"You don't," I say. I lie. She's Julie in a cheap, concave mirror. Julie in the funhouse. Attractive enough, by standards I don't share: lanky, pale, with long narrow bones; poorly nourished, by design; face like a lazy drawl, knowing and unsurprised.

She smiles again, ruefully this time, still for my benefit. "Are you staying around after? Are you coming back for the trial?"

"I have a plane to catch. I am not coming back for the trial "

"Because there are some people back there, from a publisher, and a guy from *Newsweek*. Maybe they'd like to talk to you."

I laugh, flushing laughter from her as purely ugly as my own. "They can burn in hell," I say

She nods slowly and drops the mask. "She used to talk about you, once in a while. When she got smashed. She said you were a lousy businessman."

"I don't believe you "

"It's true," she says, shrugging. "She said you blew a big chance to buy into some drugstore franchise "

"I don't believe you exist."

"Hey, Uncle J! That's exactly what she said to me. Lots of times. Her own daughter."

"Go away."

"She was a marvelous businesswoman. See those jerks over there?" She points to a huddle of men and women in navy blazers. "Her co-workers. They used to call her The Shark She specialized in newlyweds. You know, looking for their Dream House. Man, when she got ahold of them, they didn't—"

"Why don't you go rehearse somewhere else."

"Rehearse! You old creep, you don't know anything! Don't you sit in judgment on us!" She has forgotten herself. "Does this scene look rehearsed to you? Do you think we *planned* all this?" She's shaking badly, rousing me at last to pity, to sorrow, and I turn away and start down the hill.

She follows, shrieking, indiscreet in her rage. "She was a dead woman, mean and vicious and dead already. She hated every-body." I put on speed but she catches up with me, grabbing my arm. "Dad, us, everybody. Especially you. Look at me. The only thing she loved was when one of us would screw up. She loved that. Look at me. She saw us standing there, and she loved it."

"Here you are," I say. "I can't doubt you."

She is All Too True. What contempt Julie must have felt toward these needy children. How she despised their mediocrity, the ordinary stupid mess they made of their freedom. *We were lucky,* she said.

No, Julie. No, we were not. If we were lucky, then this girl is fortune's child, and your death is *the wonderful part*, and there was justice in it. And your life makes a story after all. The heartless, ironic type of thing that so pleased you.

That so suited you.

Inevitability. Destiny. Cause and effect, seeds of destruction, sense. We *make sense*, like a feather bed, and take comfort there. We tell ourselves stories at bedtime. But I loved you too much. Sleep is just not that important to me.

"She was going to send Michael to military school. Dad told

26

him he had to go, but it was her idea." She's breathing hard. "They think Michael did it." She has Julie's eyes.

"Good-bye, Samantha," I say, and this time she doesn't follow me.

But calls out bravely, her voice proud and true. "Uncle John? Uncle John, do you want to know who pulled the trigger? Do you want me to tell you a secret?"

"No," I say. "No more."

THE
HAUNTING
OF THE
LINGARDS

The Lingards were not a flashy couple, but people admired and envied their marriage, the symmetry of their mutual regard, their serene and constant intimacy. This perfect marriage was often held up as a standard against which other couples disparaged their own. In a typical argument the wife would say, "Kenneth never cuts *her* down in public," and the husband would perhaps reply that "Maybe that's because he respects her, because Anita doesn't get bombed and blab her husband's private remarks at parties. And even if Anita *couldn't* hold her booze," he might add, with somewhat more fervor, "she'd find some subtle way to let him know that they ought to leave early"; "And if she did," his wife would shout, "*he* wouldn't pretend not to notice her"; and so on.

Marital tension was high in their close-knit community, where most of the husbands and some of the wives were research immunologists, and the nonprofessional half of the couple (for there was no profession but medicine) was often lonely and alienated because the professional half worked hard and played hard, or worked hard and fell asleep. Had the Lingards not been so amiable, they would have been widely resented, like the one brilliant student who ruins a bell curve.

Common wisdom in the group (especially those on their second marriages) held that, while opposites may attract, they repel

31

in the long run, and here again the Lingards were often cited, this time as the exception that proved the rule. He was lean and fair and austere, and she was plump and dark and voluble. To relax, he devised cryptic crosswords, and she practiced her violin, which she played, semiprofessionally, with a local quartet. His intelligence was disciplined and objective, hers unruly and bluntly intuitive.

They were absolutely unalike, and yet no one ever wondered what one Lingard saw in the other, or if each Lingard sometimes yearned for the company of its own kind. They had never been known to disagree on any issue of substance, and almost never even on trifling matters of fact. When they spoke, recounting some story, arguing some position, consecutive paragraphs, sentences, even phrases within a single sentence flowed seamlessly between them. And their spontaneous behavior was so often identical and synchronous that, for instance, the Lingard Laugh, sudden and coincident, was a generally recognized phenomenon, and one not too well understood, as the occasion for amusement was often impossible for others to detect. Talking to the Lingards, as Saul Goldberg said, you often felt as though you addressed one person with two faces, like the perfect multilimbed creature of Platonic myth, or the Lingards' own freakish child. (The Lingards were childless.)

Of course no one knew what their sexual life was like— these people were not young, and the Lingards were especially discreet—but friends of both sexes imagined their marriage bed as a sunny place devoid of mystery and strife, their sex fore-ordained and utterly peaceful, and therefore oddly, and enviably, perverse.

▼ ▼ ▼ ▼ ▼ ▼ ▼

In fact, in private fact, the Lingards were so perfectly suited that they were not even aware of the joy they took in each other,

32

joy being their natural state. With other mates they might have known ecstasy, romance, resentment, the thrill and risk of sexual war; they settled, in their ignorance, on kindness and the modest pleasures of companionship. Their sex really *was* sunny, pleasant, free of effort and ambition. They were mated for life, simply, like greylag geese, and like those plain purposeful fliers they were incapable of imagining any other life but this. They hadn't the sense to be smug.

Which is not to say they were inhuman. Once, while they were driving across Florida, Kenneth told Anita to "Shut up." One morning he said "Look, I don't *want* Grape-Nuts" with absurd emphasis, in a querulous voice that saddened and diminished them both. Once when she was practicing the violin, with an all-Beethoven concert upcoming, she told him to fix his own damn dinner. But with a single exception this was the extent of their empathic failure. They were two complex individuals who made a simple miraculous whole. In the middle of a sleepless night, at a boisterous gathering, in front of a television set blaring dreadful news of the perilous world, one would reach out and touch the other lightly, unconsciously, like a talisman.

They had only one real fight in twenty years, and that very early in their marriage, when Anita made an offhand remark about her horoscope in the morning paper. "According to the stars," she told him at the breakfast table, "I must avoid undertaking any important projects today." She was trying to think of a way to turn this into a joke when he asked her to repeat herself, as he had been reading the front page. She obliged, feeling a little foolish, since she had not meant anything by it in the first place.

Kenneth, who had been up working late five nights running, and who was ordinarily the most easygoing of men, was suddenly outraged that a reputable newspaper would run an astrology column. It was just that sort of bleak, caffeine-driven morning for him: any innocuous thing could have brought on his sudden, hungry outrage. Anita, who agreed that astrology was an insult to the intelligence, made a mild remark about the public's right to get what they want, even if it's bad for them. "And anyway," she said, "it doesn't really hurt anybody."

For a long time they *seemed* not to be arguing at all, but merely carrying on an extended intellectual debate, the locus shifting from breakfast table to kitchen sink while she washed dishes, to the bathroom while he shaved, to the bedroom while they dressed, and at first they *seemed* mostly in accord, with Kenneth agreeing that people had the right to believe that the world is flat or that you can talk to the dead, and Anita agreeing that it was contemptible for nonbelievers to exploit their folly.

But it gradually emerged that they did not see eye to eye on what was folly and what was not: under the general heading of "claptrap" Kenneth included theories of ESP and telekinesis, which Anita had casually assumed were plausible; and when he refused to allow that scientists had any sort of duty to test these theories out she was unpleasantly surprised. Surely, she said, the sighted should lead the blind, and outright fraud should be exposed by those best qualified to do so.

"That takes time, Anita," said Kenneth, tying his tie. "You can't expect a Ph.D. to sacrifice a big chunk of his career just because some moron wants to believe that vegetables love chamber music."

Anita then supposed she too must be a moron, for she had more or less come to believe in the secret life of plants; and after this the argument became wildly emotional. Kenneth came from a long line of scientists, academics, and agnostics. Anita was the most rational woman in her family. Her mother and her father's sister had each had out-of-body experiences, her sister was always talking about Velikovsky, and both her grandmothers had met Jesus Christ. Yet except for her sister these women were quite

34

phlegmatic and otherwise sensible, and though she had always felt more intellectually favored than they were, she did not at all like to hear her husband call them "morons."

In the end Anita lost control and bitterly reminded him, in barely coherent, tremulous sentences, that there were other ways of looking at the world, that science would never have progressed if Galileo and Newton had been so selfish, and that her people were every bit as smart as his, even if they weren't educated.

Kenneth, white-faced and stony, delivered a frighteningly brilliant impromptu lecture on cultural evolution, the pernicious influence of Thomas Aquinas, the sheer staggering heft of human knowledge, generated only by the self-discipline and sober adherence to experimental verification of legions of scientists, who were anything *but* selfish, who were downright heroic, centurions of the enlightenment, committed to protecting and defending the truth; and he spoke, with as much feeling as if he had actually been present at the event, of the Great Library of Alexandria and its destruction by fire at the hands of an ignorant mob.

By now they were stretched out on their bed side by side, fully clothed, exhausted by the violence of their emotions. "I love you," Kenneth said, with terrible dispassion, "but I would not burn the Library of Alexandria for you"; and Anita, drily sobbing, cried, "You son of a bitch."

It was a profoundly silly fight; that is, a fight both profound and silly; it would never become a joking matter. They referred to it only implicitly, in the exaggerated care with which they attended to each other in the ensuing days, as though each were both nurse and convalescent. Privately Anita decided that they had really been fighting about something else, most likely their families, and who came from better stock.

Privately Kenneth considered and rejected this possibility. Although mortified by his own rhetorical excess, so that the echo of his speech, especially the part about centurions and the burning of the library, would, along with his "Grape-Nuts" pronunciamento, torment him for the rest of his life, he could not deceive himself about its cause.

Underneath his ludicrous show of passion lay the passion itself, the bedrock of his intentional life. He had suffered a brief indelible glimpse of his wife amid the torchlit stampede of his single enemy.

Their one serious argument became for both Lingards a warning sign posted at the verge of a precipice, a dark drop of unguessable duration; and with this sign in mind they built a marriage otherwise unbounded, which was the envy of all who knew them well.

▼ ▼ ▼ ▼ ▼ ▼ ▼

Sixteen years later, on a gray October day, Anita and Marilyn Goldberg, whose husband, Saul, was Kenneth's colleague and close friend, went together to inspect an attic full of old books that the executor of a recently deceased professor's estate wished to donate to the University Women for their annual sale.

Though both women had fortified themselves against mold and book dust with strong doses of antihistamine, the air in Professor Giddings's cluttered attic was so dry and sour that Marilyn suffered an asthma attack and had to run out to the car to get her inhaler. Drowsy Anita nestled back against a rafter, heedless of dirt and spiders, and thumbed through an old blue volume entitled *Peeps at Many Lands*.

Anita wallowed in these eccentric collections. She was an enthusiastic dawdler and without her industrious friend could easily accomplish nothing more on an afternoon like this than the further rumpling and soiling of her old woolen jumper. She liked best to imagine the lives of these dead collectors from the evidence of their books, the chatty or self-conscious inscriptions,

36

the cryptic marginalia, the abrupt vandalism of a child's crayon, the somber elegant script of the aged dead.

She was reaching lazily for *A Girl of the Limberlost* when she saw a real girl, a small child, standing in gloom at the top of the attic stairs. The child was wide-eyed and blonde, with a pale, pretty face distinguished by a small pink crescent scar in the middle of one cheek and another at the temple, suggesting that some animal, a dog, had bitten her a long time ago. "Hi, sweetheart," said Anita, but the child responded with an unchanging stare.

The directness of watchful children had always unnerved Anita, but there was something particularly disturbing about this one. She was dressed oddly, for one thing: instead of practical play clothes she wore a drab, dark-striped dress of some cumbersome material, like homespun cotton, tied at the waist with a black sash, and hanging almost to her ankles. It was a very old dress, Anita realized, or old-fashioned, anyway. No. Old. The genuine article. The child's feet were bare, but Anita would not have been startled to see them encased in tiny stiff leather boots, pointed at the toe, laced to the ankle.

"Kiddo?" said Anita. "Are you going or coming? Are you in or are you out?" But her own voice did not break the spell. Only if the child herself spoke would this happen, and Anita somehow knew the child would never speak. She held her breath, and the airless attic room ticked like a moribund clock, rocked in sudden October wind. Anita was unafraid. She regarded the child unblinking, taking in every detail, until her eyes burned; she rubbed them, and looked again, and the child had disappeared.

When Marilyn finally puffed her way back to the attic, pausing where the child had stood, to get her breath, Anita asked her if she had passed a little girl on the way, or noticed any kids playing outside. "No," Marilyn said, and Anita, herself an instant graying child, laughed with delight and clapped her hands

37

▼ ▼ ▼ ▼ ▼ ▼ ▼

Kenneth learned that his wife had seen a ghost in the worst possible way: he heard it from a third party. They were dining in their own comfortable old house, with their old friends the Goldbergs, drinking their own liquor, stoking their own fire with cherry logs they had split themselves and stacked into a sturdy wedge in their own backyard. Anita was in their warm kitchen, standing over a cast-iron stockpot they had found together at a country flea market, her round cheeks brick-red in the fragrant familiar steam of their favorite beef stew. Kenneth was a sitting duck. In fewer than three years he would kneel alone in this very room, on the exact spot where he now stood, emptying the contents of his desk into cardboard boxes from the liquor store while his gaunt bitter wife reviled him in the Goldbergs' living room, and choked the Goldbergs' big brass ashtray with unfiltered cigarette butts, and if anyone were then to ask him for the secret of a happy life, he would answer: Stasis.

"What do you make of Anita's ghost?" asked Saul, as Kenneth handed him his beer. "The little wraith," said Saul, but clearly Kenneth had no idea what he was talking about. This delighted Saul. Marilyn was the mother of his children, and on that account he loved her and would never consider abandoning her, but on that account only. Gray-bearded Saul, short and rotund, sharply dressed in clothes selected and purchased by his wife—dapper, roly-poly Saul was a zealous adulterer, discreet but ruthless, the kind that loved the capture even more than the chase; and only the Lingards made him feel, through their example, the moral weight of his infidelities, the loneliness of his married state. He always felt, beside his dear uxorious friend, a little pathetic, a little shabby. "Never mind," he now abruptly said, with a show of discomfort.

"A ghost?"

"Forget it. So. What's new?"

"What are you talking about?"

Saul leaned into Kenneth and whispered, "Your wife has had a paranormal experience."

Anita and Marilyn emerged from the kitchen with a cheese board and a can of cashews. "What's he talking about?" Kenneth asked Anita.

"I'm afraid I spilled the beans," Saul told Anita, "about the g-h-o-s-t."

"Oh."

"You didn't even tell him?" Marilyn rocked Anita with the heel of her meaty hand. "You've been yammering about that ghost for a week." Marilyn, thick-skinned and raucous, forever cuffing and prodding and nudging with her elbow, was everyone's mother. She elbowed Kenneth. "Wait'll you hear."

Anita said, "There's nothing to tell."

"You saw a *ghost?*"

Anita stammered and undercut everything with ineffectual, dismissive flicks of her hand. "It was nothing. Marilyn and I went out to the Giddings estate the other day to sort through some books, and I thought I saw something, but it wasn't worth mentioning."

To me, Kenneth said with his mild reproachful eyes.

"I knew you wouldn't be interested," Anita said aloud.

Kenneth busied himself with poking the fire. "I take it this was the shade of old Mort Giddings. How did he look?" He grinned up at Marilyn. "Did he goose you in the vestibule?"

"She didn't see it," said Saul. "*My* wife didn't see the ghost."

Anita described the attic encounter in an offhand manner, with shrugs and headshakes that were obviously supposed to belittle it. She addressed her husband but avoided looking right at him. She looked, to everyone, like a guilty wife reciting an alibi. "Probably just some neighborhood kid playing dress-up," she said, and her husband saw the lie.

For the next hour, while they ate, they talked hospital politics and local gossip, but none of them forgot Anita's ghost. Because Marilyn believed all women wanted children, she saw in the ghost child the incarnation of her barren friend's unconscious wish This, and the sudden strain between the Lingards, disturbed her. Marilyn loved her friends, and revered their marriage, in a sentimental way.

Saul shared Kenneth's pure contempt for the mere idea of ghosts, yet he had enjoyed Anita's flustered attempt to deceive her husband, the insight it had given him into the intimate dynamics of this ideal marriage. Too, he found the spectacle of Anita's wifely submission deeply erotic and wondered seriously for the first time about her round little body, and its tidal rhythms— what sounds she would make when she crested, and how she would feel when she broke. Hypothetically. Saul would never betray his friend, except now, in this way, riding his beloved wife on the gravy- and wine-stained tablecloth, amid goblets and lighted candles and plates of steaming garlicky stew, while all around them four old friends, three of them blind as bats, speculated about future trends in immunology

After dinner, over brandy, Saul told a funny story from his Cornell days, a good one with a late May blizzard and sex and frostbite, and when the laughter died down Anita sighed and said, to Kenneth, "I just wish you'd been there." No one imagined she was talking about Ithaca "I wish you had seen what I saw."

"Forget it," Marilyn said. "If God spoke to Saul from a burning bush he'd find some way to wriggle out of it. The boys have a smart answer to everything."

"That's what I want. The answer."

"To what?" Kenneth asked.

"Why was the little girl dressed like that?"

"Some kind of costume. You just said so yourself."

"Why was the old dress—I *know* it was the real thing—in such good condition?"

"It was well-preserved." Kenneth frowned affectionately at her. "Really, Anita."

"Why was she barefoot on a chilly October day?"

"Why not? What does barefoot have to do with a ghost?"

"It's *odd*, that's all." Anita, who rarely smoked, lit her third cigarette in ten minutes. "How did she just disappear? All right then, she went downstairs while I was rubbing my eyes, but why didn't Marilyn see her?" This was Anita's trump card.

"She's right," Marilyn said. "I didn't see anything."

"You weren't looking. You saw and forgot. She slipped out the back way."

"Or shot up the chimney! Kenneth, you had to *be* there. This was a strange child. She came out of nowhere and stood still looking at me, and she was, I'm sorry, unearthly, I can't help it, and that attic room, with her in it, was an enchanted place." She had no proof, and didn't see, quite, why she needed it. "You'll just have to trust me on this," she said.

Kenneth counted to ten, and when he spoke his voice was low and pleasant. "Were you on any medication?"

"Certainly not."

"Benadryl," Marilyn said. "We were sneezing our heads off that morning. Remember?"

She wanted to say "What are the odds?" but he would just ask "Against what?" and she didn't know the answer to that. She had nothing on her side but experience. Kenneth didn't have to say anything. He was attending to her now with every appearance of interest, as though she were a respected colleague, an equal, and they were hashing out some difference of opinion that could

41

go either way. He was making a great effort for her. "I surrender," she said, and felt relief.

Saul called her a pushover. "He hasn't convinced you. You're just backing off."

"It's not a question of backing off. I know my husband, Saul."

The Lingards regarded each other in that intimate, delicately exclusionist fashion that so confounded their friends, especially Saul Goldberg. They were again, effortlessly, of one mind.

Marilyn snorted. "So! Your husband tells you what to see, how to feel about it? That's cute. Does he dream your dreams for you?" She put her big square hand on her husband's thigh. "What did I dream about last night?"

"You dreamed of me, Mama," said Saul. "I was sensational."

"What I saw doesn't matter," Anita said. "There are no ghosts." She was still addressing her husband, and smiling in that maddening private way. Both Goldbergs thought of Kate the Shrew placing her hand beneath Petruchio's foot; the image affected each in a different way. "If there were ghosts, then everything Kenneth knows—and you, Saul—would be wrong."

"Or at least useless in explaining it," said Kenneth.

"My sighting of the ghost is only . . . a historical event," said Anita, recapturing Kenneth's sixteen-year-old arguments. She said, to Marilyn, "It's just like a miracle that way."

"What she means is that it's nonrepeatable," said Kenneth, "which means it can't be tested. Which is all, ultimately, that can be said about it."

Marilyn was gaping at him. "Is this what you two talk about when you're alone? What do you do, have seminars in the bedroom?"

The Lingards laughed suddenly, mysteriously, and blushed. "We have talked about it," said Anita. "The problem is the same for ghosts as for other para . . ."

"—parascientific claims," Kenneth said. "Parascientists just report these events. They have produced no theories to explain them. If there was a ghost in Giddings's attic it existed independently of all known physical laws, and probably in violation of fundamental theory."

"So?" Marilyn, outraged, rose above the derision of husband and friends. She scolded Anita. "So, you don't know what you know? You don't believe what you see with your own eyes? What do you care about known physical laws? What's it to you?"

"It's nothing to me," said her friend. "It's everything to Kenneth."

"Ah-*bab*," said Saul Goldberg

And Kenneth, blindsided, glanced sharply at Anita, who reminded him just then of the glycerin-eyed bejeweled wife of a particularly obnoxious TV evangelist. He reeled before his own gross disloyalty.

Saul raised his glass to him and murmured, "Lucky man "

"And *you*," said Marilyn, pointing at Kenneth, "what if you had seen the ghost?"

"He wouldn't have," said Anita.

"Because he's blind, or because there wasn't a ghost to see?"

"It doesn't matter."

"Yes it does!" said Kenneth, but only Saul heard him, and roared with laughter, which everyone ignored.

This was better than soccer, Saul's game of choice in youth. The true nature of the Lingards' compromise was shimmering into view, a great bubble wobbling to and fro, sinking all the while, toward its comic doom. His own bighearted, domineering wife, unaware of the trouble she was making, went on berating Kenneth and Anita. Marilyn's job was bossing children, and she never stopped to wonder if she had the right, or listen to her own strident voice; she had no subtlety and no vanity. She hunkered forward on the couch, her tight skirt twisted and straining, her big knees wide apart. Kenneth never even glanced down between her thighs; his lack of curiosity was mildly insulting.

Saul himself reached over to pour himself more wine and sneak a peek.

Marilyn had by now forgotten that she didn't believe in the ghost, so strongly did she disapprove of Kenneth's bullying and poor Anita's compliance. "How can you be so sure of yourself? You'd rather believe your own wife is nuts than be wrong about this thing. Shame on you."

"You can't expect him to throw his career out the window on my account," said Anita.

"He doesn't have to throw anything out the window! You can believe two things at once. He can believe his theories, and he can believe you. Don't think so much! Who needs it? You people are crazy."

"They're not *my* theories, Marilyn. This isn't some pet notion I have, that she has to humor me. . . ." There was something wrong. Kenneth felt discouraged, and annoyed with everyone, including himself, and some other negative emotion, so alien that he could not name it.

"You never answered me. What if you *had* seen the ghost? Never mind, Saul, shut up. Suppose you'd seen and believed. Then where would you be? It seems to me," said Marilyn, her face brightening at her own cleverness, "that you've put your faith in something pretty iffy, if this is all it would take to make your whole world fall apart."

Anita, eyes closed, trying to remember Kenneth's exact words when she herself had raised a similar argument, spoke haltingly, like a hypnotized subject. "It is not possible . . . or necessary . . . to rule out the existence of a . . . *Gegenbeispiel*." She grinned at Kenneth. "Pretty good, huh?"

Kenneth turned away from her and jabbed at the dying fire. "She means 'counterexample.' No, Marilyn, we don't live in fear of absurd counterexamples." Kenneth was *lonely*. For the first time in twenty years.

44

"All right, Smarty, but what if you *had* seen it?" Saul and Anita groaned, but Marilyn was like a bulldog with a bone. "Here you are, alone in an ordinary old attic, minding your own business, when all of a sudden presto! a little kid in weird clothes, only let's say—why not?—she's floating, no wires or anything, and there's a human head tucked underneath her arm! And you haven't taken any drugs, you pinch yourself and you're wide awake, you check everything out. I mean, what would it take for you? Okay, you've got witnesses too. And meanwhile her head is swiveling around and around like that kid in *The Exorcist*, sparks are shooting out—I'm asking you, what would it take? How would you handle *that*, Mr. Science?"

Marilyn laughed then, with the others, and for a while nothing had changed after all, it had maybe been a false alarm, and Kenneth simply enjoyed the sight and sound of his happy wife. But she didn't stop laughing when everyone else did; she would stop, and glance at Kenneth, and then start afresh. She kept saying, "I'm sorry," but she couldn't have been, because clearly all she had to do to stop was quit recharging herself, which she finally did. She stared down at her lap, biting her lower lip like a choirgirl with the giggles.

"What's so funny?" Marilyn asked, and started her up all over again.

"He'd lose his mind!" Anita said, pointing at him, pointing him out as though he were some little blob on the horizon. She saw his face and laughed harder. "Oh Kenneth, I'm sorry, but HA HA HA they'd have to cart you away!"

▼ ▼ ▼ ▼ ▼ ▼ ▼

During the next days Kenneth withdrew from Anita. He was pleasant to her, and polite, and frigid. This behavior was not entirely involuntary, as he well knew, but only he suffered from it. If he was trying to punish her, he was unsuccessful. Anita, to her astonishment, reveled in having displeased him. She was on her own and it made her giddy. She assumed that the estrangement would pass; she would make the most of it while it lasted. Although it did occur to her, when he would look right at her and decline to take her in and this would fail to move her in the least (except to a touch of admiration for his style), that perhaps she was numb.

One afternoon she picked him up early at the labs so they could go furniture shopping, and because her neck was stiff she let him take the wheel, and because one of the stores happened to be in the neighborhood of the Giddings house, Kenneth went a few blocks out of his way to drive past it: and there she was, the child, on a tricycle in the driveway next door, in Oshkosh overalls and a Cabbage Patch jacket. They were close enough to make out the little pink scars on her face.

"Is that your ghost?" he asked, and Anita could see that nothing much rode on her answer; that had this been the wrong child he would not have been embarrassed; that he was not elated now, because this was no victory for him, because there had been no contest. He had never needed proof. She could have killed him. She rolled down her window and shouted at the child: "Little girl! Little girl!" "What are you doing?" he asked, and she hissed at him, "She was trespassing, the little brat," and he said "Jesus Christ, Anita," and tromped on the accelerator, peeling away from the curb

He didn't know why he had driven by the damn house in the first place, and now he cursed the impulse that had led him there and the rotten luck of finding the damn kid What were the odds? She should have been in school at this hour, or visiting friends; she should have been inside her own house, which should have been elsewhere, at least on the next block, preferably on the far side of the moon. She was as outlandish and unnerving to him

46

in sunshine as she had been to Anita in the dusty gloom. She had made a fool out of his wife. Twice.

He told her he was sorry. He said it again that night, as they undressed for bed, and this time she answered. Forget it, she said; and the next day she brought the matter up herself, and joked about Halloween costumes and premenopausal insanity. Don't be so hard on yourself, he said. "The more I think about it the more I'd like to go back there myself and ask her just what she *was* doing there in the attic, and why the old clothes and the bare feet. . . . You know, it really is intriguing"; and she said, "Don't patronize me, Kenneth."

Then her mother, who lived alone a thousand miles away, fell and broke her hip; and though her sister lived nearby and could have taken care of her, Anita flew out to spend six weeks in her mother's house, nursing, reminiscing, mending fences. "She won't live forever," she told Kenneth as she packed. "I haven't been a very attentive daughter," she said, not having to add, "since I married you."

In her infrequent visits, accompanied by Kenneth, Anita had always suffered pity for her mother, because she saw, with Kenneth's eyes, an intelligent woman who could have had a fine mind given proper guidance and discipline; a sucker for every harebrained idea that mystics and charlatans could dream up. In the context of daughterly love and respect this had been hard: it had been hard to see her mother exposed to the thin, wintry air of Kenneth's appraisal. Now, on this visit, she rediscovered her mother's strengths, her effortless humility, her naturally good sense.

Her mother, an old woman now, had cast aside the spirit world for the spiritual. "Card tricks," she scoffed, "tricks with mirrors, scraps for the lost and the easily led. I was one of them, Anita, and your sister still is." She hefted the old Bible she now kept constantly with her. "You were the brightest one of the

47

bunch of us. You knew dross from gold." She never proselytized. Anita appreciated her shrewdness in this, the fine discretion with which, in all her enthusiastic talk of the Christian experience, she never once referred to her son-in-law, a man whose sole accommodation to her had been his love for her daughter, a man who, in the hardest sense, had taken her daughter away. She would say only: Faith is the *other* way of knowing. When Anita finally left for home she had faith, if not yet in God, then in the "other way of knowing."

▼ ▼ ▼ ▼ ▼ ▼ ▼

There was something different about the Lingards. People sensed it without realizing: a nagging little something that made their friends feel at once gratified and bereft. Occasionally, when her husband was holding forth on some abstract matter, Anita would laugh and roll her eyes skyward in mild ridicule, or fondly pat his knee and call him "stuffy." Sometimes when Anita told one of her rambling, ill-assembled stories, or talked about God, which she now often did, in a hypothetical way, Kenneth would sigh and smile at her from a distance, with tolerant affection. These were terribly ordinary events, and people easily forgot—for they had never been a flashy couple—that the Lingards had once really had an extraordinary marriage. The more poorly matched pairs still envied and resented them, and yearned to be as close as the Lingards were now.

Even the Goldbergs did not understand why these occasional dissonant moments seemed so shocking. "I don't know how Anita stands it," Marilyn said on one tipsy, rainy drive home, when all that Kenneth had done was fall asleep while Anita was talking, and Saul was quick to point out that his friend had been working overtime and besides, "He'd heard that story at least once before, because I have, too," and Marilyn said, "*So!* That gives him the

48

right to be rude?" and Saul said, "It's not rude to bore your husband?" And in this cross, distracted way they began to grieve for what their friends had lost.

▼ ▼ ▼ ▼ ▼ ▼ ▼

They had New Year's Eve at their house, with just the Goldbergs and two other couples. In midevening Anita consented to perform, so there was an unusual slapdash concert, Saul faking his way through the piano accompaniment to a couple of Mozart sonatas while Anita's violin sang melodies so lucid and so congruous that they were immediately familiar. Even Kenneth, who had a poor ear, felt he must have always known this music, these sunny, disarming melodies. He guessed that she was playing well. He admired the incline of her head, her thoughtful expression, rapt yet untheatrical. He had never admired her before. It was an awful feeling. When she finished he clapped the loudest of all. *I know that woman*, he told himself, like talking to a friend— *Hey! I know that woman!*—but he didn't, and he never had. He supposed that most people endured just this degree of solitude all their lives with good grace, even indifference. He would have given all he had to recover his durable old illusion, to spare himself the sight of his admirable wife.

Midnight came and went, with a particularly stupid ceremony. ("Good riddance," said Saul Goldberg. "To bad rubbish," cheered his wife.) Everyone but Kenneth got a little drunk Anita knelt in front of the fire, swaying very slightly in a cloud of cigarette smoke. Three or four times she caught his eye and winked and said, "I feel terrific." He supposed this was true. Lately there had been an odd, raffish air about her, as though she found adventure in the everyday solitary life. With her hair disarrayed, and firelit, and her sturdy plump body, she was an attractive woman still. She was, he had recently come to see, the image of her mother.

Once recently she had said to him, "You can quit worrying. I'm not going to find Christ." She had smiled then, her new secret smile. "I'd never do that to you," she had said, raking him with the old woman's shrewd, patient eyes.

She held the floor now telling a story that the rest evidently found greatly amusing. People liked his wife. She was a likable woman. "Honestly," she was saying, "it turned into a real knock-down, drag-out. He said, 'Plants can't think,' and I said, 'Well, *excuse me.*' But the funny thing was, it really got under my skin for some reason, so that I didn't let it go. And then—and *then*—he goes 'Isaac Newton was a saint! Einstein was the savior of humanity!' " She deepened her voice and flung her arms about in a silly way, imitating him.

Everyone was laughing and glancing his way. Saul, after laughing the loudest, protested that his friend would never have said either thing.

She said, "Whatever. This is just the gist of it, you understand. The point is that we ended up crying and yelling at each other, and I'll *never* forget—" she pointed to him, she said, "Sorry, honey," and there was nothing in her eyes but simple mischief—"I'll never forget as long as I live this deadly serious look on his face, and he says, just like this, he says: 'I love you, honey, but . . . I Would Not Burn the Abyssinian Library for You.' " All their friends screamed and rocked with laughter.

"Alexandrian," he said, but she couldn't hear him. "Alexandrian," he said again.

"Whatever," she said, then did a double take, goggling at him for the benefit of her public, whom she now addressed with an awed smile at him. She said, "You're wonderful. Isn't he wonderful?" She held out her arms to him; she knelt, in firelight, in front of the world, exacting his embrace. "I love you," she said.

Because he believed her, and because some things simply were

50

not done, he joined her on stage, held her with sudden urgency, so they were both surprised, and she, startled into joy, momentarily forgot where she was, and he pressed her face gently to his chest, to hide and shield her, from what he could not say.

Exactly then for the first time there appeared to Kenneth a woman he had never met and yet already knew, a woman as intimate as his own history. She materialized nowhere, for she had no body, although he somehow knew she would be lean and fair, and probably, though not necessarily, young. She was an invisible bundle of his own ideas; she was Athena, the daughter of his own mind. Because he needed her, she had occurred to him, and she could never, ever unoccur. She could only gather substance. He was sorry, and he put her roughly out of mind, while he still could, and he shut out the witnesses all around, and gently rocked his loving, admirable, good wife, while all the time the next one, his true companion, set out from the alien provinces, like a constant, sure-footed messenger, coming straight for him.

MELINDA FALLING

The very first time I saw her, Melinda was in midair, just below the summit of a long, winding staircase, on her way down. There were three other women on the wide carpeted stairs; two were prettier than Melinda, and all more chicly dressed—cocktail party, Newport; lawyers, bankers, brokers—but Melinda eclipsed them all, descending, as she did, by somersault and cartwheel. She was upside-down when I first caught sight of her, left profile to me, splayed hands poised above the stair upon which the uppermost chic woman was standing; long black skirt accordioned around her hips, plump pink face partially obscured by a curtain of brown hair. I thought: Oh, my. Her right foot came down first, glancing off the edge of a step, snapping free the golden heel of her plastic shoe, and, momentarily upright, she pivoted and went down the rest of the way sideways, arms and legs extended like spokes. She wheeled, in stately fashion, between the other two women, who stood motionless as handmaidens in a frieze, watching her. All watched her, all held their breath: she whirled in dignified silence, broken only by the soft thuds of hand and foot on thick red carpeting. She did not exactly defy gravity, but mastered it by the perfect rate of descent, so that, for instance, the hem of her skirt ebbed and flowed with tantalizing discretion. So deliberate, solemn, and utterly magical was her progress that it promised to go on forever. When finally she touched down on the floor, upright, there was a little collective sigh of disappointment and then spontaneous applause led, I believe, by me. "Magnificent!" I said "Bravo!" And I took her arm and led her away from the crowd I was half in love already and wanted her all to myself. "Get me out of here," she said— her first words to me—and the expression on her flushed, round face was regal, impenetrable.

Stepping out of her ruined shoes she walked beside me like a queen (though she was actually quite short), and we were out the door and halfway to my car before I realized she was trudging, uncomplaining, through ankle-deep snow in stockinged feet. "Allow me," I said, circling her midriff with one arm and stooping to cradle the backs of her knees. But she pretended not to understand and speeded up, high-stepping through the snow just ahead of me. Cursing my awkwardness I followed her, semiattached in this absurd posture, and cursed myself again when, ushering her into my Jaguar XJ-6, I heard the dull crack of her head colliding, *en passant*, against the door frame.

"My name," I began, deferentially addressing not the shadowy form beside me but the red glow of the radio, "Is Edwin Crapeau Foote. I am not a Newport Foote, but a Mattapoisett Foote. There is no ancestral excuse for my middle name; my mother just thought it sounded classy. I am a wildly successful investment lawyer, having in fifteen years made myself richer than half my clients and the social equal of the rest. I owe my present success to youthful ambition, and that ambition to precocious childhood revulsion toward the dullness and mediocrity of the smack dab middle of the middle class. I sought, you see, to move always among talented, challenging, unusual people: the witty, the sparkling, the unpredictable. Heady conversation. Candlelit surprise. I thought, you see, that there must be some connection between money and memorable experience, between rare wine and rare intelligence. In short, I was a romantic idiot.

"Dear Lady, you have just provided me with the only moment in my entire life when I was not bored almost to the point of lunacy. With a single wordless act you have shown more daring, more devastating social awareness, more sheer imagination—"

"I tripped," she said.

I was silent for a long digestive moment. "That's impossible. Nobody could do that by accident."

"I do everything by accident," she said. "That's all you have to know about me. I'm a stupid secretary, that's all, and my stupid boss brought me to this stupid party because his wife is even homelier than me. And I would just like," she said, her voice rising in pitch and thinning out into a child's cry, "to do one goddamn simple thing in my life, like walk across a room or down the stupid stairs, without goddamn making a fool of myself." At the end of this remarkable speech (which, unlike my own, I am able to render verbatim) she fell silent, or almost silent: after a while I became aware of soft gasps, breathy shudders, regularly spaced, almost imperceptible, and realized she was sobbing. (Melinda's sobs and Melinda's laughter were quiet affairs, practically indistinguishable.) And with a soothing cry I embraced the huddled bundle of her, and kissed her plump damp cheeks, and I was lost. She had astonished me twice in fifteen minutes. Are there really any better reasons for making a lifetime commitment?

▼ ▼ ▼ ▼ ▼ ▼ ▼

"God, yes," said John Rittenhouse, my partner, with uncharacteristic animation. "Jesus, Ed, she's a typist over at Flink, Spitalny and Whatsit. She's a chubby little oaf. Young, okay, cute, possibly, but marriage—Good-Lord-have-you-lost-your-mind?" Rittenhouse and I have been friends since Chicago, so I let him get it off his chest and didn't take offense. "The trouble with you, Rittenhouse," I said chuckling, "is that you have no sense of vision. See you in church."

"Oh, of course, the Acrobat," said Kimberley Swanson, with her perfected silvery laugh. She was my current mistress and had, in fact, been one of the ladies on the stairs. "The Bouncing Ball. Dumpling Descending a Staircase." She stopped laughing when I asked her to clear her little toilet articles out of my bedroom, and my last glimpse of Kimberley, as she slammed out of the house, was a flash of long legs and elegant hips, swaying gracefully even in fury. A lovely woman, splendidly fashionable, utterly boring.

▼ ▼ ▼ ▼ ▼ ▼ ▼

My mother, still alive at that time, was "tickled to death." I brought Melinda up to Mattapoisett one evening, and Mother celebrated us with pink champagne and great gobbets of her Famous Lasagna, the recipe for which she carefully copied out for my future bride on a "From the Kitchen of Mona Foote" index card, which I later incinerated. Mother was a good woman with execrable taste.

Melinda herself was more incredulous by far at my intentions than Rittenhouse or Kimberley. "All right, a joke's a joke," she said, after I arranged for our blood tests. This was at the end of a week-long courtship, during which she had received, with some apparent pleasure—Melinda was an eloquent blusher—my innumerable avowals of love. "But Darling, you accepted my proposal just the other night. We're all set. You said, 'Sure thing, Mr. Foote.'" "I thought you were kidding," she said. Delightful Melinda! What I had taken for unbecoming flippancy (I *had* been rather hurt) was really her lovable attempt to humor a crazy man. It took me some time to convince her of the sincerity of my

58

desire, but in the end she agreed, this time in earnest. "What the hell," said Melinda.

▼ ▼ ▼ ▼ ▼ ▼ ▼

Under her own power Melinda was, in word and deed, as deliberate, stolid, and graceless as a basset hound. When she walked, she plodded; when she sat, she sank; she ran as though underwater and swam as if uphill, noisily, without propulsion, like a huge, waterlogged bumblebee. Her expression was typically grave, ruminant. Her voice was pleasantly low but often so vigilantly modulated as to be almost toneless; and except for the occasional blurt her speech had a regular stately rhythm—like a sarabande—which imparted to her most casual remark the faintly ominous quality of pronouncement. She never gestured when talking, carefully trapping her hands, or busying them. Her smile was shy and pretty, transforming, but so long in coming that you could not watch its progress without conscious suspense.

Her enthusiasms were rare, bizarre, and zealously guarded. She loved two paintings, the only two with which, as far as I know, she was familiar: Hopper's "Sun in an Empty Room" and Edvard Munch's "The Shriek." Two old issues of *Time* magazine containing photographs of these were among the few personal effects she brought into our marriage. After much cajoling, she explained why she kept them, and when I presented her with decent prints, handsomely framed, she was startled into a wildfire smile. Her hands rose up and opened out like flowers. She hung them, sun and shriek, in our bedroom, side by side.

Her literary appetites were limited to doctor-nurse romances and nonfiction accounts, with photographs, of natural and man-made disasters. Fearful, wholly without cause, of my contempt she cached her paperbacks around the house in the most unlikely places. Enchanted by my accidental discovery, in the clothes hamper, of *Clinical Passions* and *Nine Horrible Fires*, I searched out the rest, like a child on an Easter egg hunt, carefully replacing them in their niches. So secretive, so unfathomable was my Melinda that I half expected also to find collections of like-colored objects, ribbons and string and pieces of glass, nestled in the chandeliers; odd cufflinks and earrings under carpet corners.

She liked these few things—the paintings, the books—and sex, which I will get to in a moment; and not much else, really. She hated only her body. "It's out," she once confided, "to get me." Because of what she misconstrued as innate clumsiness (she was spectacularly wrong), she waged constant battle against spontaneity and impulse. What appeared to the untutored eye to be lumpishness of manner was really extreme caution. She was methodical about everything she did in the vain hope of avoiding accident. Of course, this had the same effect upon her body as the command "Don't think about green elephants" has upon the mind. I could have told her this, but never did.

For Melinda out of control, obedient to only the natural laws, was incomparably graceful. She fell the way we do in dreams, lazily and in profound silence. She never degraded her falls with unseemly attempts to save herself. She did not flail, or thrash, or clutch at things and knock them over. She did not shout or make funny noises. She never wore the lonely, humiliated expression of the commonplace stumblebum. She fell *glissando*, down every set of stairs in our three-story house, on the sidewalk, in the tub (backwards into bubbles, sending up aqueous sheets, puffs of foam), down a gentle grassy hill in Nova Scotia, off a stone wall in Salem, over the lap of a grateful old gentleman on the Super Chief. Every slip, tumble, and languorous, effortless roll was as neatly executed as a movement in classical ballet.

Just how graceful, you may wonder, can a careening fat girl be? You fail to consider, for such is the tyranny of fashion, that the swan is not a slim animal; that the sea lion has no waist. You forget the patient, timeless arch of the surfacing whale.

Early on I learned to trust in the ingenuity and competence of her brilliant body—something she was never inclined to do— and I could watch her lose her balance, or rather gain imbalance, without my heart leaping to my throat. For I never knew her to acquire so much as the palest blue bruise, let alone do herself any serious damage. This is not to say that I stood idly by, a heartless voyeur, and offered her no protection from the anarchic forces which so distressed her. On the contrary. I installed extra handrails throughout the house, lowered the kitchen and pantry cabinets, laid down on tubs and tile those foot-shaped pads of ribbed rubber (so that our bathrooms looked like tiny dance studios), marred every extensive glass surface with gaily-colored safety decals (this following a sunny August morning when she joined me on the back patio without sliding open the glass door, exploding through it with casual magnificence, looking for all the world, I hardly need to say, like Danaë at the visitation of Zeus); and in general, as the sly Rittenhouse often observed, turned the house into a "paradise for shut-ins."

I wanted her to be happy. Had I been the selfish decadent my old crowd thought me to be (for they eventually hit upon the consensus that I was keeping Melinda as some outlandish sort of pet, like a capybara or potto), I would, rather than trying to help her, have gone out of my way to precipitate her lovely disasters, bumping her as though by accident at the top of the stairs, absently stretching my legs out in front of her as she passed by. I would, for example, have bought her ice skates.

Her body was sleek, compact, and rounded everywhere, each section as soft and solid as a peach. On our wedding night she came to bed in an outsized red flannel nightshirt, her brooding chubby face scrubbed and gleaming. She said, "I'll do whatever you want if you'll turn off the light." "And I'll do whatever you want," I replied, "with it on." We compromised, throughout our marriage, with indirect lighting from the hallway (and similar arrangements when we spent our nights away from home), and her skin curved in and out of shadow like dunes on a moonlit beach. "If it's all right with you, let's not do anything athletic," she said. She began, the first time and always, with terrible awkwardness, bucking, grasping, panting, without sincerity or sense, a savage if unconscious parody of the sexual technician. But in time she gave it up, and her breathing became slow and deep, and her arms circled my back, steadying me, and she took us out to sea: a night sea, some time after the passing of a storm. She moved with great power, beyond petty violence, beyond wildness, with the awesome elemental rhythm of nature in order. And though her cadence never varied, and the force of her surges never increased, at last she fell, and at the perfect moment, as if from a wonderful height. There was nothing of the flopping and hooting of her slender, acrobatic sisters. She fell with a low drawn-out sigh, smiling, her eyes wide and unseeing; her flesh and muscle rippled beneath me, and her hands fluttered against me, like wings. It was always this way. "I like that," she would say, almost as if she were realizing it for the first time. And I often wondered if she did forget, from one occasion to the next; if, in all her falls, she was in some kind of trance, or lapse.

Or perhaps, as Rittenhouse tactlessly suggested on the eve of our wedding, she was merely stupid. This is quite possible, and quite irrelevant. Melinda was the only woman I ever loved. I loved her dumpy and earthbound. I loved her floating free. It had often struck me that while we view the pairing of lovers with benign speculation, even envy, there is nothing so baffling, so grotesque, as another man's choice of wife, or a woman's of a husband. It occurs to me now that no explanation is possible.

▼ ▼ ▼ ▼ ▼ ▼ ▼

During the first year I let my half of the practice go to hell and took an extended honeymoon. We spent the last six months touring Europe at a luxurious pace. My intent was not to "widen her horizons," for I was no Pygmalion, but to give her pleasure. On balance, then, the trip was not a great success, for only occasionally did her good-natured stoicism give way to genuine interest. At first I sought out, on the basis of the paltry clues she had provided, likely objects of delight: surprising her, for instance, with a detour to the Munch Museum in Oslo. She trudged through the place without complaint, but it soon became apparent that the awful, hag-ridden lithographs and woodcuts did not move her. For all I could see they did not even ring a bell. I had better luck leaving our itinerary more or less to chance. She liked provincial French cuisine, so much that with the aid of explicit instructions she learned to duplicate it quite well when we got home. She liked the way the sheep clogged the cobblestone streets of Skye. In Paris, she coveted the voluminous dark robes and yashmaks of the Algerian women. I bought her a half dozen hideous yashmaks. (She never wore them in front of me, and I was startled to find, some months after our return, that she habitually wore them when she shopped for groceries. Whether she was enacting a fantasy or simply hiding out, I cannot say.)

Things ground to a halt in Salisbury, where, upon entering the nave of the great cathedral, she looked up at the immense vaulted expanse and, without even swaying, crashed heavily to her hands and knees. It was the only ugly fall she ever took. It was not her body's doing. "Makes me dizzy," she said, in a cranky mumble, and when I got her outside, "Can we go home now?" Overcome with remorse I begged pardon for my insensitivity, promising we would leave on the next available plane. And in bed that night

63

she patted my shoulder in one of those rare bursts of affection for which I was so grateful and said, "This isn't Europe. This is me, in Europe."

I still have a photograph, taken earlier that day by a cooperative stranger, of the two of us framed between Stonehenge monoliths: a distinguished man of forty or so, an incongruous yet convincingly hearty smile on his urbane face; and beside him, crushed against him by his circling arm, a small, stout, frumpy young woman confronts the photographer with the wistful expression of a child mauled by a distant relative

▼ ▼ ▼ ▼ ▼ ▼ ▼

We were married for five years. During the first four I was deliriously happy and Melinda—well, Melinda rolled through them, like the great globe itself, in her own inscrutable way. The trouble started one evening early in the fall, when we hosted a dinner party for the firm and a few important clients. It was partly Rittenhouse's fault, and partly mine.

Melinda had arranged a creditable feast—standing roast, mushrooms à la grecque, braised endives, and a risotto. She had also readied the fixings for crepes suzette, with the express condition that I would take care of the final preparations. She sat with the rest of us in the living room during cocktails, though she did not drink herself. In the interest of self-control, she never drank. Banal chitchat filled the air and she listened intently, or did not hear at all, and fended off the occasional polite question with monosyllables, and regarded everyone, or no one, with an unblinking stare at once vacant and portentous, like a shell-shocked sphinx. All was as usual. And Rittenhouse, as usual, regarded her with bemused fascination, for the passing of years and my continued happiness had only worsened his obsessive incredulity.

I was mired in zinc futures with old man Winthrop and so did

64

not notice exactly when and how Rittenhouse insinuated himself next to Melinda, and when I did see them he had what appeared to be her full attention and was obviously pouring on the not inconsiderable Rittenhouse charm. When I looked again they were gone—to the kitchen, as it turned out, where Rittenhouse, under the pretext of mixing himself a special drink, got her to try it. "I just wanted to see what she'd do," he told me the next morning, in a tone of mingled apology and awe. "Goddamn it," I said, too late, "She's not a toy."

They were gone a long time, and when they returned her face was flushed and happy, her brown eyes sparkled, and she carried in front of her, with monumental self-assurance, a tray holding two dozen frosted old-fashioned glasses filled to the brim with a deep amber liquid. Draped across each brim was an odorous gardenia, evidently culled from the back garden, withering visibly in its alcoholic bath. "Everybody try one," she commanded, graciously passing among us, and we all took at least one sip of her concoction, which was vile in a truly surprising way.

"What is it?" I choked, not so much alarmed as amazed at the totality of her transformation.

"A 'gin rummy,' " she said. "Jack says they make wonderful ones down at the HoHo Luau Pit." She frowned prettily. "They really should be drunk out of coconut shells." I shot Rittenhouse a look that collapsed his sheepish grin.

All hell broke loose that night, though if it had not been for the denouement I, at least, would have judged the party a success. For Melinda, who got steadily drunker throughout dinner, was the cynosure of all eyes, her body reveling wickedly in its unwonted release. There were no accidents, except for the finale: rather, she became more and more adroit as the evening progressed. Yet her unearthly competence contributed to a generally shared premonition of disaster. Conversation died as, long knife flashing in the candlelight, she carved and portioned out the huge roast with the blinding skill of a Japanese steakhouse chef. But she made up for it with a running patter of her own, commenting at length and very entertainingly upon our trip to Europe, which I had not until then realized had even registered with her, interlarding her account with aphorisms and opinions that I was startled to recognize as my own. "Neapolitans are the idiots savants of life." "When one meets the English, one understands the French."

As she glided around the table replenishing wine glasses, Winthrop leaned over and punched my shoulder with a horny forefinger. "Remarkable woman," he said.

At one point she excused herself, drove to the grocery store (she had no license), and returned in a twinkling with half a coconut, which she gutted and filled with yet another "gin rummy." Which proved to be a mistake.

For in the attempt simultaneously to propose an elaborate toast, something about "citizens of the world," and to dish out the crepes suzette, she set the monstrous drink ablaze and bowled it over, sending a river of flame the length of the table. The immediate effect was magical. We rose to our feet as one, with the hushed, appreciative cry of witnesses to a pyrotechnics display. But eventually the fire department had to be called, and though the damage was not extensive, the party broke up soon afterward.

She was disconsolate. For hours she lay face-down on the living room couch, sobbing wildly, angrily brushing off my comforting hand. When she became coherent she called herself "a freak, a freak, a freak," and threatened to run away to a sideshow. I told her that indeed, she was a freak, in a positive and glorious sense; that she was unique; that she was different, not in degree but in kind, from any other woman I had ever known; and that therefore she was infinitely precious to me. She said I was crazy. How can it be crazy, I asked her, to love someone without reservation, just as she is, and to wish for nothing more? "I don't know," she said, "but it is."

I had known all along that she was indifferent to my love, that she had married me by accident, and stayed with me through inertia, in keeping with the overall random patterning of her life. Seeing that she was now actively wretched I determined to discover what I could offer her to make her happy. Your freedom, I said, if that's what you want. She appeared to think it over, and reject it as not worth the bother. "Melinda, we have a great deal of money. Just tell me what you want. Education? A summer house? A horse?" At first I could get nothing out of her but the general wish not to have been born, but finally she entered into the spirit of the thing. "Yes, there must be something I want," she said, for I had convinced her. And for long minutes she stared into space, her brow furrowed in mighty concentration. "Anything at all," I prompted from time to time. "Animal, vegetable, or mineral." At last her face relaxed and she gave me a triumphant little smile. "What is it, Darling?" "I want a baby," she said.

As a matter of fact, across the room from where she sat was a brass newspaper rack, and on that particular night the foremost newspaper bore the prominent headline, BABY SURVIVES SUB-ZERO ORDEAL. But her desire to get pregnant, from the moment she expressed it, was, whatever the nature of its origin, fierce and all-consuming. It consumed, first of all, the great pleasure she had always taken in lovemaking, for determined as she was to conceive she did not, in bed, allow her body a moment's peace, maintaining a deadly vigilance over its every motion. There were no more sea cruises for us, ever again. For six months she could talk of nothing but temperature charts and favorable positions, and with every failure she grew more single-minded. I tried to explain to her that she was going at it all wrong, that she should relax and think about other things. But she would not, or could not, believe

67

me, and so in the end her will consumed itself, and I found her one morning, shortly after her discovery of her sixth and final failure—for I could never persuade her to try again—sitting naked, cross-legged in a square of sunlight, her face unrecognizable in fury, pounding her poor innocent stomach with knotted fists. "Stupid bastard," she called it. "Stupid idiot sonofabitch."

"We can adopt," I said.

"That has nothing to do with it," she said, with a venomous look. "This is the last straw."

She proceeded, in spite of all I could do, to punish her body with starvation and grinding, relentless exercise. It was an all-out war, having nothing to do with self-improvement, but in the process, and of course by accident, she became a conventionally pretty woman, beautiful in fact, spare of hip, bony of ankle. She achieved in time the sticklike upper arm of the fashion model: high cheekbones, knife-blade collarbones, and knobby spine emerged as her flesh dwindled and her skin tightened.

She was adopted by the Rittenhouse Gang—my old crowd—and learned, through the meddling of the chic ladies, how to dress, how to shop, how to be like everybody else. So dispirited was her pummeled, malnourished body that it could not muster so much as a single misstep, and without the blurring effect of her envelope of flesh she seemed more ungainly than ever. Though she was a mere wisp, hers were still the leaden footfalls of a giantess, hers the ponderous gestures of the ungifted auditioner. But in the eyes of her new admirers there was something terribly piquant in the physical contradictions she posed, something almost *outré* in the spectacle of a slender, petite woman with an elephantine carriage. In fact, the more fashion-obsessed ladies in the circle began, unconsciously I suppose, to imitate her peculiar style, much as idiot women everywhere once affected the *Vogue* slouch, and after a time only the hopelessly gauche were light on their feet.

And though she was as closemouthed as before, there was now a faint overlay of bitterness, of world-weariness upon her speech and manner that intrigued the men, especially Rittenhouse, my partner, my old friend, my betrayer. Rittenhouse of the impish grin and silver tongue, the most eligible of society bachelors, who had, like me, refused to settle for anything less than the perfect woman.

I knew I would lose her. After all, I had won her by working her inertia to my own advantage, through the force of my desire. It was inevitable that the combined influence of so many would pull her away from me. What I could not have foreseen was the active nature of her defection. I never imagined she would fall in love.

What could he have told her that I had not, a thousand thousand times? What more can a woman wish to hear than that she is singular, peerless, and rare? That you must have her, or die? In my blackest moods I see him snaking his arm around her pitiful waist, preening her with his hooded gaze, whispering: You are so beautifully right for this time, this place, you exemplify, typify, and crystallize, you have that certain something, you look just like that television actress. You know. The one with the hyphenated name.

▼ ▼ ▼ ▼ ▼ ▼ ▼

She did not have to tell me. I was there when it happened. I was witness, which is only fitting, since from the start I had been no less than her devout, adoring witness, and no more. I forget the place, the date, the occasion. Some awful party, a humid night, tired laughter and tireless conversation, innocent of thought. My wife stood in a clearing at the other end of the room, leaning against a pillar of pink marble. She wore a sheath of olive brown chiffon, cut in the current severe style, and her hair was skinned back into an elaborate, gold-braided knot, and the corner of one ravaged hip pointed accusingly at me. And her eyes were clear and fathomless and gave away nothing, not a trace of desire or disappointment, or memory, or wonder. She was terrible, maddening. An impossible object. My only love. I thought: Oh, my. Then she swiveled her head to face, almost, in my direction, and her mouth widened slowly into a dazzling smile, and into her eyes dawned a light of intelligence and purpose; and she stirred and hurried forward, not to me but to another. The hem of her filmy skirt lapped gently at her ankles as she rushed, with step delicate and sure. She was suddenly, irrevocably, all elegance and heartbreaking grace. And I closed my eyes and turned away; for just this once I could not bear the sight, of Melinda falling.

MY
FATHER,
AT THE
WHEEL

I remember my mother everywhere at once, my father at the wheel. I can put my mother behind the wheel, too, and in every room of both our houses, and downtown, and by the sea. But when my father wasn't driving I must not have looked at him too often, or too closely. He was, and is, a fact of great importance. Only this poor old fact, in human guise, apparently had only a right profile. Like a centaur in relief. My mythical, memory-shy father.

He drove a big black car with a running board, built before the war. He drove an old pink Nash, and then an old black and white Hudson. He drove a gold '57 Fairlane, our first new car, which we all loved, and then a gold '60 Galaxy, our first lemon. My parents said it had "ugly lines." I remember it as a Fairlane with bloat. He stayed with Ford anyway, but I don't recall the names after the Galaxy. Now his cars are Japanese. I buy American.

When I was three and a half and Mary Jane was a newborn baby, I rode in back with my panda and played with the fold-up armrest and the ashtrays. The ashtray up front was always full of brown Raleigh filters that you could peel and shred, and clouds of gray smoke issued from both my parents, settling on the baby in my mother's arms, swirling around me like weather. I loved the smell. I still do. At school my sons are taught to make rude noises when I light up, and to ask me why I don't love them. At the moment they ask, the answer is obvious. But I never smoke in the car, not even when I'm alone, not even at night.

The long slippery backseat was for children and dogs. We all liked to stick our heads out the window, and on the open highway, away from the whipping branches of trees, we were allowed to do this, with my mother watching, and our hair and fur skinned straight back, our eyes hooded against the wind. We stuck our arms out too, for the magic of air hard as a board. We threw our sneakers out the window on the Pennsylvania Turnpike. My father stopped the car and spanked me, because it had been my idea.

And sometimes, when Mary Jane and I were fighting, my father would reach around and knuckle one of us in the back of the head, or grab one of us by the arm and shake, leaving little marks. Once, before Mary Jane was born and I didn't want to leave my cousin's birthday party, my father picked me up and threw me into the car, so that I cracked my head against the door handle and stopped screaming. And there were side window vents in the back, which we could open at will, with sharp edges pointing toward our eyes. And there were no seatbelts, harnesses, or regulation infant carseats. When the car stopped short we would slam into the front seat upholstery; we learned not to sit or kneel directly in front of the ashtray, which could cut your lip. Or if I rode in front, and the brakes locked, or we ran into something, my father's arm, or my mother's, would shoot out rigid and straight in front of my face, giving me an object softer than steel to hit with my nose, to grab hold of as my body slid beneath the dash.

How tough we all were! How rubbery and intrepid! Millions of little fat kids in black and white photographs; the last of the black and white children. Twinkles in the eye of World War II. We ate white bread and spam, creamed salt cod, mashed potatoes, chipped beef on toast. Cream of wheat! And when we weren't

74

eating white things, we shared smoky air with our shameless parents; and cavernous steel boxes, traveling at lethal speeds, shook our square sturdy bodies like dice. Some of us must have died. We didn't!

▼ ▼ ▼ ▼ ▼ ▼ ▼

Here we are on the road to Galena, all the way from our apartment in New Bedford, to visit my father's people My father drives, my mother reads the maps Her hair is still long. She is still beautiful. (When she cuts it short my father will be, for almost a week, bitter and unforgiving, and I will be on his side, but not admit it.) She wears a big blue coat that will look dowdy in the old photographs, and exactly matches the color of her eyes. She is a soft blonde in blue, with hair like Dorothy McGuire's. Mary Jane and Pluto, the part collie, have the right-rear window They are hidden completely by a tent she has made out of the car quilt, one corner of it pinned by her rolled-up window, flapping outside in the light rain. She keeps asking me if I can see her, and I keep telling her I can, which is a mean-spirited lie. She is four; all she wants is not to be seen. I am almost eight, and *Tom Sawyer* is my book of the week. I am breathless in the cave with Tom, Becky, and Injun Joe.

My mother will point to the red swoop of our first cardinal, and then our first silo, our first herd of cows. Mary Jane always looks. I read. There are cows in Massachusetts. Besides, I am the sort of child for whom nothing is ever really new. My mother tells me I will ruin my eyes, and worse: that the world is going right by me while I read. I'm missing it all, she says, not quite scolding, not quite grieving.

My father defends me. If she's reading, he says, she's very much in the world. Most of the books I read are his, from when he was a boy. He asks me how I'm doing with *Tom Sawyer*, and what's my favorite part so far. I close the book. It's all right, I say. Have I gotten to the cave yet? I tell him I don't remember. Gee, he says, I don't see how you could forget that. He is so easy to fool. Sometimes, as now, my mother gives me a cold, appraising glance, a dirty look, but even she can't see into my head.

We come to our first bad accident at the Ohio state line. Traffic slows and my mother makes us lie down and close our eyes. She whispers, God. Oh no, John, look. She starts to cry. My father says what he always says: these people are good drivers but they go too fast. Fewer accidents, worse wrecks. Mary Jane and I are flat on our stomachs on the seat, with Pluto running across our backs and legs from window to window, scenting blood. We are each afraid of what we can't see; but we are not afraid for our own safety. It will be almost fifteen years before it occurs to me that I could die like that. My parents hold that thought between them, in the front seat, where it belongs.

We drive all night through Indiana. Mary Jane, who can sleep anywhere, sleeps on the floor under the quilt, with her head on the hump. I'm lying in an L with my feet on top of the cooler, my head on the middle armrest. I've brought my pillow and blanket from home. But this isn't a real bed, and after counting to a thousand with my eyes closed I settle back, wide-awake, for an interminable night. We drive in the rain through pitch-black farmland, past outcroppings of illuminated smokestacks, and then the industrial towns of the north. Gary is my father's idea of pure hell. I will always picture hell, not as a fiery pit, but as an outpost on the night horizon, iron and brick, black smoke and white steam.

My father sings to stay awake; my mother tries to harmonize, but he can never hold pitch and she ends up giggling. His voice is baritone, smoky, reverberant; even when he sings low it fills the car. He always starts out in tune and sinks, gradually, to a range where one pitch is indistinguishable from the next, at least to the human ear. They are singing "I'm Always Chasing Rainbows." I can feel his voice through the armrest. If he knew I was awake, he would make me sing with him. My father is a sentimentalist. I am not.

In the dark, at the wheel, with false dawn to his left, he has the nosy, clever profile of a fox, or so my mother says. I have an idea of what she means, although I can't see the fox, myself, except in the auburn of his hair. He is skinny and tense, well under six feet tall, light-boned, wiry. Like my husband. Like every important, hurtful lover I will ever have.

▼ ▼ ▼ ▼ ▼ ▼ ▼

My husband still looks like a fox. My father does not. While he isn't fat, he's become solid and boxy. Even his bones seem heavier. You can't see the thin man inside, not even when you look at his face, which is intelligent still, but no longer inquisitive or particularly alert. He has become the least nervous person I know, and one of the happiest.

I took the boys out to Arizona last summer to visit their grandparents. My father drove us to a ghost town near Bisbee, showed us ocotillo and mesquite, black hawks and black vultures, a vast lavender copper mine. The boys were in the backseat with geodes, and belt buckles of turquoise and sand-casted silver, and a metal detector from Sears. Up front we talked and laughed like old friends, which is what, somehow, we have become. There was never a moment of awakening, of forgiveness. All of a sudden, that summer, we had a new history.

He was in good health and he loved the Southwestern life, the dime-novel romance of the desert, the melodrama of killing heat, monsoons, flash floods. We saw a rainbow so tall and far away it barely curved. He talked about some day buying a camper and spending a nomadic year or two in the desert, taking pictures, prospecting, living the outlaw life. Your mother and I are going on the lam, he said. We'll start out at the territorial prison at Yuma, then out into the desert there, up past the Chocolate Mountains into Joshua Tree A year in the Mojave. Panamint Valley. Furnace Creek. Devil's Hole!

I said, What if you run out of gas, in the middle of nowhere? What if you break an axle or something? The sun could kill you.

Anything could kill me, he said. Something will for sure. He laughed without bravado, and the car rattled at unsafe speed across a narrow wooden bridge spanning nothing but dust, a long, dry riverbed. He was so careless that I wondered if he was really happy after all He turned and saw my face, and grinned, and for just a moment there was pity in it, and he was not my friend, but my father again. You'll get there, he said. (You'll get to where I am now.)

I spent much of that day standing on an imaginary brake My mother says he never was a very good driver. If I had complained, he would have slowed down right away. In his new expansive mood he would probably not even have been insulted. Yet it made sense (it still does) to take some risk with my own life, even my children's lives, rather than reproach my father.

▼ ▼ ▼ ▼ ▼ ▼ ▼

I didn't learn to drive until I was thirty-eight. My father couldn't teach me, though he was dead set on it. I wasn't interested. He was always yelling at me to concentrate, to get my long, straight hair out of my face so I could see in the rearview mirror. I ran an Esso tank truck off the road. My father backed down.

▼ ▼ ▼ ▼ ▼ ▼ ▼

In my teens I sat up front, next to him. He was always picking me up someplace. I waited at curbs, in front of office buildings, inside the houses of friends, watching out the front window. His car was always cutting through some obstacle to get to me—fog, rain, dark, traffic—I see it as a kind of animal, a fish, and my father at the wheel, an organic part of it. He was never late, though he often had to wait for me.

We had our most animated conversations in the car. Here was the ideal setting for talk between us. Here we could not look at each other. We listened and watched the scenery We talked about politics, morality, social change, always some abstract matter. (My mother and I talked about individual people and what made them tick.) He told good jokes and thought up terrible puns to make me groan.

These times were special to both of us. Special, that is, in a way that hung between us like a white, swollen cloud; special in a way that frightened, and made me (me, anyway) so sad that I was always turning to face the passenger window, to let sudden, irrational tears evaporate without falling. I did this so often that even now, when my husband drives, I become secretly emotional. Anything can set it off. I must imagine myself invisible there, in the passenger seat.

I thought that it all had to do with power, my father's over me. It would come to me, when he was arguing or asking about my job, that he could at any time make me sing a corny old song with him, or rap the back of my skull with his knuckles. This was false. Not merely unlikely, but false. But I couldn't see that, and I only half believe it even today. My father let go twenty-five years ago. I will hang on until the day I die.

▼ ▼ ▼ ▼ ▼ ▼ ▼

Here I am, then, at nineteen, back home for Christmas vacation. It's after midnight. I'm at the apartment of my first lover, Rudy, a downy-bearded counterculture twerp of twenty-two. Rudy is insignificant to me; he is something I have to do. I am damp from his shower, and still wet from him, and a little stoned. I stand in his dark, grubby kitchen, alone, watching out the window for my father.

Here comes that big old Ford, maroon and black vinyl I remember now, nosing through the fat flakes of an early blizzard like a faithful hound, and my father at the wheel. I float downstairs, across the snow, and the door swings open by its agreeable self. The dashboard is cheery with little red and green lights. We proceed in second gear, in silence, and there is nothing out there but blinding white snowflakes dancing in our headlights.

My father, too, has been out. Apparently he goes out a lot, and stays late. It does not occur to me, *it does not occur to me*, to wonder why. Lately he just asks me, when we're alone at the breakfast table, or in the TV room, if I'm going to Young Lochinvar's tonight, and would I like a ride home? and I say, Sure. What do I think he is doing out late at night, rolling home at one or two in the morning? Do I imagine he is working? drinking? moonlighting?

I think nothing, nothing at all. I am nineteen years old. My father is always picking me up someplace.

I'll never know who she was, or if there was more than one, or how much my mother knew, or how much it hurt her. The whole affair is opaque to me. How I admire them for that! They seem happy now. Sometimes I watch them, especially my mother, for some sign of moral advantage, or lifelong atonement. Whatever happened, it was grownup, front-seat business.

But *now*. Does he know how ignorant, how self-involved I am? He knows what I've been doing, though we pretend otherwise. Does he imagine, with me, his first daughter, an unspoken complicity, a companionship in sin? Does he therefore assume that at last we will be easy with each other?

On this night, the night of first snowfall, at Christmastime, in 1967, my father clears his throat in the dark. I'm sorry, he says.

80

What for? Suddenly so wary.

For whatever it was that I did, he says. Something went wrong a long time ago, he says, when you were little. In the Mesozoic. Your mother and I—

We're coming to a boulevard, but the brakes don't respond, and he calmly turns the wheel hard right and nuzzles us into a soft snowbank. We're stuck. Laughing like a kid, he puts the car in park and gets out. Take the wheel, honey, he says. You've got to rock it.

I am so glad for this reprieve that I welcome any responsibility, even this one, and there is my father bright in the headlights, blind and strong, and we hit a good rhythm right off, as though I am a real driver, and we have done this many times. I am competent I live, for these few minutes, in the present time, gratefully. Like a woman of forty, I put away history and worry for the pleasure of *now*. So this is one of the few perfect memories I will have of my young life. I will always be able to regain the sense of the car beneath me, rolling forward, straining back toward freedom, and the toasting breath of the heater, the smell of wet wool, and my father, still young, still lean, in white light.

Then we're free, and I move over for him. He stands outside his open door, knocking snow off himself. Thick crusts loosen from his coat and avalanche down in tall chunks. He is still laughing when he gets in. He says, Let's try that again, shall we? and we're in gear and heading home.

He is so happy this night, so easily delighted, and I can see that part of what delights him is our recent brush with calamity, the absurd almost-accident. To my mother, death and injury are only bad, near-misses only lucky. My mother never takes the longer view where we are concerned. But though he, too, would be destroyed if harm came to his children, still he has me in perspective, on this night. We are equals now. I am on my own in an unfair and unsafe place, and expected to see the loony side of it. And I do, because I am my father's daughter.

And so, with anything possible, and as though the past fifteen minutes never happened, he says, Your mother and I were your age, you know, when we got married. When you were born she wasn't even old enough to vote. Think about it, he says, inviting me to wonder, along with him, at what babies they had been, to have babies themselves. We wanted you to be the perfect child. Your mother says we were too hard on you.

No, I say. Don't be silly. Wow, it's really coming down now. Dad, do we have snow tires?

All I know is, I screwed up somewhere back then. Because when you were a real little kid, I couldn't do anything wrong in your eyes. Do you believe that? And then, all of a sudden it seemed, I couldn't please you to save my life. I don't know. I'd tell you if I knew. But I just want to say, that whatever it was—

Knock it off, Dad. I don't know either, and I don't care. That's just history, Dad.

Exactly, he says. I can hear the smile in my father's voice. That's exactly what I was about to say. It's all in the past. I can't change it. I would if I could, honey. He takes my hand from my lap and squeezes it hard, with fierce love, his eyes straight ahead on the slippery road. He has the right to do this. He relaxes his grip, allowing me to choose. You know I love you more than anything.

I know he does. And I take my hand away.

▼ ▼ ▼ ▼ ▼ ▼

I had understood how to hurt him since before I could read and write. He took it, my best shot, with grace, and said no more on the drive home. In a while he was humming softly, for his own benefit, a tune from the forties, when he and my mother were children in love

I never took less pleasure in my cruelty than on that night.

82

This was my bleak duty, as it was my father's to entreat forgiveness. It hurt me, as they say, more than it did him. In my grief, with my hand still warm, I thought that some day at least the mystery would clear and we would make peace with each other. We are at peace now, but the mystery survives, with my father's innocence, not guilt, at its foolish heart. If he had truly needed forgiveness we would be fighting still, to the death. And not mine. He was hopelessly overmatched, as fathers of women ought to be. (This is a very old story, the one about daughters and fathers. It ends in marriage, and the promise of renewal So it must be a comedy.)

My father hummed "Moonglow" and ferried us both through snow and ice toward Home, whether either of us wanted to go there or not; Home being where it always ends. He was a born driver, my father. Not a good driver, maybe, but born to it. Born to take me home safely, and then die, disappear, take up hobbies. How humble he was that night, and happy in his work! He turned off the boulevard into the neighborhood, where streets became inevitable, and their invariant sequence had an inane Mother Goose rhythm, and had long ago become the Family Poem He turned,

> Left on Seneca
> Right on McIntosh
> Straight past Mapleview
> Left at the light
>
> On past Alcott,
> Wildflower, Hillary,
> Left at the willow tree,

Home for the night, said my father.

And in a better world than this one, stopped at the willow

tree, backed from the driveway, took us to the boulevard, headed us west. We drove due west through a thickening storm, and then past the place it began, and angled south toward the place where winter itself began, and past that, at last, into the outlaw territory. We stopped where we wanted to, and when, and never spoke. We drove at night through endless desert, where there were no landmarks, and all perspectives were alike, and the air was so brutally pure that we cast shadows in starlight alone. And sometimes we sang together. And sometimes I drove, and my father slept, safely, in my care.

FATHER
OF
INVENTION

At the age of three she creates, for the first time, a better world than this one.

That is, this is the first time for *her*.

Maybe she was four. Certainly no younger than three. You have to be able to talk first. People need words to say. Words also help to anchor things so that they don't disappear on you, or shift shape. You can't have a gorilla one minute, and then a pirate king, and then your father, home from work. You can't make up a world that way.

"Better" world may not be quite right. "Alternative" is more accurate.

But "better" is better.

▼ ▼ ▼ ▼ ▼ ▼ ▼

At the age of three she is the harried mother of bad girls. Their names—Darla, Giggy, Ellemer—are useful mainly for listing, like the days of the week. Her daughters are beautiful and bad. They will not eat their soft-boiled eggs. They take dangerous risks and tell lies and break things with bold malice. They are defiant, nasty, and rude. She does not know what she did to deserve such children.

She really doesn't know. She is getting tired of them and often,

87

even though they have names, they disappear for long stretches of time.

She tells them: Wait till your father comes home.

She does not know who their father is.

She loves them only when their father is home and they are tucked in bed and she sits by them in the dark and sings them to sleep, while their father fills the doorway behind her. She can't see him, but he fills the doorway. She sings, in her true voice,

> Lover, when you're near me
> When you're near me honey honey
> Softly little baby
> Little girl.

▼ ▼ ▼ ▼ ▼ ▼ ▼

Then (age eight, maybe, or nine; the ages don't matter, except to the child; the ages don't matter to the woman) three men lie in the sand at her feet. They are trussed like chickens and they buck furiously and curse her through neckerchief gags. A cowboy in white rides toward her out of the sagebrush, kicking up a straight line of dust under the wide blue sky. "Whoa, Nellie. Whoa, girl." He jumps down from the still rearing horse. "What in tarnation—! I heard gunshots clear across the mesa!"

"Bandits," she says, and nudges one of them with her boot. "This one's got a flesh wound."

"Where's your family?"

"They killed my mommy and daddy," she says, trying not to cry. "I'm an orphan now."

"What's your name, little girl?"

"I'm not a little girl. My name is Claire Rose Stella Dagmar Elizabeth."

"That's a beautiful name." He takes off his big white hat "Give me the gun, little girl."

"Why should I?"

"Hand it over here right now, young lady." She turns and starts to run; she is going to do something dangerous. He grabs her around the waist and carries her kicking to his horse "You're coming with me!" She rides in front of him on the saddle. "I'm your daddy now," he says, "and don't you forget it!"

Sometimes he finds her in the Comanche Indian camp, bargains for her with Cochise, scrubs the buffalo grease off her face and body with harsh soap. They sit around the campfire with other cowboys and cattle drivers, and he plays the guitar, or someone else plays and she sits on his lap and they sing duets. "The Yellow Rose of Texas," "The Rose of San Antone." He is usually angry with her, because she is so brave and disobedient, and sometimes he spanks her, and she says she's sorry, but she never really is. They have many adventures. Each time in the end she saves his life, often by rescuing him from a lynch mob.

▼ ▼ ▼ ▼ ▼ ▼ ▼

Her name is Felicia Elizabeth Jamison and she has long fine jet black hair and a beautiful figure. She is much too young to run her own ranch, but she commands fifty surly, trail-hardened cowboys with her iron will and ingenuity. Also she associates with known outlaws, and the townspeople of Virginia City disapprove of her and try to throw her into jail She works part time in the Golden Slipper Saloon and wears a low-cut silver dress with black and white petticoats showing underneath. She sings and dances on top of the long mahogany bar and all the men go wild.

A family of brothers, four or five, who own the biggest and most prosperous ranch in the valley, befriend her and warn her about the murderous outlaws, and try to stop her from dancing in the saloon. They do not know this—that she does everything for a dark purpose: to avenge the death of her father. Also she has to run the ranch and work at the Golden Slipper so that she can become independently wealthy, because her family is gone, and she doesn't want to need anyone ever again. She has been too badly hurt. Her heart is stone.

She escapes from jail! Her cattle stampede! The dam breaks! Alone she turns the herd away from the flood, runs them hard just ahead of the thundering wall of water until at last it recedes. Exhausted she faints but does not fall. The ranch hands receive her in awed silence, lift her gently from the horse and carry her inside. She has earned their undying respect. At some point the outlaws learn that she is the daughter of the man they killed. They confront her after midnight in a bleak forest clearing and torture her. Though afraid she does not cry out, but works steadily on her bonds until she frees one hand, grabs a knife from the belt of one of them, and slashes them all to death, shrieking Murderer! Murderer!

Streaked with her own blood and the blood of the men she has killed, half crazy and in shock but fiercely determined, she staggers through the woods (owls hoot, coyotes yowl) and collapses on the brothers' doorstep. Inside is warm and firelit, gleaming with polished oak, and on the walls hang the hides of great animals. The brothers carry her to a massive bed and the oldest brother gently removes her dress, ignoring her mumbled protests, and treats her wounds. They make her stay with them. They all love her, especially the oldest one; she loves him, too, though she constantly opposes him and refuses to give up her own ranch or quit dancing in the saloon. Sometimes he happens on her bathing in a stream and hides her clothes. Once they plan to get married, but for some reason it doesn't work out. When she isn't fighting with the brothers she takes care of them and fights along-side them.

The part where she regains consciousness after her ordeal in the woods is always the same. She lies propped up painfully on her elbows. ("Don't move, lie still and rest." "I must. Don't you understand?") The brothers gather around her, some sitting on the ample bed; she speaks in a strained, weary monotone, her eyes lifeless.

Her story never varies: that her family came West on a wagon train; that something happened to her mother; that one day her father was standing on a footbridge spanning high cliffs and she was walking toward him; that she heard gunfire and saw her father slump, sag against the single rope railing; that she ran and ran as he lost his balance and his feet left the bridge floor, that she caught his hand in both of hers and held his full weight, suspended over air, as her shoulder muscles tore and her arms came out of their sockets; that she would have held on forever but he slipped from her, somehow, and fell away, his white face upturned, imploring, calling her name, and she watched until he was a pinpoint against the gray rocks below and finally disappeared. She cries, true tears, and cannot be consoled.

▼ ▼ ▼ ▼ ▼ ▼ ▼

Her name is Anne. Her last name doesn't matter, since she is in the wrong century, and even her kind of name is obsolete. She is, in a sense, the oldest living human being. Just before the car in which she was riding crashed and burned she was, through some kind of error, teleported into the future. Scientists on a distant planet, descendants of her contemporaries, confine her in a hospital. She is their laboratory subject. They are keenly interested in her because she illustrates the extent to which man has improved himself through planned evolution. Physically she is plainly inferior: though beautiful, her features are irregular (eyes a little too close together, face a shade too narrow; there is a small star-shaped mole on her left breast). Though young and healthy, her body is much smaller than the average, and significantly weaker. She has less than half the normal life expectancy and is not cancer-immune. What really excite the scientists, though, are her primitive mental and emotional characteristics.

Her mind is brilliant but undisciplined, her intelligence unspecialized, diffuse. She is prone to emotional disorders, especially depression. She is apparently, illogically, disgusted with herself and her new world. Hotshot academicians report their findings at intergalactic anthropoidologists' conventions, in bright white seminar rooms the size of football fields. They lecture using holographs (taken without her knowledge or consent), which show her pacing the contours of her sterile room, upsetting food trays, refusing to cooperate. They refer to three-dimensional graphs and X-rays. "Note particularly the disparate cerebral hemispheres; the right lobe shows *marked* something something something, possibly indicating an ancient, tenuous connection between something and something . . . irrational behavior patterns . . . not adaptable to productive life in present state . . .," and so forth.

The decision is made to modify her, to conform her to their standards, through a series of painless, mind-altering operations. But first they force her to view scenes that they have recorded in her own century, in a last-ditch attempt to shock her out of her depression. She sees her own funeral (everybody thought she was in the car), the mourners sobbing, unaware that here she is, still alive, a prisoner. She sees her mother's grave. She sees her father: querulous, senile, incontinent, indifferently tended by strangers.

This practically drives her insane with grief.

She escapes, stows away on a spaceship, a great big thing, labyrinthine. The captain discovers her and locks her up until they reach the next way station. (They are on a long-range exploratory mission.) She drinks heavily and does not eat or sleep.

She sits at one end of the long dining table at the officers' mess. At the other end the captain sits, and on both sides are communications officers, engineers, medical personnel, all in sleek dress uniforms, color-coded according to rank. She is exotic in frayed blue jeans and a T-shirt full of holes. She regards them coldly over the rim of her iridium snifter. What was it like, they want to know, to be alive in the mid-nineteen hundreds: a particularly savage era in human history. Yes, we were all savages, she tells them. We wore fur pelts and ate our young. She goes on like this, and eventually passes out and is carried to her room. The captain sits on her bed, brushes loose strands of unkempt golden hair away from her face, caresses her in troubled sleep. He decides not to put her off the ship after all. To keep her with him at any cost. She is so sad, so beautiful.

He gives her various jobs: tending the ship's extensive garden, helping out with the library, and so on. Everybody tries to make her feel necessary, but she can see through them. The prospect of being nothing more than a mascot, of living without purpose or function, is insupportable to her. She transports herself to a barren planet, and when they follow her she tries to kill herself, usually by jumping from a high place. The captain saves her, and beats her, and drags her back to the ship.

She becomes the captain's mistress, although she never experiences any strong feeling for him, or indeed for anyone else. She is loved, admired, enjoyed. She could not love the captain, really, as there is little about him to distinguish him from the others. He is just the one who loves her, and who forces her to live, and who punishes her for her stubborn refusal to believe that she is worthy of love, or respect. Her strangeness is forever a burden to her, a melancholy enchantment. Though unhappy, at least she is not bored, because their mission takes them to dangerous, unknown places.

▼ ▼ ▼ ▼ ▼ ▼ ▼

She arrives at the office early. The outer door is still locked, but once inside she sees that Mr. Hathaway is already here. The translucent glass of his closed door is bright with artificial light. She fixes him a mug of black coffee, knocks routinely before pushing open the door, screams! (the cup bounces on thick carpeting, splattering her ankles with scalding coffee) at the sight of him hanging, turning, somehow suspended from the ceiling (his belt, his tie), his face and protruding tongue purple-blue, the highly polished toes of his black shoes pointing down, inches above the mahogany desktop. She sags against the doorframe, shields her eyes. "Oh, you poor bastard."

Behind her she hears Miss Warden's brisk morning footsteps. "Oh, he's in. Let me just—"

She pushes the old woman back, slams the door behind her. "Don't go in there. Call the police." (Somehow she is not surprised. Such a cold, remote, unsmiling man.)

▼ ▼ ▼ ▼ ▼ ▼ ▼

She has come into a lot of money and has used most of it to renovate an old warehouse in downtown Manhattan into a kind of nightclub. She employs excellent young rock and folk musicians. Often she performs with them, singing and dancing, and while not really talented, she has an ironic and witty presence; her audience appreciates that she performs out of generosity and daring; that there is nothing at stake when she performs. With the rest of her money, and with her profits, she is able to let the club double as a home for lost kids (runaways, misfits, delinquents) whom she hires in various capacities. They have their own rooms

94

in the loft and plenty of money, so that they won't have to steal or prostitute themselves, and to the extent that they allow her to mother them, she does. There is Jack, a black ex-junkie, the oldest, who holds himself aloof and hides behind an impassive mask, but who for reasons of his own is always there, always reliable. And Angelica, a vacuous, amoral little girl whom she tolerates, she supposes, because she is so pretty and her behavior so amusingly transparent. And sweet, bashful Jimmy, the stutterer. And Rudolph, who is searching for a handsome prince ("*Toujours gai* is my motto, kid") but meantime settles for motorcycle crazies and paunchy, sad-eyed truck drivers. And many others, every one of them distinct and intricately made. Especially there is Beano (no one knows his real name; Jimmy suggested "Beano" and it stuck), a retarded man in his thirties or forties, placid, moon-faced, trusting. A balding angel. She finds him early one morning in the alley behind The Warehouse, peeing against the brick wall, his pants around his ankles. He is more startled than she: he says "Uh oh," his mouth a perfect O in his bland pink face. He hobbles away from her, without the sense to pull his pants up, and shakes his head back and forth ("I'm in big trouble now!") and she catches up with him, laughing, takes him inside, cleans him up and feeds him, and gives him work to do. He is in charge of the broom. Every morning he sweeps out the rooms upstairs, and every evening he sweeps the club spotless after closing time. Beano is really as much of a unifying force as she. He is everybody's baby.

Her lover is a police lieutenant, a hulking, taciturn man of Russian descent. He is honorable, incorruptible, but dangerous and tough and quick-tempered. There is a long, puckered knife scar on his left thigh, another much uglier scar on his left shoulder, from a bullet wound, wide and deep enough to accommodate the tips of two fingers, the tip of a tongue; the ring finger of his right hand ends at the first joint, sliced off clean. His body is heavily muscled, fleshy, with a stevedore's massive shoulders and rounded back. On his chest is a luxurious pelt of black and gray and white.

She visits him in his small, sparsely furnished apartment on the Upper West Side. There is no question of her moving in, although occasionally she spends the night. He has a fraying, comfortably sprung sofa, a battered coffee table, a handsome old bookcase with glass doors, half-filled with ragged, leather-bound classics, and on the bottom shelf a carved teakwood box containing photographs, of his parents, brave, grim-faced young immigrants, of his many brothers and sisters, of his children from a failed marriage, all grown now; an ancient gas stove, Philco refrigerator, heavy iron pots, canisters of coffee beans and herbs, pint jars of wild thyme honey, tiny jars and cans of exotic spices; and in the bedroom no curtains, nothing on the pale green walls, no carpet; two bureaus, cheap and functional; a steel-frame single bed.

They never go out. They have little to say to each other. His dominion over her is total within these walls. Outside, her life is her own. She takes care of the people at the club; he takes care of her. If he is ever brutal, even vicious, it is her doing. They understand this.

She sits at one end of the old couch, her slippered feet propped on the coffee table. He lies asleep along the length of the couch, his head cradled in her lap. He looks tired. Grave. Disappointed. In her? Or is he dreaming? And how can she ever know, when he is only . . .

Oh, how she wants.

She brushes his forehead with her fingertips, her dry lips. He smells of honey, tobacco, and horses. She lets her head fall back, closes her eyes. Sleeps.

(And remembers a story she read when she was very young, really young, still young, about a woman who spent all her time in front of mirrors. Her house glittered with fabulous mirrors of

96

every description. Gold-leafed Sheratons, girandoles with candle sconces, Chinese Chippendales. And one night, when she was pirouetting before them in a long white dress, she danced right inside a cheval glass and was never seen again. She wonders why this story ever frightened her.)

▼ ▼ ▼ ▼ ▼ ▼ ▼

The time is now, and with two vivid exceptions there is not much to choose between the worlds. She does not know how this happened. One world is slightly more hilarious, and populated, occasionally, with famous, challenging people. But mostly she sees there people she truly knows, true friends, true enemies. She just sees them more often, that's all. And in more brilliant circumstances. Sometimes the police lieutenant drops by, but she can never get him to stay for long. Not a very bright man, really. Not interesting. His brooding, humorless face makes her sad. Like running across an old friend selling Fuller brushes. Or a ghostly dinosaur.

Still, she would have kept him with her, if she could.

▼ ▼ ▼ ▼ ▼ ▼ ▼

And yet, here is this ridiculous *airplane*, which is *going down*. Sick, sputtering engine sounds, fire on the wings, screams. Men and women screaming. Should she be screaming too? Not if she has to think about it. The ending of a pointless life hardly calls for such display. Delayed stillbirth. She keeps her eyes wide open, looks left and right, back and front, at fellow passengers, at gaily colored airborne flight bags, at the uprushing ground, registering everything. This much at least she will experience in full.

Somehow they are safely down, but not safe: everywhere flames and thick smoke from burning plastic. She is nervous but knows better than to battle for the exits, so she sits, as if in a theater when the movie ends, and watches through acrid haze as the others scramble and scuffle and tumble. No class, no style. There's a woman with her elbow in an old man's eye.

Everyone is gone and it's her turn now, which is a good thing, as she is starting to panic. Fire has spread to much of the carpeting and upholstery. She coughs, breathes through a paper napkin. Almost free, she crouches in the emergency exit, at the summit of an inflated yellow chute. In the distance she can see people running toward the shelter of the terminal. She'd better hurry. But then (whimpers, wails, angry infant squall) she is not the last after all, there are all these *children!* Children! abandoned, every-where she looks, pinned under twisted armrests, piles of fallen suitcases. Furious naked baby in the luggage rack!

To the survivors in the terminal she is an oddly shaped dark speck against the background of the burning silver plane. A human being, they realize. A woman, running with bulky parcels. Drop them, you idiot! No, wait, those aren't—children! My babies! She'll never make it, it's going to blow! Stay back, She's on her own, Come on, Lady!!!

Live TV coverage (how?), wild cheering. *Great* background music. The news story of the century. "Graphic Message of Hope for a Dispirited World." Talk shows? Movie rights?

No. She hobbles, loaded down with children. She sails, buoyant with children. One under each arm, one hanging on in back, baby in a sling around her neck. Somebody's *pet dog*, released from its carry-case, yapping at her feet. She runs on silly high-heeled shoes, pumps poorly muscled, sooty legs; thin silk skirt bunched high between her thighs; reddened, sweaty face distorted with effort. A ludicrous figure, grotesque, foreshortened through the rippling heat. She has never been so happy. If she lives she will tell them only, I am grateful. How lucky I am, to have had this chance! And *then*, to have done the right thing! How lucky I am, and silly, and so happy.

98

▼ ▼ ▼ ▼ ▼ ▼ ▼

And, at the same time, a small crowd has formed on the twilit city street. At its center lies an old, old man, emaciated under layers of Salvation Army coats. His head and hands are caked with layers of dirt and filth. Wens and scabs cover his hairless, unprotected scalp. One dirty yellow eye is almost obscured by a livid, knobby growth. He smells so terrible that people move away or edge back in according to the direction of the shifting wind. He moves his arms and legs feebly, and from his throat comes a low, liquid rattling. It is bitter cold. Whatever is wrong with him he won't last much longer this way. Someone drops a woolen scarf over him, hastens back to the circle. Someone leaves to call an ambulance. The crowd whispers. Disgusting old wino, Isn't that awful, Somebody's baby once.

She steps forward, reluctant. No choice, though. Nothing brave about this: she must. She kneels beside him, gags, hovers above him until she is accustomed to the stench. Foul reek of sick breath, excrement, ancient sweat. She lifts his head, nestles it on her lap. Her leg, bent awkwardly under her, scrapes against icy cement. He speaks: her name? She can't quite tell. Honey? Honey? I'm right here. His hands scrabble at her coat front. She lets it fall open, admitting bitter cold. His frozen fingers work the buttons of her blouse. His yellow eyes are avid, bright. He coughs with frustration. Sighing she opens her blouse and frees one breast. The nipple blooms in the freezing wind. He can raise his head by himself, but she must bend low to let him feed. He is toothless. His crusty lips abrade her skin. His eyes are shut tight, oozing milky tears. Maybe he isn't really dying. Wouldn't that be funny. If he winked at her and gave her a pinch, Gotcha, Little Girl. What difference would it make? She spreads her coat out, sheltering them both together, cups the bony skull in her hands, and rocks him, humming Moonglow.

The crowd is gone, the street empty, silent.
No one sees this:
A nameless old man and a childless, middle-aged woman, an
unremarkable woman, slowly rocking, crooning nonsense, achiev-
ing some kind of peace.

—▲—
ANTICIPATORY GRIEF
—▼—

When her father died he was fifty-one, and her mother fifty, and her husband fifty-four, and she was twenty-nine. Her father was a charmer, immature, monumentally self-centered, an irresponsible, forgetful promiser, a good and honorable man. All his life he sold the products of Ralston Purina, Stokely-Van Camp, and the Mason Jar Company to the grocery stores of southern California. He knew the names of all the managers of all two hundred seventy-eight stores in his region, he knew their wives' names and the ages of their children. He believed in his products, and liked his customers, and never did anything underhanded. "Which is why," Rebecca's mother often said, "the company does such good business. Your father doesn't cheat on his taxes or offer bribes, or deceive people, ever. Your father is an unusual man." Rebecca's mother inspired both her children with pride in family, in both its history and its living members, and as a child Rebecca believed her father to be a figure of legendary accomplishments. "My father has integrity," she told her friends at school. "My father can charm the birds out of the trees." Long before he died, of course, she knew he was not really so extraordinary.

He had just sat down to supper. "I feel funny, Martha," he said. Her mother's back was to him—she was at the counter pouring tea into two glasses of ice—and when she turned around he was

JENNY AND THE JAWS OF LIFE

on his feet, bent forward, massaging his left shoulder; he fell to the floor before she could move, and he was dead by the time she got to him. This much she told her children, and no more; nothing of what she said, or did. She may have rocked him in her arms. She waited for some time after the ambulance left before calling them: Charlie, who lived down the street, and Rebecca, her first-born, a continent away.

▼ ▼ ▼ ▼ ▼ ▼ ▼

Rebecca lay in the yellow bathtub, her hair pinned up to keep it dry. She was thinking of nothing in particular. She lifted the cake of Ivory soap from the water and held it under her nose, enjoying the smell; she drew letters and spiral designs on its waxy white surface with her fingertips.

"Hello," said Simon, poking his head around the shower curtain, and then he stepped into the tub, long and naked and graceful, and sat down cross-legged at the faucet end.

She drew up her legs to accommodate him. "Hello," she said, idly stroking his bony calves with her big toe. "You sure are pretty," she said, and to her he was, although she spoke this time out of habit, her mind unengaged.

He soaped himself vigorously, methodically, splashed his face with water cupped in his long hands. "The Celtics blew it in the last minute," he said.

She rolled her eyes and flopped around in a parody of shock.

"Smell my foot," he said, sticking his big pink foot in her face.

"Smell this," she said, and the phone began to ring as her foot cleared the water. Only cranks called after midnight. "Obscene phone call," she said, "It's for you."

He arose dripping, with a sigh and a smile, grabbed a towel and went into the bedroom. He was so good to her. "Yes, Martha," she heard him say, and she was on her feet.

"Is it Charlie or Dad?" She stood next to him, shivering; he balanced the receiver between ear and shoulder and wrapped his towel tight around her, tucking in one edge to hold it in place.

He listened, his face expressionless. "Martha," he said, "I'll put her on. She's right here."

He handed the phone to her. "It's about your father," he said. His gray eyes watched her; he was waiting for a sign.

"Is he dead, Mom?" She regarded her husband unblinking, proud, as she listened to her mother's calm voice. After hanging up she asked him, "Do you want to fly out with me?" and heard with small surprise the pleasant, almost musical sound of her question. He nodded, and took her by the shoulders and shook her a little, very gently; he smiled and his face was full of love.

While he made plane reservations, and arranged for someone to take his classes for the next week, she packed, deliberating brightly over each article. It's warm out there in December, she thought; we won't need heavy coats. She packed his good gray three-piece suit, and white shirt with blue pinstripes, and wrapped his shoes in plastic bags. For herself she chose a dark green woolen dress that she never wore because they both thought it dowdy. She folded nightgowns, blue jeans, blouses, underwear, with uncharacteristic precision, stacked and restacked everything in the suitcase in quest of the optimum arrangement. She filled his battered old toilet kit with shampoo, toothpaste and brushes, razor and soap. She glided smoothly through the apartment; her body felt light and well oiled. "Do you think you'll want to swim? In the pool? I'll pack your suit."

He shook his head no, his eyes a little wary, as he waited for someone to confirm their reservation. He held a pencil poised above a note pad, a column of times. He looked his full age, sitting there on the edge of the bed, watching her, all the lovely creases in his face deep hollows in the dim light.

105

She hurried to the dining room closet and pulled a Filene's box down from the top shelf. "Open this," she said, as he hung up the phone.

"We're flying out at 7:30 this morning, with connections in New York and Chicago."

"Go on, open it. I got it for you for Christmas, but it's just a little present, and I want you to have it now." He lifted off the cover and revealed beige pajamas with light blue piping on the collar, nestled in white tissue paper.

She sat down beside him. "See, they're just like those old ones you had that frayed through in the seat."

"Very nice," he said, and did not look at her

"I want to pack them. All your old pj's are so ratty-looking."

He lowered the box to the floor. "Oh, honey," he said.

Untying her terry robe she lay back on the bed behind him. It took him too long to turn his head and see what she had done. A quarter second would have been too long, so abrupt was her need of him. She pulled him down, filled with the sense of her own selfishness. She gripped him, she mauled him, and he seemed a small and sacrificial thing, a long thin animal, pale-skinned, defenseless. This is shock, she thought with some satisfaction, proud of her body's capacity for textbook response, and of her ability to recognize it; she had read that death often produces such reactions. But her desire was too sharp; it raced through her in stingy narrow stabs, unconnected to him and scarcely connected to her, it made her frantic, inhuman, and ugly: she gathered him to her and into her and through her like an implacable machine. She could not be satisfied; he held still, finally, resisting her in silence, to tell her this; and she subsided. She lay beneath him, her head turned away from his pitying regard. It had been the proper thing to do, the one perfect thing to do, and she resented his failure to take her where she needed to be. She thought, I could have cried then, I could be crying right now, and he comforting me, and we would be together now, and not like this.

▼ ▼ ▼ ▼ ▼ ▼ ▼

It was late afternoon of the funeral day. Rebecca stood in her mother's golden kitchen, in a broad ray of orange sunshine, washing dishes and glasses with tireless efficiency. The guests had all left, well fed and well impressed with the dignity and competence of the two women. Her father's business partner had given her brother an awkward embrace in farewell: "Take good care of them, Charlie," he said, when it must have been clear to all that Charlie was the one who needed tending. He looked more than ever like his father, she thought, tall, long-limbed, and frail now, weak from crying. She had always loved her brother. Even when they were children he had seemed to her innocent, and herself corrupt and wise. As far back as memory went she had known when the truth would serve, and when was the best time for silence or a lie, and he knew nothing of the arts of tact and subtle manipulation. He had his father's instinctive charm and none of his mother's patient reserve and detached analytic curiosity.

Rebecca had grown up believing that all men were optimists, credulous and clear-eyed and in need of vigilant protection; she and her mother had always known that some day the axe would fall, had squirreled away part of themselves for just such a moment as this. She was proud of her mother, and never more so than today: they had stood on either side of Charlie, beside the open grave, gripping his hands in their cold ones; had borne him through the worst of it, so that the three stood erect and proud; and Simon had seen it all.

When she turned off the faucet and wiped down the counters and stove top she heard the men's low voices in the living room.

Her mother was resting. Evidently Simon, who during the past three days had moved among them like a benign ghost, correct, discreet, was now with her brother. She listened to the faint reverberation of their alternating voices, her husband's moderate tenor, the deeper husky tones of her brother. It must be hell for Simon, she thought—he was as self-contained, as private as she; more so, in fact; he would hate to witness such unashamed display. Unlike her mother she had married a man much like herself, exactly like she wanted to be. Rather than complementing her he provided her with a standard to work toward, perhaps to surpass. From the beginning she valued his strengths, and saw that she must either seize advantage of them—let him take responsibility for her, as he was inclined to do—or reject the shelter they offered and so strengthen herself. She chose to be his equal.

The conversation stopped. She stood for a minute listening, then straining for the barest sound. Unable to contain her curiosity, and intending to extricate Simon, she walked to the living room door. Simon held her brother in a tight, one-armed embrace; her brother's chest rose and fell with dry sobs, his face was pressed against his hand; she could not see her husband's face, turned away from her as it was, toward her weeping brother. There was nothing stilted or formal or embarrassed about the embrace. He comforted Charlie simply, naturally, with straightforward generosity. She could not bear the sight. She steadied herself against the doorjamb, recovering balance; then stepped back, and briskly away, and they disappeared.

▼ ▼ ▼ ▼ ▼ ▼ ▼

Her mother looked very young, lying curled up on the pale yellow comforter, in the middle of their new bed, a huge low rectangle that half filled the bedroom. Maybe it was the room itself that made her look that way: she had recently

108

redecorated—they had planned, she told Rebecca, to make the whole house over—and the walls and carpet were an even paler yellow, almost white; and on the two marble-topped nightstands stood deep burgundy vases filled with daisies. Except for the bed, it was a young girl's room. Her mother opened her eyes and smiled, like a young girl, at Rebecca standing in the doorway. "I'm not sleeping," she said.

Rebecca picked up an old wedding picture from the bureau and sat down beside her mother. "He was awfully skinny, wasn't he? You always said he was handsome, but I think he got much better looking than this." The picture was not as yellow as the walls. Her parents smiled shyly at her, foolish and happy. "You haven't changed much." This was a lie; she was softer now, and plump, and her wispy golden hair was cut short.

"He looks a little like Simon there," her mother said.

"I don't see that at all." She lay the picture on the nightstand.

"You know, your father liked Simon very much. A couple of years ago, when you phoned and told us about him, he was a little upset. 'Why, he's my age,' he said. 'What the hell does she want to marry an old man for?' Well, he liked him right off when you brought him out here. Liked him the minute he saw him. You know your father."

" 'A man's character is written all over his face. You just have to learn how to read it.' "

"Actually, I think he got to like the idea, too, of Simon's age. When he stopped to think about it, he took it as a compliment."

"He took everything as a compliment." They laughed, and Rebecca briefly squeezed her mother's cold hand. They had always been so easy together. Touching was never important to either of them. It was their men who were affectionate; the men had more literal minds.

"I'm taking it very well," her mother said. "I surprise myself."

"It's horrible. It's the worst thing that could have happened."

"No. If it had been me, leaving him . . that would have been worse." She pushed herself up into a half-sitting position, resting her head on her crooked-back arm. "And if he had to die, I'm glad he went this way."

"For his sake, yes. But you had no time to prepare. Sudden death is always—"

"Prepare," her mother said. "How would I have done that, I wonder." She spoke softly, with her eyes closed, as she often did when she was tired or had a migraine. "I have heard there are people, doctors, who specialize in grief, who claim that when you know someone is dying, you begin to grieve right away. The more you grieve beforehand, the less you will afterwards. You give yourself a kind of credit, I guess.

"Imagine," she said, "being a grief specialist." There was a long silence. She opened her eyes and regarded her daughter without any expression at all. Her stare chilled Rebecca. But then she relaxed into a slow smile.

"What are you thinking about?"

"About when you were a baby, and we were afraid there was something the matter with your legs because you weren't walking, and then we found out you were practicing secretly in your room."

"I just wanted to get it right." This was one of Rebecca's favorite stories

"Oh, yes. And then that Sunday when we had all those people over to the house, and you decided to go public—just got up and walked across the floor, just as nonchalant as you please. I never saw your father laugh so hard." She grinned, and pain skittered across her face.

"I love you."

"Is anything wrong between you and Simon? You don't seem close somehow."

"Everything's fine." The question shocked her. It wasn't like her mother to pry. And there was nothing wrong, she was just cold. These were cold times. She stood up. "Try to sleep," she said, and walked to the door, and turned around. "Mother? Are you all right?"

"No," her mother said.

▼ ▼ ▼ ▼ ▼ ▼ ▼

Rebecca broke at the last minute. An hour later and she and Simon would have been boarding their plane at San Diego International. In retrospect, the timing of it provided her with still further evidence of her own amazing competence.

Her mother was already at the garage, starting the car; Rebecca, Simon, and Charlie roamed the house making a last-minute check to see if they had left anything behind. She went into the yellow bedroom for a brief glance around and suddenly felt her knees turn weak. It's coming, she thought, with perfect certainty, though she had had no idea what form it would take. She stared at the wedding picture, held it straight out in front of her, and this helped; soon she could not see his features for the tears. Good, she said to herself, here I go, but then it was not good; pain appeared, flared out with astonishing power, with the force of nausea. She clapped her hand tight over her mouth and shook with fear and the worsening pain, and when Simon found her she was pacing the room in panic, fighting it, on the edge of it; and when she saw him standing close by, his arms extended toward her, she exploded into rage: "Look at this," she hissed at him, pointing at the huge yellow bed, feeling her face and body harden, contort, and was fueled by the sense of her own ugliness and utter irrationality: "Look at it! She has to sleep there! Look at it!" She pounded her thighs with the knuckles of her clenched hands. He caught her, and she did break then, and in her last act

111

of will wrenched away from him and ran through the house until she found her brother. With profound humiliation and crazy spite and sincere generous impulse she gave her little brother this gift, the awful spectacle of her grief And she cried at last for her poor father, a good man, silly and self-important, fragile, human; because his death was such a cheat; because of the ignominy of his last words, of his death fall to the kitchen floor; she cried out of pity, and because she would miss him, and because she would not miss him more. Then she let Simon take her to the car, and slept on the way to the airport, and all the way home.

▼ ▼ ▼ ▼ ▼ ▼ ▼

A month went by before she was conscious of the strain between them, so eagerly did she submerge herself in the December holidays, and in newfound enthusiasm for thesis work, an ambitious project she had abandoned the year before. Full of nervous energy, she did the Christmas shopping for both of them, ranging through department stores and specialty shops, agonizing over every purchase. She was as pleased with her final selections, and with the elaborate dishes she prepared for him, as she would have been about the success of far weightier enterprises. She was fascinated with minutiae, she fairly hummed with content, like a well-tended motor, until she realized that Simon was unhappy.

He was sleeping far too much. He napped when he came home from school, and often for an hour or more after dinner, and always on Saturday afternoons, and Sundays after their morning country walks. He was always lying down. "Something's the matter with you," she said, the instant she recognized it, jogging him awake with her voice. "Are you sick? Don't you think you should see a doctor?" She made some attempt to appear solicitous, but really she was furious. She knew him; withdrawal from her was his way of reproach, his only way, though he had never done it

112

on such a grand scale before. "Do you know you've been doing this for weeks—just sleeping, like a lump? I've been worrying about you." "Have you," he said, a sardonic mumble, and he was asleep again, before she could say, "God, you annoy me sometimes." It was the old game, guess your offense, and this time at least she was innocent.

Simon didn't withdraw to make her feel guilty. Simon, she knew, was never petty. Rather, he had always and consistently refused to insult her and demean himself by articulating the obvious. If the offense was not apparent to her he would wait until she saw it for herself, and corrected it, or defended it, and he never expected apologies. He was older, and more patient; he could always outwait her; and he was rarely, if ever, unreasonable.

In the face of his gentle supine rebuke she could not sustain her December sense of purpose, and dropped into immediate and serious depression, a state that she had, she saw, been avoiding by means of mindless enthusiasm and activity; the inevitable cost of her family's tragedy. She wrapped herself in mourning; she grew as dependent upon its habits, as comfortable with its routine, as does an invalid with his favorite quilt. Now she slept as much as Simon—noticed this, too, with no small satisfaction. She attended to their needs perfunctorily. She shut him out on purpose, making her intentions clear. Their home fell under siege. They did not speak of it.

She cried a great deal, thinking sometimes of her father, prodded by sudden recollections of happy times, more often of childhood misunderstandings, broken promises on both sides; thinking sometimes of nothing at all, crying like rain. She cried soundlessly in the bathroom, with the door locked. Once Simon tried the door; she watched the brass knob rotate once clockwise, once counterclockwise; he stood outside saying nothing; watching, she was bitterly offended. Many nights she left their bed, stealthy

113

and wide awake, and cried in the spare room, secure beneath the cheap, garish coverlet of the cheap and narrow bed.

Until one night in late March he woke her there; she had fallen asleep and awakened to harsh light and the snap of a switch, and he stood over her, gray, hopeless, strange. "I can't stand it any more," he said.

She had, for the first time ever, outwaited him. He looked tired and sick; she saw at once that she had done this to him, and was frightened. "I'm sorry," she said, choosing her words with care, "I just get blue sometimes. I don't want to bother you, so I come in here."

"I don't believe that, and neither do you. You can't be that stupid."

She had not looked at him in so long. She became conscious of a tiny horror, steadily growing, as a parent must feel when, emerging from glorious rage, he sees blood and bruises on his only child. "Look," she said, sitting up, keeping her voice calm, "we're too alike. We've always known about this problem. When things go wrong between us, which doesn't happen often, we take forever to come out of it."

The spare room was functional, impersonal, like a motel room, only worse: cartons were stacked in corners, bedspreads and curtains were ill-matched castoffs, and on the walls she had absently hung trite prints, faded calendars. They deserved better than this room, sitting in this room at this most terrible hour of night. She caressed his shoulder. He was still warm. "This has been a bad time for me. I'm sorry I haven't taken it very well." He did not return the caress.

"Do you want to tell me now why you're angry with me?" he said. She didn't answer, keeping her eyes down. "This started the minute your mother called."

"You never liked him," she said, almost blurting it out. It might

114

be the true explanation. It made sense. "That time I brought you out to meet my family you were bored, terribly polite. You acted like a goddamn aristocrat." She managed anger. "Because he liked Mantovani records, and golf, and none of them are educated. I don't come from class, like you, you made me ashamed of him. . ." Simon sighed with disgust and left her there. She followed him into the bedroom. "I don't mean I blame you, you didn't do it on purpose. It's just that naturally I resented you a little when . . . when he died." This was so obviously a lie that she watched without protest as he got into bed and turned his back to her.

"What is it?" she cried, climbing in beside him, hovering over him. "Tell me now. I can't stand any more either. I'm scared."

"Rebecca," he said finally, calling her by name for the first time in years. "You can stand anything. But you can't control it all." And after a while he said, in a dry voice, devoid of sympathy, "Winter's over now. Three months wasted. That's three months gone."

She let him sleep then, or perhaps he lay awake too. She gave herself up at last to honest mourning, to frank despair, and of course he could not help her. She had killed him in her mind a thousand times, and he had watched her do it.

▼ ▼ ▼ ▼ ▼ ▼ ▼

The next morning, Sunday morning, was sunny and warm. She could see it was warm from the soft blurred edges of the shadows outside, the powder-blue sky. False spring, she thought, without hope. But they left for their Sunday walk as usual, on schedule, with a minimum of discussion, and drove to an old favorite place, an Audubon sanctuary a half hour from home.

They had never come here this early in the year. The oaks, maples, and birches were bare, and the blackberry bushes, and there were still large patches of grainy snow in the thickest part of the woods. But the evergreens were lush in contrast, their damp needles giving way pleasingly underfoot, and song sparrows and fat, handsome chickadees broke the clean silence with friendly buzzes and high, thin pipings. Simon walked ahead of her on the trail, setting her an easy, loping pace. She followed, hands in pockets, though it was not cold, looking occasionally left and right, seeing little. They covered a mile this way, effortlessly, without a false turn or an unnecessary word. They moved as gracefully together as they always had, only their silence now was not companionable. It is terrible, she thought, how the bodies move so well in their old accustomed patterns, undirected.

And with this thought, the thought of bodies, she wanted him. At first it was a mere idea, but almost at once her body took it up, sang with it, with marvelous urgency. She had not wanted him since the night her father died, and that dark frantic desire was only the faintest shadow of this. He was stopped a few yards ahead of her, gazing through binoculars at the top of a far-off maple. He stood bent forward, back straight, one long sneakered foot propped weightlessly on a moss-covered rock; the elbows of his old red flannel shirt were frayed through in ragged circles, revealing chapped pink skin. He might have been a young man, except that slender shafts of light, filtered through pine, exposed the fine leather of his neck and ears, the eggshell skull beneath thinning, charcoal hair; a wise innocent, he was; an aging faun. A passing crow sounded alarm, but he did not hear; and she laughed silently at the thought of her own menace. She opened her mouth to tell him but could not speak; she was shy of him; alive for the first time in so long, she could not take the risk. So when he moved forward, leaving the yellow-marked trail for the blue one that would lead in another mile to the water, she followed, keeping her own counsel by a desperate act of will. She tracked him through damp sunny clearings and shaded snow, past holly trees and silver birches and thickets of mountain laurel. Utterly distracted, single-minded, she stalked him, and saw herself an absurd ungainly animal, like a great lovesick bird who, on account of some tragic nestling misapprehension, desires only impossible union, outside its own species. Halfway to the water she knew she must tell him, and searched, left and right, hanging back and catching up again, for a place they could go. She looked for a pine needle bed, but all secluded spots were ruined with white crust. And when she finally found a spot—a large flat rock set somewhat back from the trail, not too visible, with only a thin film of snow upon it—and drew a deep breath to call for him, she heard voices, high, excited giggles and a sharp answering baritone, a father and son, somewhere nearby. And still she would have dared, on the rock, anywhere, if she could just have determined where the people were, and in what direction they were heading. But there were so many trails, yellow, blue, green, and red, coinciding here, diverging there, circling and crossing one another. The voices receded and returned, sometimes with startling clarity, as she shadowed Simon through the maze. Finally she hung back for a full minute, deciding to disappear for a time into the woods alone and take care of herself. Her skin was feverish, she breathed in shallow gasps. But out of sight of him her body saw no point to it. A degree of reason came to her as she wandered toward her goal, just enough reason to discourage, not enough to calm; and with a sigh she turned back and headed down the trail.

She came upon him at the marsh's edge. He knelt in high grass, binoculars trained on white specks sitting on the water far away down the shoreline. He was absorbed and happy, his face relaxed in an unguarded smile. The sun was at his back: his smile was real. He smiled at what he saw, and with simple momentary pleasure in the warm morning of a false spring. He was an optimist,

117

like Charlie and her father, but with a rare intelligence somewhere at the source of his durable hope. She knelt beside him, silent, on fire, and he turned to her for a brief look, smiling, agreeable, put the binoculars in her hands, saying, "Look over here. Egrets. Is that possible this time of year?" And at his touch she broke, came sweetly apart, staring down at a velvet oval of forest-star moss, a bright green constellation in miniature; and she leaned lightly against his shoulder for support, to steady her rocking, while he scanned the shoreline, unaware; and after a time she raised the glasses to her eyes, to search with him for what could only, after all, be herring gulls.

THE
BEST
OF
BETTY

Dear Betty:

I'm only forty-two years old and already going through the Change. I tried for twenty years to get pregnant and now I never will. Also, I get horrible cluster migraines now. The worst ones feel like a huge tarantula is clamped to my head with his legs sticking into my eyes and ears, and I have to scream with the pain. Next Tuesday I'm going to have all my teeth pulled, because the hormones have rotted my gums. I'm forty-two years old and for the rest of my life I'm going to sleep with my teeth in a glass by the bed. I hate being a woman. I hate my life. I hate Iowa. If I didn't believe in hell I'd kill myself.

Hopeless in the Heartland

Dear Hopeless:

What's the question?

Sorry, Readers. It's broken record time again. (1) Seek the aid of a competent therapist or clergyman; (2) Keep busy; (3) Above all, don't think about yourself so much; because (4) WHINING DOESN'T ADVANCE THE BALL.

For starters, Hopeless, why don't you rewrite this letter; only instead of cataloguing your complaints, include everything you have to be grateful for. You'll be amazed at how well this works.

121

Dear Betty:

Calling all Tooth Fairies! Don't throw away your kids' teeth! Save them up until you have a good third cupful, then scatter them around your tulip beds come spring, and you won't lose one bulb to marauding squirrels. Scares the dickens out of them, I guess!

Petunia

Dear Petunia:

I guess it would! Thanks for another of your timely and original gardening tips.

Dear Betty:

Lately, at parties, my husband has started calling me "Lard-bottom." I know he loves me, and he says he doesn't mean anything by it, but he hurts me terribly. Last night, at the bowling alley with some of his trucker buddies, he kept referring to me as "Wide Load." Betty, I cried all night.

We're both big fans of yours. Would you comment on his cruel behavior? He'd pay attention to you. Tell him that I may have put on weight, but I'm still a

Human Being

Dear Human:

Yes, a human being with an enormous behind. Sorry, Toots. If I read correctly between the lines, hubby's worried sick about your health. Try a little self-control. Quit stuffing your face.

Dear Betty:

Last winter my sister and I moved out here to Drygulch, Arizona, for her health. She's doing well, but I've developed tic douloureux, of all things, and the spasms are unpredictable and

122

agonizing. Our nearest doctor is fifty miles away, as is, for that matter, our nearest neighbor. I can't help feeling I'd be better off in Tucson or Phoenix, near a large medical center, but my sister, who's quite reclusive, says that if we moved her emphysema would just kick up again. Should we split up? Do I have the right to leave her, on account of a disease which, though painful, is not life-threatening?

Dolorous in Drygulch

Dear Dolorous:

Why not join a tic douloureux support group? If there isn't already one in the area, why not start one? (The company might bring Sis out of her shell!)

Dear Betty:

Isn't it about time for a rerun of "Betty Believes"? I'd love to get a new copy laminated for my niece.

Happiness Is

Dear Happiness:

Of course. Here goes:

BETTY BELIEVES

1. That everything has a funny side to it.
2. That whining doesn't advance the ball.
3. That there's always somebody worse off than you.
4. That there's such a thing as being too smart for your own good.
5. That there are worse things in the world than ignorance and mediocrity.

6. That it takes all kinds.
7. That nobody's opinion is worth more than anybody else's.
8. That the more things stay the same, the better.
9. That everything happens for a good reason.
10. That no one ever died from an insult to the intelligence.

Dear Betty:

My Grandma Claire used to read your column every morning with her first cup of coffee and cigarette of the day. She called "Ask Betty" the real news. She said that following the progress of your career over the years was her only truly wicked pleasure, and that it was like watching a massacre through a telescope. What did she mean by that? She got throat cancer and died, and the last thing she said to me was, "There are too atheists in foxholes." My mom says she was out of her mind. What do you think?

Fourteen and Wondering

Dear Wondering:

That your Grandma Claire will not have died in vain if you will heed the lesson of her life: *Don't smoke.*

CONFIDENTIAL to *First Person Singular:*

Is it worth it, kid? Is it really?

Sure, on the one side you have money—obscene amounts of money—not to mention job security, reputation, celebrity. But . . . what about the numbing boredom? What about self-respect? What about, you should pardon the expression, honor? Huh, Toots?

I mean, who's really contemptible here? Them, or you?

Hint: Who's got the ulcer?
Who's got the whim-whams?
Who's got the blues in the night?

Dear Betty:
This is going to sound ridiculous, but hear me out. My husband smacks his lips in his sleep and it's driving me batty. If he were only snoring or gnashing his teeth, but this is a licking sound, a lapping, sipping, slurping sound, like a huge baby gumming pureed peas in the dark, and it makes my flesh crawl. I've tried nudging him awake, but he just looks at me so pitifully, and then I feel guilty. Imagine how he'd feel if I told him what I really want, which is my own bed in my own separate bedroom! Help!

Nauseous in Nashville

Dear Nauseous:
Sounds like hubby has some deep dark cravings, or so my sleep disorder experts tell me. Why not fix him up a yummy bowl of butterscotch pudding (from scratch) just before bedtime?
By the way . . . you mean "nauseated," dear.

Dear Betty:
You want to know what burns me up? Inconsiderate bozos who jam up the speedy checkout line with grocery carts loaded to the brim, and moronic bimbos who let their children rip open bags of candy and cereal boxes and knock over jelly jars, and don't even have the decency to tell the stockboy to clean up their disgusting mess. I just got back from two hours at the grocery store and my new pumps are covered with mincemeat. What do you think of these lunkheads?

Burned Up

125

Dear Burned:
These people are not bozos, bimbos, or lunkheads. They are trash.

Dear Betty:
I am 135 pounds of screaming muscle in crepe-soled shoes. I groan under enormous trays laden with exotic delicacies I shall never taste, as they are beyond my meager economic means. Having seen your face once I am able to connect it with the food and drink of your choice. I smile when you are rude to me and apologize when the fault lies in the kitchen. I walk the equivalent of five miles each night on throbbing feet to satisfy your every whim, and when you are stuffed and have no further need of me, I act grateful for a substandard tip, if at all. I am
Your Waitress

Dear Waitress:
Thank you.
What's the question?

Dear Betty:
You hear from so many unfortunates with serious problems that I feel a bit ashamed to take up your time this way. I am an attractive woman of 59; my thighs are perfectly smooth, my waist unthickened, I still have both my breasts and all my teeth; in fact I am two dress sizes smaller than I was at eighteen. My three grown daughters are intelligent, healthy, and independent. My husband and I are as much in love as when we first were married, despite the depth of our familiarity, and the, by now, considerable conflation of our tastes, political beliefs, preferences in music and art, and, of course, memories. He still interests and pleasures me; miraculously our sexual life remains joyous, inventive, and mu-

126

tually fulfilling. I continue to adore the challenge and variety of my career as an ethnic dance therapist. We have never had to worry about money. Our country home is lovely, and very old, and solidly set down in a place of incomparable, ever shifting beauty; our many friends, old and new, are delightful people, amusing and wise, and every one of them honorable and a source of strength to us.

And yet, with all of this, and more, I am frequently very sad, and cannot rid myself of a growing, formless, yet very real sense of devastating loss, no less hideous for its utter irrationality. Forgive me, but does this make any sense to you?

Niobe

Dear Niobe:
Certainly. You're lying about the sex.

Dear Betty:
Why not scissor the cups out of your old brassieres and set them out in your annual garden as little domes to protect fragile seedlings? It looks wacky but it sure does the trick!

Petunia

Dear Petunia:
Why the heck not? And hey, don't throw away those brassiere *straps!* Kids love to carry their schoolbooks in them, especially once you've disguised their embarrassing identity with precision-cut strips of silver mylar cemented front and back with epoxy, then adorned with tiny hand-sewn appliques in animal or rock-star designs. Use your imagination!

CONFIDENTIAL to *Smarting and Smiling:*
What you describe is not a "richly deserved comeuppance" but

a sexual perversion, which, aside from being your own business and none of mine, is harmless enough and, if I read accurately between the lines, apparently works well for both of you.

You might just try these thought experiments, though: Imagine the effect upon your sex life of: a business failure; the birth of a child; rheumatoid arthritis (his); a positive biopsy (yours); the death of a child; a sudden terrifying sense of vastation that comes to either of you at three in the morning; a Conelrad Alert. In what ways would it differ from the experience of a couple for whom the concepts of integrity, maturity, valor and dignity retained actual relevance and power?

Dear Betty:

You deserve a swift kick in the pants for your bum advice to *Fretting in Spokane.* Where do you get off telling that lady to iron her dustcloths? Dollars to doughnuts you've got a maid to keep *your* rags shipshape, but most of us aren't so lucky.

And another thing. These days there's getting to be a snotty, know-it-all, lah-dee-dah, cynical tone to your column. I can't put my finger on it, but I'm not the only one who thinks you're getting "too big for your britches." Don't kid yourself. You need us more than we need you. So bend over, Betty, if you know what's good for you, and get ready for a

Washington Wallop

Dear Wallop:

For what it's worth, I agree with you about the dustcloths. But I sincerely regret having ever unwittingly encouraged your brand of coarse familiarity. And may I suggest that you take yourself to the nearest dictionary—you can find one in any public library—and "put your finger" on the distinction between cynicism and irony. Think about it, Wallop. And tell me how it turns out.

128

Dear Betty:

Many years ago you ran a column that started off "The Other Woman is a sponging parasitic succubus. . . ." I clipped it and kept it magnetized to my freezer, but it finally fell apart. Do you know the one I mean? Would you mind running it again?

Sister Sue

Dear Sis:

Not at all. Here goes:

"The Other Woman is a sponging parasitic succubus, a proper role model for young people, a vacuous nitwit, a manic-depressive, a Republican, a good mother, an international terrorist, or what-have-you, depending, of course, upon the facts of her particular character and life.

"Though this much should be obvious, there are those who believe that any woman sexually involved with a man she is not married to can be, for social and moral purposes, reduced to a cheap stereotype. *This is dangerous nonsense. This is a terrible habit of thought.* For who among us has fewer than three dimensions? In the history of the human race, has there ever existed a single person, besides Hitler, who could slip beneath closed doors, disappear when viewed from the side, and settle comfortably, with room to spare, between the pages of a bad novel?

"Therefore let us rejoice in our variety! Let every one of us celebrate the special homeliness of her own history! Let us wonder, and be surprised, and admit to possibilities, and get on with it, and *stop being so damn stupid!*"

Dear Betty:

Are you nuts? You can't get away with this. Even if you do, what's the point?

First Person Singular

Dear F.P.S.:
The point is, watch my smoke.

Dear Betty:
I need you to settle an argument. My brother-in-law says
you're not the original Betty and that you're not even a *person*.
He says Betty died two years ago in a car wreck and they covered
it up and this column is being carried on by a committee, hush-
hush. I say he's all wet. (He's one of those conspiracy nuts.)
Anyway, what's the poop? (Hint: There's a lobster dinner riding
on this.)

No Skeptic

Dear No:
This is a stumper. I've been staring for so long at the wonderful
phrase "original Betty" that the words have become nonsensical
and even the letters look strange. Who, I wonder, is or was the
"original Betty"? I'm not making fun of you, dear. I honestly don't
know what to say. If it's any help to you, I do have the same
fingerprints as the infant born prematurely to Mary Alice Feeney
in 1927, and the vivacious coed who won first prize in the national
"My Country Because" essay contest of 1946, and the woman
who put this column into syndication in 1952. So I suppose you
deserve the lobster; although how you're going to convince your
brother-in-law is anybody's guess. I wonder what he'd take as
proof. I've got to think about this.

Dear Betty:
It's *him* I can't stand. In *bed*! And he knows it, too. I just don't
want him *touching* me, I can't bear it! And *I still love him*! But there's
nothing left any more, and how the hell is homemade butterscotch
pudding going to help that? My God! My God! And don't tell

130

me it's just a phase, because I know better and so does he. God, I'm so unhappy.

Nauseated, All Right? in Nashville

Dear N:

That's much better. Awful, isn't it? The death of desire? And you're probably right, there's no help for it. Though if you can stomach the notion that intimacy is nothing more than a perfectable technique, you might try what they call a "reputable sex therapist."

Of all the foolish, ignoble, even evil acts I have committed in my long life, including the "My Country Because" essay, the single event that most shames me, so that I flush from chest to scalp even as I write this, was when I sat, of my own free will, in the offices of one of these technicians, and in the presence of a pink, beaming, gleaming young man, a total stranger, took my husband's hands in mine, and stared into his face, his poor face, crimson like my own, transfixed with humiliation and disbelief, and said—oh, this is dreadful; my husband of twenty-three years!—and said, in public, "I love it when you lick my nipples."

My God! *My God!*

Dear Betty:

Our family recently spent a weekend in our nation's Capital. While there we visited the moving Vietnam Memorial. Upon our return home I penned the following lines, which I would like to share with you.

You Could Have Been a Son of Ours

You could have been a son of ours
If we had ever had a son,

You could have been our pride and joy
    But someone shot you with a gun
        And now your work is done.

You perished in a jungle wild
    So that our freedoms might be insured.
You risked your life without complaint
    You laid it down without a word.

And now upon a long black stone
    Are chiseled words that give you fame;
You could have been a son of ours—
    We're proud to say, "We know your name"

Emily

READERS:

Policy change! Policy change! Pay attention, now, because I'm not kidding around. Hereafter this column will continue to run the usual advice letters, recipes, and household hints; but we will no longer publish original verse. There will be no exceptions. Don't even think about it.

Dear Betty:

I guess you think you're pretty funny. I guess you think we're all hicks and idiots out here.

Well, maybe you're right, but I'll tell you one thing. That old letter I asked for about "The Other Woman"? It's not the one you ran before, even though you said it was, or you changed it in some way. I may not be super intelligent but I've got a good memory, and what's more I know when I'm being made fun of.

You know what? You really hurt me. Congratulations.

Sister Sue

132

Dear Sis:
I am ashamed.
I, too, have an excellent memory, and for this reason my record-keeping has never been systematic. And very occasionally I confuse genuine mail with letters I have concocted for one reason or another. This is what happened in your case. I had you down as a fiction.
I can't apologize enough.

Dear Betty:
Aren't you taking a big chance, admitting that you make up some of this stuff? Also, you haven't dealt with Sister Sue's real complaint, which is that now, inexplicably, after spending three decades securing the trust and affection of middle American women, you expose yourself as a misanthrope, misogynist, intellectual snob, and cheat. What are you up to, anyway?

F.P.S.

Dear F:
Look, nobody reads this but us gals, so I'm hardly "taking a big chance." And it should be obvious, especially to you, that I'm "up to" no good.

Dear Betty:
Do you believe in God? I don't. Also, do you ever sit in front of a mirror and stare at your face? My face is so blobby that I can't figure out how even my own parents can recognize me. Lastly, do you think we should be selling weapons to Jordan?

Fifteen and Wondering

Dear Wondering:
Take five years off after you graduate from high school. Move

133

away from home, get a menial job, fall for as many unworthy young men as it takes to get all that nonsense out of your system. Don't even think about college until your mind is parched and you are frantic to learn. Don't marry in your twenties. Don't be kind to yourself. *Keep in touch.*

Dear Betty:

I was not "lying about the sex"; nor do I for a minute imagine that you thought I was. You simply could not resist making a flip wisecrack at my expense.

I was lying about my friends, who have gradually lost their affection for me but continue to socialize with us because they value my husband's company. He is aging well. I am turning into a fool. I'm one of those handsome old beauties with a gravelly, post-menopausal voice and a terrible laugh. I never had much of a sense of humor, but once I had a smoky, provocative laugh, which has now somehow become the sort of theatrical bray that hushes crowds. Strangers, accosted by me at parties, attacked at lunch counters and in elevators, shift and squirm in alarm: even the most obtuse knows he's about to be mugged, that he will not be allowed to pass until I have exacted my tribute. I am all affection, obvious need and naked ego: just that kind of horrible woman who imagines herself an unforgettable character. I tell off-color jokes and hold my breath after the punch line, threatening to asphyxiate if you fail to applaud my remarkably emancipated attitude. During the past forty years I have told countless people about the stillbirth of my son, to show that I Have Known Great Sorrow. I parade my political beliefs, all liberal and unexamined, as evidence of my wisdom. I am a deeply boring, fatuous woman, and strangers pity me, friends lose patience with me, and my family loves me because it never occurs to any of them that I know it I am the emperor in his new clothes, who knew perfectly well he was naked, who just needed a little attention, that's all,

134

merely the transfixed attention of the entire populace, not an unreasonable request, just unlimited lifetime use of the cosmic footlights.

Don't try to tell me I can change. Of course I can't. And don't for an instant presume that I'm not all that bad. I am. Believe it.

Niobe

Dear Niobe:

Yes, but on the other hand your astonishing self-awareness makes you a genuinely tragic figure. And, Honey, cling to this: you're not ordinary. Commonplace sufferers find themselves trapped in homely, deformed, or dying bodies; you're trapped in an inferior *soul*. You really *are* a remarkable woman. Bravo!

How about it, Ladies? Isn't she something?

Dear Betty:

Just who the hell do you think you are?

Washington Wallop

Dear Wallop:

I am 147 pounds of despair in a fifty-pound mail sack. Though overpaid I groan with ennui beneath the negligible weight of your all too modest expectations, and when I fail to counter one of your clichés with another twice as mindless I apologize, even though the fault, God knows, is yours. I am

Betty

Dear Betty:

Temper, temper.

F.P.S.

Dear F:

I can't help it. That broad really frosts my butt.

135

Dear Betty:

Do I have an inner life? I think I read somewhere that women don't. Also, what does it mean? Do you think we're capable of original thought?

Fifteen and Still Wondering

Dear Wondering:

I love you, and wish you were my own daughter. I have in fact two daughters, but neither of them has an inner life. I am what they call nowadays a "controlling personality." (Believe me, dear, that's not what they used to call it.) I was one of those omniscient mothers—the ones who always claim to know what their children are thinking, what they've just done, what they are planning to do. Not for any sinister reasons, mind you, but I got so good at guessing and predicting that, without intending to, I actually convinced them both of their utter transparency. They are each adrift, goalless and pathetic. They are big soft women, big criers, especially when they spend much time with me. I think I should feel worse about this than I actually do. Do you think this is Darwinian of me? (Hint: Go to a good library, and take out some books on Darwin.)

Dear Betty:

It's me again! Do you have any suggestions as to what I can do with a ten-foot length of old garden hose?

Petunia

Dear Petunia:

Do you ever just sit still? Do you ever just sit in front of a mirror, for instance, and stare at your face? It's none of my business, but—and I say this with no snide intent, I am trying to be good, so that my teeth are literally clenched as I write this—I

136

seriously think you should calm down. Petunia, even the Athenians threw things away. Let the garden hose be what it is, a piece of garbage. Now sit very very very still and try to think of nothing but the weight of your eyelids. Come to rest. Let your muscles slip and slide. Easy does it, girl. Easy. *Shhhhhhhhhhhh.*

Dear Betty:

Maybe you should stop "trying to be good" if that's the best you can do. If I were Petunia, I'd rather get a wisecrack than a lot of patronizing advice based upon a snap analysis of my character and the circumstances of my life. You're a fine one to exhort them to wonder, be surprised, and admit to possibilities. On the basis of little evidence you've turned the woman into a cartoon. You don't see her as a person at all, just a type Early thirties, right? Hyperthyroid, narrow-shouldered, big-bottomed, frantically cheery, classically obsessive-compulsive; a churchgoing, choir-singing, Brownie troop mothering Total Woman with a soft sweet high voice, darting panic behind her deep-set eyes, an awful cornball sense of humor, and an overbite like a prairie dog Am I right? Boy, how trite can you get! And how presumptuous you've become! I've tried to see it your way, but it's no go. I say, bring back the Original Betty.

F.P.S.

Dear F:

Look, we know for a fact she's a cornball. No one who asks what she should do with a ten-foot length of hose could possibly have a sense of humor. As for the rest, well, I stayed up half the night trying to imagine another psychological context for her question (which, I must object, is hardly "a little evidence"), so that if I have failed it isn't for lack of trying

Oh, all right, I admit it. I did see her as a type But it becomes so difficult to believe that Petunia, or any of them, has any kind of independent existence. Remember, these folks are just words on a page; of course they're full-fleshed and complex, but I have to take this on faith. Most of them probably think they're revealing their true selves, whereas really they tell me almost nothing, and with every letter I'm supposed to make up a whole person, out of *scraps*.

I don't like to complain, but this doesn't get any easier with practice, and I'm tiring now, and losing my nerve. I can live with not being nice—nobody nice would do what I do—but what if I'm not any *good*?

READERS:

Do you think that failure of the imagination can have moral significance? I mean, is it a character flaw or just an insufficiency of skill? Is triteness a *sin*? Or what?

Dear Betty:

Last night my husband woke me up at 2:00 A.M. with a strange request. Then after awhile this old song started going through my head that I hadn't thought about for thirty years. I must have gone through the darn thing ten thousand times. It got so I was following the words with a bouncing ball, so that even when I blocked out the sound that old ball was still bobbing away in my head and I never did get to sleep until sunrise. The question is, does anybody out there know the missing words?

> Herman the German and Frenchie the Swede
> > Set out for the Alkali Flats—Oh!
> Herman did follow and Frenchie did lead
> > And they carried something in, or on, their hats—Oh!
>
> Now Herman said, "Frenchie, let's rest for a while,
> > "My pony has something the matter with it—Oh!"

138

Now Frenchie said, "Herman, we'll rest in a mile,
  "On the banks of the River Something—Oh!"*

> (*If I could get the name of the river
> I'd be all set here)

Now Hattie McGurk was a sorrowful gal,
  Something something something.
She had a dirt camp in the high chaparral
  And a something as wide as Nebraska.

There's more, but I never did know the other verses, so they don't matter so much.
  Betty, we sure do love you out here in Elko.

Sleepytime Sal

Dear Betty:
  One time I was at this Tupperware party at my girlfriend's. Actually, it was just like a Tupperware party, only it was marital underwear, but it was run the same way. Anyway, everybody was drinking beer and passing around the items, and cutting up, you know, laughing about the candy pants and whatnot, and having a real good time. Only all of a sudden this feeling came over me. I started feeling real sorry for everybody, even though they were screaming and acting silly. I thought about how much work it was to have fun, and how brave we all were for going to the trouble, since the easiest thing would be to just moan and cry and bite the walls, because we're all going to die anyway, sooner or later. Isn't that sad? I saw how every human life is a story, and the story always ends badly. It came to me that there wasn't any God at all and that we've always known this, but most of us are too polite and kind to talk about it. Finally I got so blue that I had to go into the bathroom and bawl. Then I was all right.

Partly Sunny

Dear Betty:

When I was first married you ran a recipe in your column called "How to Preserve Your Mate." It had all kinds of stuff in it like "fold in a generous dollop of forgiveness" and "add plenty of spice." I thought it was so cute that I copied it out on a sampler. Time went by, and I got a divorce, and finished high school, and then I got a university scholarship, and eventually a masters degree in business administration. Now I'm married again, to a corporate tax lawyer, and we live in a charming old pre-Revolutionary farmhouse, and all our pillows are made of goose down, and our potholders and coffee mugs and the bedspreads and curtains in the children's rooms all have Marimekko prints, and every item of clothing I own is made of natural fiber. But I never threw that old sampler away, and every now and then, when I'm all alone, I take it out and look at it and laugh my head off about what an incredible middle-class jerk I used to be.

Save the Whales

Dear Betty:

This is the end of the line for you and the rest of your ilk. We shall no longer seek the counsel of false matriarchs, keepers of the Old Order, quislings whose sole power derives from the continuing bondage of their sisters. Like the dinosaurs, your bodies will fuel the new society, where each woman shall be sovereign, and acknowledge her rage, and validate her neighbor's rage, and rejoice in everybody's rage, and caper and dance widdershins beneath the gibbous moon.

Turning and Turning in the Widening Gyre

Dear Betty:

I did what you said and sat real quiet and let myself go. Then you know what happened? I got real nutty and started wondering if I was just an idea in the mind of God. Is this an original thought? 'Cause if it is, you can keep it.

Hey, are you all right?

Petunia

Dear Petunia:

No, since you ask. My mother is dying. My husband's mistress has myesthenia gravis. My younger daughter just gave all of her trust money to the Church of the Famous Maker And I, like Niobe, am not aging well. My ulcer is bleeding, I can't sleep, and I'm not so much depressed as humiliated, both by slapstick catastrophe and by the minute tragedy of my wasted talents. To tell you the truth, I feel like hell.

Dear Betty:

I can see you have problems, dear, but whining doesn't advance the ball. Why not make a list of all your blessings and tape it to your medicine chest? Or send an anonymous houseplant to your oldest enemy? Why not expose yourself to the clergyman of your choice? Or, you could surprise hubby with a yummy devil's food layer cake, made from scratch in the nude.

Or, if nothing seems to work, you can put your head down and suffer like any other dumb animal. This always does the trick for me.

Ha ha ha. How do you like it, Sister? Ha ha ha ha ha.

Bitterly Laughing in the Heartland

Dear Betty:

See? They're closing in. You had to try it, didn't you, you got them going, and now all hell's breaking loose. You took a sweet racket and ruined it, and for what? Honor? Integrity? *Aesthetic principle?* Well, go ahead and martyr yourself, but leave me out of it.

F.P.S.

READERS.
For what it's worth,

BETTY REALLY BELIEVES

1. That God is criminally irresponsible
2. That nobility is possible.
3. That hope is necessary
4. That courage is commonplace.
5. That sentimentality is wicked.
6. That cynicism is worse.
7. That most people are surprisingly good sports.
8. That some people are irredeemable idiots.
9. That everybody on the Board of Directors of GM, Ford, Chrysler, and U.S. Steel, and every third member of Congress and the Cabinet ought to be taken out, lined up against a wall and shot.
10. That whining, though ugly, sometimes advances the ball.

How about it, Readers? What do *you* believe?

Dear Betty:
Does anybody have the recipe for Kooky Cake?

Kooky in Dubuque

Dear Kooky:
Forget the cake. The cake is terrible. What we're trying for here is a community of souls, a free exchange of original thoughts,

an unrehearsed, raucous, a cappella chorus of Middle American women.

A Symphony of Gals!

Kooky, for God's sake, tell me your fears, your dreams, your awfullest secrets, and I'll tell you mine. Tell me, for instance, why you use that degrading nickname. I'm sending you my private phone number. Use it. Call me, Kooky. Call me anytime. Call collect. *Call soon.*

That goes for everybody else. All my dear readers, the loyal and the hateful, the genuine and the fictional, the rich and the strange. Call me anytime. Or, I'll send you my home address. Drop in. I'm serious. Let's talk.

Serious? You're critical. These people are going to kill you.

These people are my dearest friends. I love them all.

You do not! You don't even know them!

What's the question?

But . . . sentimentality is wicked.

But cynicism is worse.

UNDER
THE
BED

On November 6 of last year, at around 8:15 P.M., I was beaten and raped by a man named Raymond C. Moreau, Jr., who had entered our first-floor apartment through a living room window while I was taking a shower. This is neither the most significant event in my life nor the most interesting; nevertheless it is a fact, around which cluster many other facts, and the truth is always worth telling. As I approach forty I am learning to value the truth for its own sake; I discover that most people have little use for it, beyond its practical applications, except as the glue that holds together rickety constructs of theory and opinion. As a rule the brighter and better educated select their facts with great care.

I teach philosophy at our mediocre state junior college. My husband teaches physics at the University. He is the real philosopher, like all good scientists, although, like most good scientists, he amiably resists this description. We self-styled philosophers window shop through metaphysics, epistemology, and ethics, until we settle on those views that suit us, and then we tailor them to fit our idiosyncrasies. The more cynical among us deliberately choose unpopular or bizarre philosophies the more easily to establish a reputation. My husband is a born verificationist. He does not ask unanswerable questions; he does not whine, or posture, or plead, or shake his fist at the stars. His agnosticism, unlike

147

mine, is consistent throughout, utterly free of petulance and despair. It is he who taught me to hold the truth in such high regard, as he has taught me so many things. He believes in a rational universe. How I love him for that! He is worth a hundred humanists, a thousand priests.

My husband was at an evening seminar on November 6 (or, as we now refer to it, with some humor, "The Night of the Thing") and did not return until 9:00, when I was again alone in the apartment. Of course he blamed himself, especially at first, for having been away, for not coming right home when the seminar concluded. I am very glad he stayed for coffee. Had he interrupted us he would have had to do something, as would Raymond C. Moreau, Jr., who had a gun.

As it happened, and for reasons I shall try to explain, when he came home I was under our double bed, asleep. He did not notice that our television set was missing, there were damp towels on the living room floor, and on the bed the comforter was rumpled and askew, but this did not alarm him so much (for I am not very neat) as the apparent fact of my absence. He was smiling when he opened the front door—I know this, because I am usually there to meet him, and he always smiles—but when he sat on our bed to puzzle out where I might be he was not smiling. I imagine that at that moment he looked his age (he is older than I) and that he let his shoulders sag, and that his expression was blank and vulnerable. I cannot imagine how he looked when, bending down to untie his shoes, he saw the fingertips of my right hand protruding from behind the comforter. Thank god he has a good heart. He dropped to his knees and took my hand and lifted the spread, at which point I woke up. A farce ensued.

I immediately realized, from the way his voice cracked when he called my name that he was badly frightened, as who wouldn't

148

be; since I did not want to frighten him further I determined not to let him see my face, which was bloody and ugly with bruises. "I'm fine," I said, idiotically, in an exaggerated reasonable tone.

"What the hell do you mean," he said, and yanked on my arm. "Come out of there."

I braced my other arm against the rail. "I will in a minute. I have to tell you something." Then, unfortunately, and rather horribly, I began to laugh, at the picture we would have made to an impartial observer, at our outlandish dialogue. This is usually called the "hysterical laugh," to distinguish it substantially from genuine laughter.

Now my husband—and good for him—wasted no time, but gave the bed a hard, sideways push. It flew on well-oiled casters and thumped against wall and windowsill; and for the second time in an hour I was well exposed. A pitiful and wrenching sight I must have been, clutching my old red bathrobe tight around me like a cartoon spinster, hiding my ugly face in the dusty green shag. (To this day a breath of dust makes me flush a little, with artificial shame. The body remembers.) Well, then there was reconciliation, and explanation, and generally the sort of behavior you would expect from lovers to whom such a thing has happened. These events were not extraordinary, except to us, and I shall not record them, here or anywhere else. These are private matters. We are very private people.

▼ ▼ ▼ ▼ ▼ ▼

Raymond C. Moreau was twenty years old and looked thirty. He had long, sand-colored hair, which hung in greasy ropes; small, deep-set eyes, I don't know what color; thin lips and receding chin; and a rough, ravaged complexion: the right side of his face especially was seamed and pitted. I gave this information to the police artist and he drew me a picture of Charlie Goodby,

149

a paperboy we had in Worcester when I was a little girl. He—
the rapist—wore a soiled yellow windbreaker, an undershirt, beige
chinos, and jockey shorts. Obviously he must have worn shoes,
but I never noticed. His breath was terrible. He looked, as you
would expect, like a bad man and a loser.

During the fifteen or so minutes of our association he said the
following:

> Get it off. Drop it.
> In there, lady.
> On the bed.
> You got a husband? You all alone, you stupid bitch?
> Spread them, bitch.
> You're all alike. All alike. All alike.
> Shut up. I'll kill you.
> That's right.
> Oh. Love. Love, love, love, ahhh, love. Ahhh.
> Stay there. Stay away from the phone. I'll come back and I'll
> kill you.

That he said "love, love, love" at the point of orgasm does not,
in retrospect, strike me as ironic. On the back of his windbreaker
the initials CHSE and the numerals 1983 were stenciled in brown.
CHSE 1983 is heavier with implication than "love, love, love." CHSE
1983, now that I think of it, is eloquent as hell.

He never looked me in the eye. But he did not, I think, pur-
posely avoid my eyes. He was not nervous, or ashamed, or fearful.
It just never occurred to him to look there.

▼ ▼ ▼ ▼ ▼ ▼ ▼

I used to be afraid of everything. That is, I was a functioning,
relatively happy person with a great deal of fear. Spiders, heights,

150

closed-in places—I had all the phobias in moderation. I never answered the phone without first composing myself for bad news—I always waited a beat before I picked up the receiver. (The ring of a telephone on a late sunny afternoon was particularly menacing to me.) Every time I got on a plane I knew I was going to die; and I was ever aware of the dangers inherent in any form of transportation. At night I never let my hand or my foot dangle over the side of the bed. If I had to enter a dark room I hurried to the light switch, even though my night-vision is excellent.

Once or twice a year I would experience a few days of serious dread, touched off by something Dan Rather said, or a remark overheard at a sherry hour. Once a colleague mentioned a Roman Catholic legend to the effect that the last Pope would be the first non-Italian. "Then what," I asked him, with a false conspiratorial smile. "The end of the world," he said, and lifted his glass as if to toast this hideous prophecy. Oh, I despised him then, and all the laughing doomsayers, who spread terror all unmindful, precisely because they do not know what terror is. Cassandra never laughed.

It is not that I have ever believed the holocaust inevitable, or even probable; rather, I was forced on some occasions to admit the possibility. And on these occasions suicide had a certain appeal for me. I would lie beside my sleeping husband and try to think about a universe purged of human beings—surely there was some comfort in this concept; but then, I would be reminded, there would be no concepts either. A universe of particles, morally neutral: black, a pitiless black whole, with no memories, not even of the finest of us. I kept imagining the moment of purging, the dying, the knowing, and terror froze me so I could not even cry. I feared most that we would see it coming, that we would be spared nothing; that I would be separated from my husband, unable to get to him in time—in the last moments of time; or that we would be together but helpless to end in our own way. Plans must be made, I would think: emergency rations of cyanide. But even then we would not both die at once; once would have to endure alone, for however long it took. . . .

When I had had enough of this I always sought to calm myself, with craven prayer, and with the warmth of my husband's body, and the cool, dry cross-grain of his skin; and magically, on the third or fourth sleepless night, the terror would slip away.

And other nights, when nothing weighed on me at all, and fearless as a movie hero I lay in wait for sleep, I would suddenly have to rise on one elbow, just like a robot, and strain to hear the sound of my husband breathing; and if I could not be sure of it I would brush and push against him, as though by accident, until I had drawn out a sigh or shaken him into motion.

I was not so much neurotic as superstitious, as though through occasional ritualistic suffering I could save us all. I carefully hid this, and only this, from my husband, my talisman, because I did not want to worry or disappoint him; and if he ever suspected the depth of my perverse irrationality he kindly left me to it.

I am not superstitious now. Whatever else he did to me, Raymond C. Moreau measurably improved the quality of my life. My body sometimes jumps or shrinks from the unexpected casual touch, and this can be awkward. But I know no fear. I don't worry anymore.

▼ ▼ ▼ ▼ ▼ ▼

I used to have a good friend. Regina Montgomery is the only woman outside my family for whom I have ever felt affection. She is an Amazon, sturdy and large-breasted, with plain coarse features; she smiles like a big cat and is made beautiful. We are opposites physically, emotionally, politically; she is ten years my junior. She pleased me. She was exotic in her proportions and in her strength; earthy, passionate, intense—everything I was not.

She gave me two weeks to start talking on my own about my experience with Raymond C. Moreau. Actually I did not let her see me the first week, until the marks faded; and when she came to the door it was she, not I, whose eyes were red-rimmed and puffy. I remember she had part of a foil-wrapped fruitcake in her hand, and that she kissed my husband on the cheek and hugged him fiercely—it was so strange to see them embracing, she had always been so shy around him; and that she waited for some sign from me and didn't get it, for she kept her distance, hovering, saying how wonderful I looked. I was cruel to her, surprising myself; I was bland and cheerful and gracious, serving up the fruitcake, making light, maddening conversation, meticulously avoiding even oblique allusion to the single topic she had come to discuss. Her anxiety, so ingenuously displayed, was as comical as it was touching I kept thinking that at any moment I would let down, but after a while she left, unsatisfied and bewildered.

"I understood," she told me later, when we finally had it out. "You couldn't stand to be touched in any way." I let her think this. The truth is, I have a mean streak. Obvious people bring out the worst in me. I was not proud of having tortured her like that; I loved her for her genuine concern, her simple candor, her trust. I made a gift of my confession, describing the attack in detail, answering all her questions. It was not enough for her. "You talk as though this—this horror—happened to someone else. How do you feel? Or don't you even know?" "A total stranger invades my home, hurts me, rapes me, calls me names, turns my life into a melodrama. How do you suppose I feel?" She opened her mouth, shut it again. She had decided, I could see, that I was still not "over it." She would bide her time.

As she watched me closely, obviously, over the next few months,

153

impatiently waiting, I suppose, for me to start drinking, or break into sobs at a faculty meeting, or something like that. Amateur psychoanalysis has always annoyed me. I deeply resented such presumption on the part of a friend.

We went out for wine one afternoon and had an awful fight. Our friendship has not recovered.

"All you can say is, you're not changed, not outraged, not afraid, not anything. Christ, you make it seem like a—an embarrassing *incident!*"

"Or a shaggy dog horror story?" I said, smiling, and poured us wine from our third carafe. Wine makes me happy and reckless.

"But you have changed," said Regina, who was not happy at all. "You're icy. Icy. Not like your old reserve. You've become rude, do you know that? Well, not actively, but I swear you look at people with such—I don't know—contempt—"

"You're just a bad sport," I said, teasing her. The difference in our ages was never more apparent. She was flushed, earnest, and drunk, and childishly adamant. "Reggie, look. He just got me on a good day, all right? You know how sometimes a movie will make you cry, and other days you laugh yourself sick—"

"That's disgusting! You were violated! Violence was done to you!"

"You say that with such an air of discovery."

"And not just to you. To me. To all women."

"Oh, really?" I was angry now. We had argued the political point before, but this was personal. "Then why don't you tell me about it, Regina? It must have been a ghastly experience."

"You *are* bitter! You see." She was triumphant.

"Only about you. You want me to be a martyr, a role I find repellent in the extreme. I was victimized, yes, but I am not a victim. And I am not a symbol. I am not in the symbolizing business."

154

In the end I said she was no different than Raymond Moreau. Always willing to take a metaphor and run with it, she stared up at me, stupid and open-mouthed, trying to understand in what way she had been "raping" me. I could see clear into her skull. I threw my money down in disgust and left her there. I had meant only, she thought we were all alike, all alike. All alike.

▼ ▼ ▼ ▼ ▼ ▼ ▼

I padded on damp feet into the living room, wrapped in a big yellow towel, another towel on my clean hair I was going to turn on the television, for the comforting noise. He was winding the cord around its handle; a nice breeze came in the open window. I said, "Hello." I thought to say, "I've been expecting you," for this was true; I had been expecting him all my life. I thought to scream, but then the gun was out. Another woman—Regina— might have screamed without thinking first. I never do anything without thinking first.

I let my body have the fear. Bodies are designed to handle fright. It rippled and shuddered, the heart panicked, the blood scampered in terror. I watched. Really, it was not so bad. It was nothing like the end of the world.

He lay me on my back, arranged my legs this way and that, pushed against me like a vacant idiot child; his belly was soft and slack, it rested on mine light and warm and unmuscled; when my flesh shrank away it followed, spread thick, a cloying, intimate layer of skin and fat. His upper body he kept to himself, propped up on rosy eczematous elbows. I could see each row in the machine-weave of his undershirt, the irregular rows of tiny hairs and diamond-shaped skin segments in his neck and jaw, the arch of his upper teeth, filigreed with silver. If there is a god, I remember thinking, he certainly attends to detail. He hit my face, alternating open palm and knuckles, with precise unhurried rhythm; and from

155

my mouth came a terrible sound, as from a grunting pig. But I did not make the sound. I could never make a sound like that.

At no time did I need to remind myself that this was happening, and not a dream. There was no feeling of displacement. Nor did I wonder why he did it. After all, he never wondered about me.

Where is the tragedy here? He did not touch me. Of course, it was unpleasant and wearing, but I have been more deeply hurt by rude bus drivers. It was just a collision of machines.

When he left I was faced with the problem of how to tell my husband. It does not seem now like such a great problem but then I had been under a strain and could not think clearly. Once, when I was in college, I was playing bridge with some friends in my dormitory room when a girl from down the hall—a secretive, nervous girl, a bare acquaintance—shuffled in, in nightgown and slippers, and asked if she could sit and watch. She was very pale, apparently exhausted from crying. She sat still for half an hour, peculiarly ominous but circumspect, until finally, blushing with shame, she confessed, in an offhand way, that she had taken a lot of pills and didn't know what to do. There is just no proper way to inform a roomful of strangers that you have attempted suicide. There is no way at all to tell your husband that you have been raped. Should I stay as I was, naked, unseemly? This seemed a gratuitously cruel method, almost amounting to accusation. Look what's been done to me! I put on my robe and wandered through the apartment, looking for a place to light. Well, I could sit down, on the couch for instance, with a single dim lamp on, and greet him that way—but with what words? For a while I thought seriously of cleaning up, combing my hair; I could stay in shadow, avert my face, never mention it at all But now my body, which had served me so well, let me down: I was tired and could not even lift a cloth to wash to myself. I needed a hiding place, where decisions could be held in abeyance; a place of noncommitment.

Intending to rest for only a minute I slid underneath the bed, where the monsters used to be; and there were no monsters there, just me; and I slept without dreaming.

▼ ▼ ▼ ▼ ▼ ▼ ▼

To say the least I have never been effusive or easygoing, but before the rape I got along well enough with my colleagues. There was mutual respect. I have no respect for most of them now; they have shown little for me. We live in an age when self-control, competence, discretion—all are thought abnormal, symptomatic of dysfunction. "But how do you *feel*," they all want to know; their eyes betray them, they are so obvious; some of them dare to ask. "I'm sorry," said our Kant and Leibniz specialist, a man I had always credited with sense. "*I'm sorry!* What for?" I asked him, infuriated by his gloomy, hangdog look. "Are you responsible in some way? Did you once have adolescent rape fantasies? Do you believe in common consciousness?" Shoddy, second-rate thinkers; bullies. Sentimentalists. *Why, look you now, how unworthy a thing you make of me!*

A police detective came to my office with a high school photograph of Raymond Moreau. After I identified him the detective told me he was dead, shot dead by some woman better prepared than I, a woman with her own gun. (What a stupid criminal was Raymond Moreau!) "Well, that's convenient, isn't it?" I said, and shook his hand. And even he, this stolid, unimaginative fellow, even he paused, surprised, disappointed, waiting for some further response. Tears of relief, perhaps; a primitive whoop of joy.

There are so many like Raymond Moreau.

My disgust is not unreasonable. I know, because I have talked to my husband, and he agrees with me. He does urge me, from time to time, not to be too harsh: they mean no harm, he says. He contends that people usually do the best they can. I suppose

157

he is right, although I do wonder if this is not really a tautology in lush disguise. He has always been a compassionate man. He alone sees me as I am, and loves me as he loves the truth.

We are closer now than ever. We seldom go out; neither of us spends unnecessary time at school. Evenings find us here, laughing, talking into the night. We seem again to have as much to say to each other as when we first were lovers. I have fixed up the apartment quite differently—the bedroom is completely rearranged, with all new linens and a white bedspread and a thick white carpet. (I happen to like white. White does not symbolize.) Often we have picnics, as we did when we were young, only now we hold them indoors on the living room floor; and we drink good wine, '66 Burgundies, '61 Bordeaux, rich wines of every hue from purple-black to brick-red. And I have never been so content.

But lately, and too often, as we lie in the dark, I curled away from him, peaceful and fearless, he rises, stealthy, gentle, and leans over me, watching my face; I can feel his breath on my cheek; and I must give him a sign, a sigh, a dreamy moan to ease his mind. Just like a robot he must rise, prompted by my old, foolish impulse, unworthy of him, as though by watching he could keep me safe; as though the universe concerned itself with us.

There's the violation. There's the damage. There's the tragedy.

JUSTINE LAUGHS AT DEATH

At 3:00 A.M. the phone rang and rang, extracting him like a stubborn, healthy tooth from the maw of a garish dream, a complicated one with melting scenery, shifting shapes, wheeling, screaming birds. In confusion and nascent outrage he reached for the instrument beside his bed. His hand, still dozing, held the receiver like a toddler's, first with the earpiece to his mouth, then turning it so clumsily that the business end bruised his upper lip. "Why?" he said. This wasn't what he meant to say, but it was a good question.

The voice was a woman's: sweet, motherly, unfamiliar. "I know what you've been up to," she said. "I've got my eye on you, Sonny." Click. Dial tone. He replaced the receiver and stared at it for quite a while.

He owned six ordinary telephones, one for each other room in his apartment, but this bedside one, the one most often used, was a novelty model, bought recently in order to add an ironic dimension to his private life. So that now, in the grudging light of a new moon, he contemplated the emergent features of an obnoxious duck. For the first time it occurred to him that irony might not be the best thing for a man in his business to fool around with.

For his business was Evil.

161

He was a specialist, concentrating on Pleasure in the Monstrous
—depravity, sadism, and gratuitous mayhem— uninterested in,
say, hypocrisy, greed, or false witness. In his experience, general
practitioners were gasbags, all talk and no action. Evil is noto-
riously inconsistent, so that the orthodox believer, pulled in sev-
eral different directions, is often left at square one. One has only
to study—as he had, in depth—the confused philosophy and
pathetic life of the Marquis de Sade. Long ago, having zeroed in
on the essentials of his faith, he had ruthlessly junked all corol-
laries not directly on point. For instance, he was not a racist; and
if he had ever taken the time to file a return with the IRS, he
would not have cheated on it.

But he had time and attention for nothing but predatory delights. From the beginning, in 1887, his prey were exclusively
women, his pleasure raping, maiming, torture, murder, and scaring
the living daylights out of the entire sex.

When he first made his mark, in the Whitechapel slums of
Victorian London, he revealed to the world its first pleasure killer.
He was still the champeen. He raped, maimed, etc., not for re-
venge or wealth, not for love of Art or Science, nor in the name
of State or Church, but simply for the sheer dirty thrill of it.
His style quickly caught on worldwide, so that he had many
imitators—more every day—but all of them, to a man, got caught.
Such was his genius that he never even came close to discovery,
and never would. He was the Babe Ruth, the Art Tatum, the
Secretariat of murderous heterosexual perverts.

He followed lonely women down dark alleys and into singles
bars, or capered and skipped ahead of them, letting himself into
their apartments so that he could greet them properly, once they
had closed and triple-locked the door behind them. (He loved
to wait for her gentle sigh as she shot the deadbolt home.) He
plucked schoolgirls from playgrounds and gave them long, lei-

162

surely country rides. He stalked big-boned, apple-cheeked hikers, unwrapping them from their backpacks, flannel and denim like granola bars. Every woman he chose was transformed in some permanent way—mentally, into, say, an agoraphobic, or a giggling lunatic; physically, so that she was in some measure smaller than before, or her face had become literally unforgettable; ontologically, so that what had been a living woman was now a pile or piles of organic matter.

He made them do terrible, degrading things with the false promise that he would spare their lives. He made them do terrible, degrading things with the candid threat of certain slaughter whether they did them or not. (Hope being one of his minor themes. He loved to watch it die, and he loved even more to manipulate the hopeless, to test the limits of their endurance when their only certain reward was another few seconds of life.) Even the solitary recipients of his 3 A.M. telephone calls (always 3 A.M., their time) were altered thereby. The hardiest ones got unlisted numbers; most had their phones disconnected, and refused ever to speak into one again.

Seriously. Every time a sex crime went unsolved it was his and his alone. Every serial killer who ever tantalized the press was this actual man. He was the unknown perp of the most voluminous open files in the police departments of every major city in the world. His was that intimate omniscient whisper in the dead of night, his the moving finger writing bloody valentines on flowered wallpaper, his the footprints cast in plaster, crumbling into powder on the evidence shelves of police warehouses. Every unclaimed torso, every writhing, bandaged horror, every pitiful seminude body discovered by Boy Scouts in a litter-strewn ravine was the work of his hands. And make no mistake, he was only human. Terrific genes, it's true: easily passing for a man of half his age (he was one hundred and eighteen), and strong as a minotaur.

But only human. He was finite in height and girth, commonplace in weight and glove size. He occupied one space at a time, just like you and me, submitted, as we must, to the natural law, and put on his pants in the age-old way. And his name was Robert L. Ripley.

▼ ▼ ▼ ▼ ▼ ▼ ▼

Ripley pulled on his terry robe and fuzzy slippers and shuffled out to the kitchenette. He fixed himself a club sandwich, the main ingredient of which, for reasons of prudence and pity, I shall not disclose, and ate it at the counter, and washed it down with buttermilk. He supposed there was a funny side ("THE BITER BIT") to this midnight alarm. He supposed this, but didn't really feel it. He smiled, broadly, just for practice, as though he *did* feel it, and his open-mouthed, bare-toothed, meat-flecked smile was at that moment the ugliest thing in the universe. Its object was a sweet-voiced motherly woman with indistinct features. He gave her thigh- and buttock-flesh by the handful, adding billowy white skin and the sturdy forearms of a breadmaker, and he was trying to decide which to subtract first when the telephone rang. This time, at least, it was an ordinary harvest-gold wall model.

Anonymous again, and female, but much younger. She was thirteen or so and spoke, when she could get her words out, with an orthodontic lisp. From background squeals and whispers it was obvious she was not alone, but in the company of her coltish, spring-scented kind. Probably a slumber party. "Have you got—" she squeaked, and then peppered him with giggles, the crowd around her tittering like a flock of geishas. "Mister, have you got —" Again, no go. Hee hee HA-ha-ha-ha-ha. The sunny, burbling descent of a house wren. A happy little tune, and infectious, to anyone not naturally immune.

"Have I got *what*, Dear Heart?" A slumber party. . . . He concentrated on that winsome thought and tried to ignore the unprecedented affront. His fingers tightened on the receiver, indenting it a tad.

"Have you got—shut *up*, I'm *doing* it—have you got Aunt Hee hee HA-ha-ha-ha!"

He bared his lips in a smile no primate could misinterpret, and a large spider, viewing the grin eightfold, dropped legs-up onto a nearby windowsill and shriveled like fatback on a griddle. "Little girl? What's the name of your street, Dear Heart? Precious? What's the number on your front door?"

"Have you got Aunt Jemima by the box?" Hilarity erupted at the other end, emerging at a pitch that scalded his eardrums.

"NO!" he cried, the phone starting to deform in his hand like a surrealist watch, the children laughing, happy, *safe*. "No, my little squab, but I'd surely love to have *you* by the—" Click. Dial tone.

▼ ▼ ▼ ▼ ▼ ▼ ▼

After taking two sets of pills, some for sleep, some for blood pressure, he lay wide-eyed in bed, clenching and reclenching his fists and jaw, and his lips moved soundlessly in the dark. Sleep was out. He had been grievously wronged and his entire musculature cried out for justice. He switched on the light, took the duck in his lap, and began thumbing through the special black loose-leaf binder that he kept in the nightstand drawer. There were two sections to the notebook, both roughly alphabetical lists of names, numbers, addresses, comments; the first list of past correspondents, the second of future prospects. He picked a name, Lucy Garney, from the second list, letting her image coalesce as he removed his pajamas, wadded them behind his tense neck, slid down supine, threw aside comforter and satin sheet, splayed on the square bed like a peeled pink starfish. Lucy Goosey, plump and juicy, maybe old, though, with a name like that, no Jennifer she, no Adrienne, Kristin, Michelle Ma Belle Quail-stout, doughty old Lucy, comes right out in middle age with her nickname for the world to see, none of this L. Garney nonsense. Looking for a husband, Lucy? Looking for love? He closed his eyes and felt out her number, touched her very tones, his fingertip hovering for a sensuous moment above the final digit. He rang her chimes. Even now she tottered, sleep-stupid, to the telephone, wondering Who has died in the night? Who, *in extremis*, thinks of silly old Lucy?

Someone at 8 Buena Vista Circle picked up the phone. "Speak," said Lucy Garney.

She didn't sound flustered, although he couldn't tell much from a monosyllable. Maybe she worked nights. "Miss Garney? This is Omni-Research, Inc., calling with a brief survey questionnaire? I hope I didn't disturb you?"

"No problem."

It was almost four in the morning. "All righty. We deeply appreciate your cooperation, and I can tell you right now that soon, very soon, a surprise package will be hand-delivered to your very door, especially for you, Lucy Garney. Now, are you ready?"

"Shoot."

"All righty. Now, repeat after me. No. 1. Rubber baby buggy bumpers."

"Rubber baby buggy bumpers."

"No. 2. Blooming boughs of bearded bats."

"Blooming boughs of bearded bats."

"No. 3. Brutal bloody blubber burgers."

"Brutal bloody blubber burgers."

"Excellent! Now listen hard, Lucy Garney. Here's your question. Which of these three sentences—No. 1, No. 2, or No 3—would you have the most difficulty enunciating if I were to come over

166

to 8 Buena Vista Circle right now with a straight razor and cut off your upper lip?"

Utter silence. Not even the sound of breathing. Often they forgot to breathe

Ripley, grinning in the dark, wriggled his bottom like an ecstatic baby. "Lucy, dear, would you like me to repeat the choices?" Silence. "This isn't a memory test, Dear Heart. I love you, Lucy." Silence. "All righty, let's try a different one. Number One. Thready throats of throttled thrushes—"

"I guess Number Three."

"*What?*"

"The one about the blubber burgers."

The grin felt plastered across his face; his left hand froze in mid-caress, contracting to a claw, producing agony. "Are you deaf, woman?" he shouted. "Are you feeble-minded? You—you—I'm going to *kill* you, you half-wit sow! Death by fire will seem like a month in the country by the time I—"

"Gotta go now. 'Bye." Click.

Ripley, who in infancy had neither smiled nor cried, threw his first tantrum. He ripped the duck phone from the wall, along with a fist-size chunk of plaster; he clawed the sheets and comforter to shreds, upended his mattress, tore it in half like a joker's telephone book, tore it into quarters, eighths, and so on, scattering feathers and foam. He attacked his pillow with an ice pick, cursing at full roar with every thrust, so that his neighbors banged on wall and ceiling and threatened to call the law. He grabbed his black notebook and ran into the kitchenette, stood by the phone turning pages with such violence that they ripped and scattered like handbills in a parking lot. He found a name, Violet Bone, misdialed her number, awakening a furious *basso profundo*, misdialed again, awakening an answerphone belonging to Jim&Sally Hamper, said something so hideous at the time of the tone that, had his voice not been unintelligible with rage, the Hampers would, post-playback, have sold their house at a loss and left the country. Finally he got the number. As it rang, he tried to get his breathing under control, which was difficult since, in addition to all other provocations, the receiver in his hand was so disfigured by his earlier fury that he couldn't hold it to his ear and mouth at the same time, and was going to have to keep twisting it into position. "Hello?" said Violet Bone.

"Is that Vi?" he asked, in a not-so-hot approximation of good-natured geniality. "Is that really you? Lawks, Child, I can scarce believe my ears."

"This is she," said Violet Bone.

" 'This is she!' Ho ho ho. That's rich, Vi." He was on the verge of enjoying himself. "Well, this is *I!* And I bet you haven't recognized my voice! Come on, Vi. Guess Who."

"You lose."

"Huh?"

"Look, Ripley, the telephone is not a toy. Grow up or shut up." Click.

▼ ▼ ▼ ▼ ▼ ▼ ▼

He looked every bit as stupid as he felt, standing there in his trashed kitchenette, in a mulch of obscene memos, one dull finger on the telephone cradle. His thoughts were looped and fragmentary. All he knew for sure was that he was not crazy. On the other hand, he was afraid to release the plunger because Violet Bone, She Who Knew His Name, might be lurking in the telephonic ether. He dialed 0 and got a man named Burt. "Yeah, Burt, I'm having trouble with my phone. It's kind of . . . look, I'm going to be honest with you." Ripley took a deep breath. "I may be the victim of a conspiracy. I mean a joke. The butt of a joke. Heh heh. Probably a bunch of my nutty friends. What I'm wondering

168

is, is there any way you could put a temporary trace, or whatever you call it, on my phone?"

Burt was quiet for a moment. "Do you own your own phone, sir?" Ripley said he owned all his phones. "Because you could put the trace on, yourself."

"Really? How?"

"Phosphorescent paint would do it. Or garlic."

"Huh?"

"Either way, you'd always know where it was." Burt had a cruel, barking laugh. "Look, Mr. Bozo, nobody who wants his own telephone traced at four forty-five in the morning has any friends, nutty or otherwise. You are a conspiracy loon, and if you think I have to humor you, forget it."

Ripley turned eggplant-purple, the cords in his neck standing out like buttresses. "This is an outrage! I'll report you to the phone company!"

"Phone company! What phone company?" Burt laughed bitterly. "This is Anarchy, buddy. This is Chaos you're talking to."

"I know your name."

"I lied. Go trace yourself." Click.

Ripley dialed 0.

"City Information Justine Speaking May I Help You?"

Ripley cursed the divestiture of the Bell System at such volume and with such force that millions of tiny circuits disintegrated and the local weather outlook began inexorably to awaken everybody on the immediate eastern border of the city park. This was the first time he had ever expended his rage on a nonsexual target. It was a terrible waste. Midway through he remembered what he was talking to, and focused his wrath personally upon Justine, and called her names so dreadful that only a handful of men had ever uttered them aloud, and one in particular so foul that it has never even been written down, although everybody knows

169

what it is, and even indecent women, upon hearing it, lose their minds.

Justine's response—a laconic "You ready to talk, Ripley?"—affected him more or less as the hundredth galvanic shock affects a Skinner animal. In other words, having by now acquired that combination of paranoia, sophistication, and lugubrious self-pity peculiar to the white rat, he caved in. He leaned against the sink, staring out the kitchen window with burning eyes at the noisome rebirth of day, held the phone tenderly against his ear, as though nursing both it and a migraine, and said, "Yeah. I'm ready to talk."

Justine lost her professional monotone, breathed too close into the receiver, teased him like some moist, silly preschooler. "What *about?*" She sounded like she was digging her toe into the dirt.

"Who you are? How you know each other? How you know about me? What you want?"

"Your worst nightmare. Psychic resemblance. You stand out in a crowd. To have a few laughs."

"Psychic resemblance? What the hell is psychic resemblance?"

"We're all alike, Bob."

A huge bird landed in the winter-stripped maple tree in the courtyard below his window. First he thought it was a crow, but it was too big, and perched ramrod-straight, with a military, uncrowlike posture. It sat still, ruffling its feathers in a rhythmic, self-soothing way, as though telling itself a bedtime story. Its big round head swiveled back and forth a couple of times like a tank turret. It dwarfed the tree that harbored it. Watching it helped, a little. "All alike?"

"All alike."

"Justine. Dear Heart. That's just an expression."

"Yes, and one of your favorites, Dear Heart. In fact, it's not unfair to say it's a basic tenet of your creed."

"So what?"

"So, you ought to be delighted. You're vindicated. You are our first initiate. You now know What No Other Man Has Known."

"That you're all alike?"

"All alike."

"In the dark. Yessssss. In the pitch black, alone and helpless, your thin hands beating, fluttering like wings ..."

"And in the big fat light of day. All alike. Interchangeable. Omnipresently coincident."

"Omnipresently my buttocks!"

Justine giggled like a thirteen-year-old.

"All for one, eh? I'm supposed to believe that whatsoever I do to the least of you my sisters I do to all. Well, get this: ———" (Here he said something for which there is no euphemism.)

"You got it backwards, Bob. What you do to all you do, repeatedly, to one. One with, I must point out, a by now substantial grudge." Justine sniffed. "Namely, me."

"Justine?" Ripley, watching the big bird, the Great Horned Owl, fast asleep, limned in shell-pink light, concentrated mightily, breathed slow and deep. "I'm thinking now of an ordinary pair of pliers, the kind your home handyman buys in any hardware store. Do you wear nail polish, Justine? Are those cuticles ship-shape?"

"I thought you wanted to talk. If you're just going to horse around—"

"I am talking, Justine. And I'm thinking about a belt sander. ..."

Justine sighed. "Call me when you're ready to get serious. Any old number will do."

"Wait." How he surprised and hated himself for begging! *How she would pay.* "Explain yourself. Please. You're a coven of feminists, you've got ahold of a computer and rigged up some kind of network. We'll start there."

"Wrong." Justine made a rude blatting sound, like the loser's

171

honk on a game show "The technology is totally uninteresting, and forget politics. This is personal, Bob. I Am Woman, get it? I take everything personally."

"You're sticking to this ridiculous story, then. You're all the same person because that's the way *my* mind works. Justine, honey, this is the real world. This is Planet Earth. That kind of stuff only works in cheap fiction."

"If I were you, Bob, I wouldn't take that line of reasoning any further."

Ripley unaccountably began to sweat. He didn't take that line of reasoning any further. "So. Revenge, eh? You're plotting vengeance for my crimes against you."

Again, with the game show blat. "No punishment could possibly be, as they say, 'appropriate in this instance.' Why, you'd bankrupt the Furies themselves. The Eternal Agony of Prometheus would amount to a slap in the face. I mean, really, how in hell are you going to pay me back?" Involuntarily, tenderly, Ripley massaged the region of his liver. "See, what I have in mind is more like what I said before. Having a few laughs. And, well, keeping in touch. Do you have any idea how lonely I get?"

"I can fix that, Justine. Tell me where you are."

"No, no. Not *that*. Bob, do you know, this is the first time we've ever really talked?"

He had been admiring the owl for so long, and the light had been so slow in coming, that he had failed to note the arrival of the others. He saw that the maple branches, which he had dimly supposed were laden with some sort of small ovoid fruit (God, he was tired!) were full instead, to flashpoint, with scores of tiny birds. Perhaps as many as a hundred. And scores were perched everywhere below, on the low brick wall, in the arbor vitae. It was a huge winter flock, a city mix of sympathetic foragers— nuthatches, titmice, chickadees. Mostly chickadees. But they weren't foraging: they were sitting stock-still, a rapt congregation, attending upon the owl. Who slept, oblivious. "What did you mean," Ripley asked, "when you said you were my worst nightmare?"

"Just that. Your worst nightmare, Bob. A woman with an inner life."

Ripley let out his breath, then laughed with relief. "But that's what I count on! Your inner life! Your fear, your longing, your wild hope! You haven't learned much, Justine, if you think this is just about sex. Why, I could get an inflatable doll, I'd buy 'em by the gross, I'd stay right here in my own head and not *do* anything at all, if sex were all I wanted. What would I need you for, if not your inner life?"

"Not a doll, Bob. A robot. A synthesizer. Press one key for FEAR and another for TERROR and a third for ABJECT HORROR and so on. A crude and primitive instrument, for your trite, monotonous music."

"I terrify you!"

"True."

"I give you endless, exquisite pain!"

"Sure."

"I take your precious life."

"You bet."

"I fill your mind!"

Blaaaat.

The owl opened his round yellow eyes, took in his audience, its size, its nature, showed no fear. Did not, for instance, cringe comically like a surprise party stooge at the moment he switches on the light. Ripley could almost see him suppress the involuntary start, gather his great dignity around him like a purple robe. The animal could not, however, control the reflex behavior of his feathers, any more than Ripley could keep the little hairs on the back of his neck from standing up. Layers of down and feather lifted, fanned, bristled. The owl, unmoving, grew tall and fat. The man, for all his goose bumps, grew not a micron.

"Do you remember that time in the laundromat?" Justine asked.

"Which laundromat?" There had been so many laundromats. He tried to remember a woman, any woman, but all he could get were smells, sharp detergent, clean lint, dryer heat. He hated laundromats.

"The Helpy Selfy in St. Paul."

"Got you." Ripley couldn't remember her at all. He didn't even want to remember. He didn't *care*. He was desperately tired and he felt vacant, cavernous, with only dread and apathy where his hunger should be. He was *depressed*. "I feel awful," he thought, then realized, to his horror, that he had spoken aloud.

"I was bottle blonde, forties, little potbelly in light blue double-knit stirrup pants. I was monopolizing the drycleaning machines. Remember?"

"Yeah. Sure."

"So, what do you suppose I was thinking about, there, at the end?"

Something was happening outside, in the trees. No one had moved, but he could hear, through the glass, the sleigh-bell jingle of a hundred cheeping throats. The tiny birds were scolding, en masse, at full throttle. The sound on his side of the glass was unpleasantly insistent, like the cry of an infant, about which, regardless of how you feel about infants, you must do *something*. Outside it had to be deafening. The owl, with his so-sharp ears and no hands to cover them, swiveled his great head back and forth, scanning, patient, every inch the monarch, back and forth again and again in the same ponderous rhythm, getting nothing new, no purchase, like a monarch-machine, robotic and stupid and dull.

174

"I was thinking, believe it or not—" Justine caught her breath, laughed a rueful laugh, "—this is right at the *end*, remember, just before I died. I was thinking about cigarettes, and how much I wanted the one I dropped when you came up behind me. I could just taste that Lucky. God. But that's not all, and this is really wacky. I remembered this time when I was a kid, and I was Christmas shopping by myself for the first time, at Woolworth's, with a ten dollar bill to cover everybody in the family—imagine *that*, Bob!—and I had two whole dollars left to spend on my Mom, and I wanted to get her the most perfect present, and then I *saw* it. On top of a glass counter, a painted statue of the Virgin Mary. It was the most gorgeous thing I'd ever laid eyes on."

"You lie! You were in mortal agony! If you could think at all, you thought of me! 'Why is he doing this to me? How have I offended him? What can I possibly offer him to make him spare my life?' "

"And when I got it home I looked at it for hours on end—well, minutes, anyway—and it was even more beautiful when I owned it. And every little detail, every eyelash, every fold in the robe was painted in. Of course, machines turn those things out by the pantload, but I was just a kid. I kept picturing my Mom's happy face when she unwrapped it from the tissue paper—"

"WHO CARES?"

"Well, of course, she wasn't happy at all. She tried to look thrilled, but even I could see that something was wrong."

"WHAT DOES THIS HAVE TO DO WITH ME?"

"So, she acted thrilled, but the next day she called me into the kitchen and there, at her feet, were the smashed remains, no piece bigger than the nail on my little finger. She said she was washing it and it slipped out of her hands and she was very, very sorry. I told her I'd get her another, but she said, No, no, and her cheeks were bright red and her face was like a mask, like she was hiding

175

something. I don't want another one, she says, I'll always remember *this* one; and in the next room my father snorts like you do when something funny happens in class. So suddenly I get the big picture. It was a bad gift for some reason, she'd broken it on purpose, they were laughing at me. God, I wanted to kill them. I was so embarrassed." Little swarms of chickadees, still scolding, left their perches and circled the owl. Like participants in some confrontational therapy group they took turns screaming in his face and He, who could have reached out one yellow taloned foot and plucked out a life, pretended he was alone. He looked ridiculous. "The point is," Justine was saying, "we were Presbyterians."

Ripley grabbed a fork from the counter and began to rap on the glass, which cracked prettily, like ice. Again he thought aloud. "What's going to happen? Why won't he fight back?"

"It's a common natural phenomenon," Justine said. "It's called 'mobbing.' Most birds do it."

"Are they going to peck him to death?" Ripley shuddered. Death in a million tiny bites.

Justine laughed. "Nah. They're just having a little fun. See, owls are dangerous only when they're feeding. The rest of the time, there's nothing special about them, except they're huge and hard to camouflage They're very, very good at what they do. But they're not terribly bright."

"WHO ARE YOU?"

"This one's especially stupid because he tried to hide in the city. But even in the deepest, darkest forest they have a hell of a time getting fifteen minutes of uninterrupted sleep."

"WHAT DO YOU WANT?"

"They never dream, you know. And they always feel crummy."

Ripley's fork shattered the window. Deafened and distracted, the owl below ignored noise and raining shards. A chickadee

176

swooped up onto the sill, inches from Ripley's white knuckles, regarded him with frank, good-humored curiosity, and addressed him in its little buzzy voice. It said: *"Dee dee dee dee dee."*

"But at night," said Ripley, "at night . . . they terrorize and maim and kill. . . ."

"And in the morning they hunt, in vain, for a quiet place to sleep, and just a little respect."

The chickadee was quick but Ripley was quicker. He pounded it, with one lightning fist, into a distant memory. Another jaunty bird, identical in every particular, instantly popped onto the sill, like toast from a slapstick toaster. He took in Ripley with one wise black-button eye. He said: *"Dee dee dee dee dee."*

Ripley saw it all then, the infinite assembly line of chickadees, the joyless, dutiful, mechanical pounding of his fist, the stinging jangle of a million midnight telephones. His comic, boring future. "I'll never stop!" he screamed, whirling in hopeless fury, ripping the cord from the wall. "Do you hear me, Justine?"

"Everyone hears you, Bob."

"And tonight, and tomorrow night, and every night you'll suffer and cry and beg for an easy death! You'll *bleed* and you'll . . . I don't know . . . *bleed* . . . and—"

"I know, I know," she said, like comforting a baby, and stifled a little yawn. "Bob? Listen. I'll call you." Click

And he would, too. Never stop. Below, the owl spread its great gray wings and lofted up and out across the courtyard, majestic, pretending no hurry; his little torturers followed him up, darted around his head like bees, chirping with derision. The owl circled the tree deliberately, twice, as though seriously considering going back there, then turned himself north and sailed away, oh so slowly, as though he had all the time in the world and were just acting on a whim. As though he weren't Grand Marshal in a capering parade of hooting, nose-thumbing hors d'oeuvres. Ripley tried to admire the elaborate pretense, the grandeur of the act. But sentimentality was not one of his faults. The owl, really, looked like the big stupid idiot it was, and they'd ruined *everything*, and a single bitter tear tracked down the side of his nose and plopped onto the receiver in his hand, which buzzed in its perky, tireless, impossible way, and he was already so very tired.

MR. LAZENBEE

Mr. Lazenbee was an old, old man with watery eyes and a shriveled, bashed-in chin, so that his face sloped right back to his neck from the tip of his big purple nose. Viewed from the side, hunched over the green metal wastebasket under Miss Milliken's desk, shuffling down the corridors behind the huge waxing machine, he looked just like a vulture, with his bald head and his beak and his scrawny old red neck. Marsha was the first to recognize this likeness. Soon after, all the girls called him "Vulture Man," sometimes in his hearing, behind hands damp with giggling. Astonished to have thought up a popular joke, Marsha took to bragging about it. Miss Milliken, who always stopped talking whenever Mr. Lazenbee came into the room, whose knees could be seen to flinch when he emptied her wastebasket, who never looked directly at Mr. Lazenbee at all but addressed the air in front of him, scolded the whole class one day for calling him "Vulture Man." "Cleverness," said Miss Milliken, looking straight at Marsha, "in the service of unkindness is a sin." She dropped her eyes and frowned, to herself, not at the class. "This is inappropriate behavior, children," she said, in a tone less sure.

▼ ▼ ▼ ▼ ▼ ▼ ▼

Marsha walked the O'Brien twins to their house. She skipped ahead of them and drew a big heart on the sidewalk with red

181

chalk. "Miss M. + V. Man" she printed inside the heart. "Don't," whined Sheila O'Brien, scuffing out the mark with her toe. "That's dumb," said her sister Val.

Marsha guessed that the heart joke was poor. Even the skinny, rat-faced O'Briens could, without effort, tell the laughable from the lame, a distinction Marsha continued to find elusive. "What if he grabbed her by the *leg*," she said, in her excited voice that carried. She doubled over and pretended to vomit. The twins ignored her. "Mr. Lazenbee!" she shrieked, in a silly old-lady voice, and then cackled, "Come wiz me to zee boiler room, *girly*!"

"Grow up," said Val, who had laughed with the whole class the time he called Miss Milliken "girly." She and Sheila, in fact, were the ones who had first pointed out to Marsha that Mr. Lazenbee always looked at the girls' chests and their laps when they passed him in the corridor or playground, that he called them all "girly" and laughed in a foolish, nasty way; that he was a dirty old bum. Marsha never even noticed Mr. Lazenbee before that. She thought it was unfair and typical that now they changed the rules so that she was once again a pariah for the exact same reason she had been briefly, and tentatively, included.

Marsha tried again. "Mr Lazenbee smells like a brewery," she said. "He's utterly repellant."

"He's Borderline Retarded," said Sheila She and Val stood on their front porch. They were not going to invite her in.

"He is not," Marsha said. The door slammed shut. "You don't even know what that means," she yelled after them, then walked away, muttering, "So what if he is."

That night at dinner her mother explained that Borderline Retarded meant slow-witted and childlike "Such people are almost always harmless," she said Marsha thought Mr. Lazenbee was more like a cunning, crippled animal than a slow child. Her parents did not make her tell them why she asked; but, "I trust," her father said, "that whoever it is, you haven't been tormenting him or her."

▼ ▼ ▼ ▼ ▼ ▼ ▼

Miss Milliken was unusually tense and preoccupied. "Children, put away your quizzes and sit still. We're going to have a little talk." She pulled her swivel chair from behind her desk and around in front. She perched there, looking smaller and older than usual, and very uncomfortable. She studied a booklet that she held before her with one hand; the cover read, "Sixth Grade Facilitator: For Your Eyes Only." The class was wary, for Miss Milliken, a formal and old-fashioned teacher, never left her desk except to write on the board or collect papers. She glanced up at them. "I am sitting like this," she said drily, "to put you at your ease and encourage a frank and open dialogue." She looked back down at the booklet and after a long pause began to read in a clipped, expressionless voice.

"Everyone has feelings," she read. "Good feelings and bad feelings. Happy feelings and sad feelings. Sometimes we feel sorry, and sometimes we feel guilty. When do we feel guilty?" She paused but did not look up. Crystal Van Meter said we feel guilty when we do something bad. "And when do we feel excited?" Sheila O'Brien said, "When something, like, exciting happens." "And sometimes," Miss Milliken said, "we get what we call a 'funny' feeling. It is easier to give examples than it is to explain exactly what this means. When do we get a *funny* feeling?" "When we do something funny," said Barry Levin. Barry was the class wise guy and Miss Milliken usually dealt with him ruthlessly. Marsha was shocked now to see her lips curl at the edges. "It is hard to fault your answer, Barry," she said, regarding him mildly, "but it was not the one we were looking for." Claudine Fortin said, "When we throw up," and everybody in the class laughed. John Block said he sometimes got a funny feeling in the middle of the night. "We get a funny feeling," said Marsha, "when we know something is wrong but we can't explain it."

"Marsha has given us the correct answer," Miss Milliken said. She lifted her glasses and massaged the spot between her eyes with two fingers. She stayed quiet for so long that Marsha began to wonder if she had fallen asleep.

"Now the easiest feelings to identify are physical feelings," Miss Milliken read. She stopped and looked out at the class, brightening momentarily. "The verb 'to feel' can, of course, be transitive as well as intransitive." She looked down at the booklet again and read, "We get feelings of pleasure or pain when our bodies are touched What are some examples of touches that make us feel good?" A couple of the boys snickered. Miss Milliken did not even give them a dirty look. Three girls raised their hands, looked around, and put their hands back down again. Miss Milliken sighed. "Hugging and kissing and squeezing and embracing and caressing and fond pats on the head," she said, her lips in an angry purse. "These are the kinds of touches we all love."

The class was nervous because Miss Milliken was acting strange and it was impossible to tell what she wanted from them. Marsha understood that Miss Milliken was in her own world now, as her parents often were, but felt terrifically complimented rather than left out. Miss Milliken was letting the class see that she was angry about some adult matter; she was *sharing*, Marsha thought, without understanding exactly what this meant. Marsha loved the way she said "hugging and kissing and squeezing" in a deliberate monotone, the way she said that "we all love" these things and let her cross voice and face say the exact opposite thing. She thought this was so funny that she could hardly keep from laughing. Marsha liked Miss Milliken very much, even though Miss Milliken did not like her.

Miss Milliken got a more enthusiastic response when she asked for examples of painful touches. The boys were especially inventive and graphic, and Miss Milliken let them run on, trying to outdo one another in violence. She finally stopped it by agreeing with Jason Adams that no one liked to be hit in the face with a hammer.

"Now some touches," she said, "make us feel 'funny.' They give us that 'funny feeling.'" She regarded the class with weary, sympathetic eyes as the children tried to imagine what this could possibly mean. One said "tickling" and another "when someone pretends to crack an egg on top of your head" ("Yes, Elvira," Miss Milliken said, "that certainly would feel funny") and another "when someone trips you and makes you fall down in front of everybody." The longer it went on the more tolerant of the class and angry at something else Miss Milliken got. It seemed to Marsha that she was putting on a performance just for her. Marsha got very excited; she wanted to clap for Miss Milliken. She started giggling to herself, and then, without meaning to, she laughed out loud. Miss Milliken inclined toward her, gazing at her with neutral curiosity, and waited. Marsha had to say something, and she had to say it through her own convulsive giggling. "Vulture Man," she said. The class stared at her. Children in the front rows swiveled around in their seats to get a look. Miss Milliken, studying her from a great distance, turned to stone. Marsha was drowning in laughter. She snuffled and snorted like a pig. "Vulture Man gives me that funny feeling," she said.

Miss Milliken looked at the space where Marsha was. She did not look *at* Marsha at all; she looked through her, and Marsha felt herself disappear. Miss Milliken turned away from the empty space and regarded the class for a moment. She ripped the booklet into four neat pieces. "This is not my job, children," she finally said, and then dismissed them for lunch, ten minutes early.

▼ ▼ ▼ ▼ ▼ ▼ ▼

When Marsha got home Aunt Reba was there. Aunt Reba was her father's older sister, a fat, pale, doting woman with a vacant laugh. She always hugged Marsha, and kissed her with peppermint lips, and squashed Marsha's face and boneless unresisting body against the jello of her bosom and stomach. She was the only adult who paid close attention to the things that Marsha said; she listened greedily to her opinions and especially to her accounts of the day. She seemed to live through Marsha in some awful intimate way that she was powerless to prevent; Marsha's adventures, such as they were, were no longer her own once Aunt Reba had extracted them from her. Marsha despised Aunt Reba, and not just because she was a leech who invaded and plundered what little privacy she had. She hated her because Reba was the family member whom she most resembled, and she saw her future self interned within that flabby, freckled body, mocked by those stupid and glittering eyes.

Marsha sat beside Aunt Reba at the dinner table and picked at her mashed potatoes and roast chicken. She usually took third helpings, but the sight of Reba's plate, piled high with food and gravy-drenched, disgusted her. Aunt Reba warned that she would dwindle down to skin and bone if she ate like that. Marsha's mother pointedly replied that this would be "highly unlikely." Aunt Reba tittered, "oh-ho-ho," this being her standard response to the most innocuous statements. Marsha's father, who was ashamed of his big fat sister, often privately referred to her as "the global village idiot," inevitably complaining in the next breath that her IQ was "within normal limits." Marsha's father was a child psychologist.

Aunt Reba's moon face loomed over Marsha. "What did we do in school today?"

186

Marsha began to shovel mashed potatoes into her mouth. "Answer your Aunt Reba," her father said.

"I made everybody hate me," Marsha said.

"Oh-ho-ho," laughed Aunt Reba.

"Marsha has problems relating to her peer group," her mother said.

Reba laughed and said she couldn't imagine such a thing. "She's smart as a whip," she said.

"She's brilliant," her mother said, "but she socializes poorly."

"She's working on it," her father said. "We've discussed the problem with her many times, and she understands what she has to do."

Reba nudged Marsha with her dimpled elbow "Maybe we march to a different tune," she said. Marsha made a fat moon face in her potatoes with the bowl of her spoon and submerged it in milk gravy. "How did you make everybody 'hate' you?" Aunt Reba asked. "Oh-ho-ho."

"She doesn't have to tell us. We respect her privacy." Marsha's father turned and addressed her in a tone that pretended there was no one else in the room. "Are we going to hear from Miss Milliken about it?" he asked.

Marsha thought about Miss Milliken's cold and final stare at the empty space where she used to be. "I think it's highly unlikely," she said.

▼ ▼ ▼ ▼ ▼ ▼ ▼

Miss Milliken introduced the lady as "Mrs. Johnson, our special guest speaker," then sat down at her desk and folded her hands in front of her, her face a polite, expectant mask. Mrs. Johnson wore blue jeans and a green checkered shirt rolled up to the elbows, and her hair was red and down to her shoulders, like Crystal Van Meter's. She smiled broadly at each member of the class, and told them to call her "Judy," and to drag their desks out of their straight rows and into a half circle around her. She stood up and leaned against Miss Milliken's desk, hugging her elbows against her chest, so that she had poor posture. She was younger than Marsha's mother, and she didn't wear makeup.

"Now," said Judy, when the room was quiet, "everyone has feelings. Good feelings and bad feelings. Happy feelings and sad feelings." Judy did not read from a booklet, but spoke as though the words had just occurred to her and every sentence was new and exciting. The other children seemed willing to pretend that they had not heard this before. When Judy asked for examples of touches that feel good they were much more cooperative than they had been with Miss Milliken, and they pleased Judy by giving her the right answers. ("When *who* hugs you?" Judy asked. "When your mom hugs you," said Merilee Spoon in a lisping whisper, and Judy smiled at her.)

Judy had to help them out with "touches that feel funny." She said that sometimes hugs and kisses don't make us feel good at all; she asked if they knew what she meant. Merilee Spoon said that one time a man was going to hug her but he got stopped by a policeman. She was less audible than usual, and everyone, especially Judy, leaned toward her to hear the story. Miss Milliken came out of her private world and attended to Merilee. She looked alarmed and sad, very different from her usual distant self. Marsha had a sudden dizzying vision of Miss Milliken, with her fragile old-lady bones and sculptured silver hair, a woman made entirely of words and ideas, standing guard over Merilee Spoon, shielding her with her actual body.

Judy nodded gravely all during the story, and when Merilee was done she looked out over the whole class to make sure they had been paying close attention and understood how important it was. Then she told them about bad touching, and about saying

188

"no" and screaming as loud as you can when someone grabs you. "Your body belongs to you," she told them. "Nobody, not even a grownup, has the right to touch you if you don't want to be touched." She told them what to do if anybody said or did something that made them feel "guilty and embarrassed, without knowing why." She made them all write down a phone number they could call at any time of the day or night.

Marsha wished she could see Judy the way the other children did. If she could just understand why they liked her and believed everything she said she would not have to work so hard just to get through her life. Angry and fatalistic, she raised her hand. "If it's somebody in your own family," she said, "you have to let them touch you. They can hug you and pinch you and follow you everywhere and you can't help it. If you screamed you'd just get in trouble." Judy was staring closely at her with that special alertness her father often showed, when he listened, not to what she said, but to what she meant. Marsha's voice rose. "They can fix it so you don't have any privacy at all. They can crawl all over you like . . . they can eat you up." She knew this last bit was melodramatic, but the arresting image of Aunt Reba leaning over her with a knife and a fork seemed a righteous one, and clever, too.

Judy, in the charged silence that followed, never taking her eyes from Marsha, leaned back, inclining her head toward Miss Milliken, who said "Probably nothing, nothing at all" in a calm voice but she, too, regarded Marsha closely and with the beginnings of interest; and the other children were watching her, only a few of them looking derisive or skeptical. "When you talk about being 'followed everywhere,'" Judy asked with an encouraging smile, "do you mean, within the house?"

"Certainly," said Marsha. She was trying hard not to enjoy Judy's concern, but she could not help her heart pounding.

189

"What rooms in the house?" Judy asked. "Is there a particular room or rooms where he follows you?"

"It's not a man," Marsha said, and thought for a despairing moment that here was the eliminating answer, but Judy made her face blank, the way adults tend to do when they get excited, and asked which rooms the *woman* followed her into.

"Perhaps after class," Miss Milliken said to Judy in a low voice. "I shouldn't pursue it here."

"The bathroom," Marsha said, watching Judy's eyes, and saw she had gotten it right. "The basement," she said.

Marsha was not conscious of doing wrong until she sat in the big leather chair in the principal's office with just Judy and Miss Milliken and Mrs. Kelly, the nurse. There had been the confusion of Judy's questioning, and then the bell ringing, and the dismissed class dawdling on their way out, reluctant to leave her. But even before Judy and Mrs. Kelly indirectly made plain the specific nature of "bad touching," Marsha knew she had deceived them so seriously and so thoroughly that if they ever found her out they would not even bother to hide their disgust. The cool leather against the backs of her thighs, the important hum of the principal's air-conditioner, three pairs of adult eyes that never left her—this was all wrong. She didn't belong here. Miss Milliken asked her if she would like some chocolate milk, and Marsha, who never cried, could not answer for the tears that froze in her throat.

Aunt Reba was nasty, but not in a way that anyone cared about. In class Marsha had briefly come to believe that she had been treated as badly as Merilee, that if people knew what her life was really like they would want to shield her, too. But Aunt Reba was only an unpleasantness, as her father often told her, and life was not a carnival, and Marsha was not the center of the universe.

Marsha was a good, defensive liar, cautious and canny, and

gave them enough to justify their faith in her. She made them promise not to tell her parents, and even so she was careful to emphasize that Aunt Reba never hurt her and did not frighten her. When Judy said she was going to drive her home, Marsha wondered that the woman could know how very tired she was, how gratefully, and deeply, she could sleep, and she almost liked Judy then, for her kind perception. Miss Milliken stood up to see them off. "My dear," she said, and Marsha turned and ran, stumbling, from her teacher's foolish compassion.

▼ ▼ ▼ ▼ ▼ ▼ ▼

There was a scene on Marsha's front lawn, when she pleaded with Judy not to tell and screamed at her retreating back as she marched up the front steps. Her father, home with the flu, opened the door before Judy got to it and welcomed her in, Marsha running in after her, and there was another, louder scene when he agreed to see Judy alone and tried to shut the study door. Marsha's mother had to help pry her daughter's fingers off the inside doorknob. Marsha had never made so much noise. She had the power only to deafen. Her mother tried to pull her upstairs but she kicked her hard in the shins, ran into the coat closet, and shut the door.

When her father opened it she was kneeling in a pile of boots and coats yanked from their hangers, her mother's fur, her father's Burberry, and her arms ached from the pressure of stopping up her ears. Judy was gone. Her mother was gone. There was no one but her father and her. He said something she couldn't hear. She planned to keep her ears plugged forever; she planned never again to explain or listen. He seized her by the wrists and pulled her to her feet, his violence astounding them both. He was pale and sweaty from illness. For a moment he was speechless, and his face showed confusion, even self-doubt, a look so alien that she wondered if he were having some kind of attack. Then, to her amazement, he asked, "Is it true? Is any part of it true?"

"Of course not!" Marsha said. "Don't you know anything?" She started to laugh, because, really, he was as big a fool as the rest of them, and when she heard him ask, "What am I supposed to do with you?" in a helpless whine, she laughed even harder, and she was still laughing when, after much awkward maneuvering, he tucked her head and shoulders under one arm and began to spank her.

He hit her very hard, but held her lightly in place. She could stop the spanking any time, she could simply straighten up and walk away. The thought made her light-headed even as the blood rushed to her face. Here she was, at the end of a terrible day, and here was her father, and they were doing this curious, intimate thing. She was not angry anymore, or frightened, and the pain was unimportant; she felt, oddly, as if she could forgive him anything. She had such a longing to forgive. But the arm around her waist was gingerly, not gentle. He held her with distaste, and in his grudging dutiful embrace she closed her eyes and turned herself, for good, into an orphan.

After supper she used her bedroom phone to call the hot-line number in her notebook. She told a woman with a pleasant grandmotherly voice that her father had held her still so she couldn't get away, and then had touched her where he shouldn't have. She felt guilty and embarrassed, she said, and she didn't know why.

▼ ▼ ▼ ▼ ▼ ▼ ▼

Marsha stood on the second-floor landing, in robe and pajamas, looking down at her parents as they helped the child abuse couple into their coats. There had been a great deal of talk, and she had answered all their questions with scrupulous honesty. *Are you afraid*

192

of your father? No. *It was just a spanking, nothing more?* Yes. *Why did you call us, Marsha?* I wanted to see what would happen. *I think you must be very, very angry with your Dad.* That's not a question. *You're a clever girl, aren't you?* Yes, I am.

"Sorry about this, Dr. Potter," the man was saying, and the woman said, "We have to check everything out."

"Of course, of course," said her parents. Everyone was laughing and talking at once, and pretending not to be upset. Marsha hated them too much to feel guilty, although she supposed she should. All she wanted was to fall asleep and wake up in a hundred years, some place where no one knew her.

"You know," said the man as he opened the front door, "I wish they were all this simple."

"So do I, George," said her father, shaking his hand. "God, so do I."

"What a world," said the man.

Outside two car doors closed, and the car started up and drove off. Her parents stood very close together in the dark front hall. They held hands. They were wary, skittish. if she were to cry "boo" and stick out her tongue they would jump like rabbits. "Psychopath," her mother said, to him. "Sociopath," said her scrupulous father.

▼ ▼ ▼ ▼ ▼ ▼

A week later she slipped down to the boiler room during recess, when she knew he was outside sweeping leaves and picking up litter with a pointed stick. It was warm down there and very dry, not musty-smelling, like her own basement: the pale walls and gray floor were free of obvious dirt, and there was plenty of light from a bare bulb hanging from the ceiling. There was furniture, too: a cot with a bare, discolored mattress, a beat-up table that swayed when Marsha pushed against it with one finger, with a long drawer full of mostly empty bottles. It wasn't as bad as it could have been, though there was an air of expectancy here, as if the room held its breath, and she thought of the robber bridegroom, and the lairs of predatory beasts. But that was silly. She was overexcited, she knew, from lack of sleep, and secret planning.

Next day she came back down after school, carrying her mother's old canvas tote bag from the garden club, and wearing her nicest blouse and skirt. Mr. Lazenbee didn't hear her over the throbbing hum of the boiler. He lay on his back drinking liquor out of a bottle; his legs were stretched out straight in front of him, and he lifted only his head to drink, with his shoulders flat against the dirty mattress. Marsha was sure that if she tried this she would spill the liquor all over her chin and neck. If Mr. Lazenbee were buried under sand, with just his head and right arm sticking out, he could still drink his liquor. This seemed extraordinarily innovative for a man as stupid as Mr. Lazenbee.

Mr. Lazenbee caught sight of her during a long pull from his bottle. She was quite close to him by then. He swallowed wrong and sat up in the throes of a choking cough; he capped the bottle and stuck it partway under the mattress. He was not happy to see her. "You lost, girly?" he said. Marsha shook her head. He squinted at her, his old mouth hanging open so long that she was going to tease him about catching flies. He got an idea. "*She* send you?" he asked.

Marsha hesitated. He could mean either Miss Milliken or the principal, Mrs. Schwab. "Yes," she said. "She wants you to fix this place up." She pulled the orange afghan Aunt Reba had made out of the garden club bag and put it on the bed beside him. She unpacked the cracked teacups and jelly glasses and the two Nancy Drews, and her framed picture of the harlequin. "She says you don't have to live like this."

"She's nuts," said Mr. Lazenbee. He spoke in a series of progressively indignant afterthoughts. "I don't live here. She say that? You tell her, I got a home, just like everybody else. Tell the fat cow to stick it."

"Do you really live somewhere else?" This was unimaginable to Marsha. "Where do you live?" she asked, trying to catch him out.

"None of your beeswax." Marsha giggled at a grown man saying such a thing. Mr. Lazenbee narrowed his rheumy eyes and studied her. "She didn't send you," he said.

Marsha reached into the canvas bag. "Want some peanuts?" she asked.

"I'll give you peanuts, girly. You get out of here now." Mr. Lazenbee lay back down on the bed, and, when she didn't move, raised his head and scowled at her. "Beat it, I said. Rotten kids." Marsha stood the harlequin picture on the table top, propped against the cement wall. "You're going to get in trouble, girly," said Mr. Lazenbee. He smiled in a nasty way. "I'll tell 'em you were down here. You'll catch it good. Stuckup little piggy." He looked at her everywhere, her chest and bottom, everywhere but her face, and showed her his long brown teeth. Marsha's skin felt toasted. She turned her back to him, barely breathing, and unbuttoned her turquoise blouse, and shrugged it to the floor, and swiveled to face him in her embroidered cotton slip. "Jesus God," said Mr. Lazenbee.

Mr. Lazenbee scuttled backwards on the bed and off onto the floor, moving with impressive speed considering how many tries it took him to get to his feet. "What are you doing?" he screamed, and then lowered his voice to a terrified whisper. "Jesus God, kid, don't *do* that." Marsha stepped out of her woolen skirt. "What do you want?" he cried.

Marsha started fussing with the afghan, unfolding and smoothing it onto the mattress. Mr. Lazenbee's reaction, and the intensity

195

of it, had stunned her into blank confusion. She had taken his cooperation for granted. Not once had she put words into his mouth. This had been stupid of her; but even if she had given him credit for a will of his own, she would never have had him ask, "What do you want?" "You're the one who wants," she said, under her breath, terribly embarrassed. She looked at him, held out her arms away from her body, hopelessly toward him, showing him her self, whatever there was to see and want. "You're the one," she said.

"Oh no I ain't!" He sidled to the door, then edged away from it toward the center of the room beneath the light bulb. He did this again and again, moaning with fright. "Never gonna believe me," he said, and then he looked at her with pure loathing and called her a dirty name. But it was not "sociopath."

"I can come every Friday," Marsha said, "and Wednesdays for a little while."

"Jesus God," said Mr. Lazenbee.

"It'll be just us," Marsha said, using as few words as she could, but there had been too many words already, and everything was ruined.

He made a dash for the heavy door, yanked it open. Once on the other side of it, holding it against his body like a shield, he looked at her for the last time, as it shut out his ugly, knotted face. "Rotten kid!" he screamed, and left her down there, alone.

▼ ▼ ▼ ▼ ▼ ▼

"So," her father said. He was slumped, gray and exhausted, in his leather swivel chair in the study, regarding her across his desk. Her mother had just left. "Here we are again. Right, Marsha? The whole adult world, dancing attendance on you." He sighed through grimly pursed lips, steadily, with low force, as though inflating a black balloon, and doodled on a lined pad. Doodling gave him

MR. LAZENBEE

something to look at besides Marsha. "It seems to me," he said, "that you're getting better at this all the time. You've got your mother crying now. You've got the principal of your school stuttering, like . . ." He shrugged angrily, smacking his pen down on the pad.

"Porky Pig," Marsha said.

"Don't you wise off at me!" His eyes widened, to take her in, she thought, and her heart began to race. But then she slipped right out of focus. There was some mechanism in his eyes that adjusted itself, and soon he was not angry at her, but at someone in back of her, visible through her. "I'll tell you a little something, Marsha," he said. "You think things are funny that aren't funny at all. Just because you laugh at something, don't expect other people to laugh with you. You're not funny."

"I know."

"No, you don't know."

Marsha was thinking about Vulture Man, and how she never had understood why the girls laughed, when to her it was just an accurate description; and about the red heart she had drawn on the sidewalk, with her corny joke inside, which wasn't funny. "Yes, I *do* know," she said.

"No, you *don't!*"

Marsha made her face flat and smooth.

"You do *not* know, Marsha! But you are going to *learn*. And I am *not* going to give up." He closed his eyes and leaned back.

Marsha leaned back too.

"Worst of all," he said, "you've taken a poor old man with half a mind to begin with, and frightened the hell out of him. He quit his job, did you know that? Does that mean anything to you, Marsha? Do you even know what a job *is*? You do? Wonderful. Let's hear it."

Marsha was trying to keep her face pale and her lips from

197

curling. There was no reason to laugh. Her father slipping in and out of control was the sort of thing that should have been funny, but wasn't anymore, really. She tried to picture something serious and sad, which should have been easy, and up popped Mr. La-zenbee, which was horrible. *None of your beeswax.* She snorted, pink and piggy.

Her father did controlled breathing. When he spoke, his voice was calm. "It's not working, Marsha. I'm not going to lose my temper with you again, ever. Do you believe me?"

Marsha nodded. He never lied to her. He didn't believe in it. Judy had lied to her. Judy had been in this study, with her father. Judy Sing-Song, who talked down to children, and her father, who didn't, because he didn't believe in it. Marsha watched her father get up and walk to the window, and stand there for a long time, looking out.

"Your mother is worried," he said, "and I am too, about exactly why you did what you did, and what you thought you wanted from the old man. We know, of course, that it was a cry for help, and I want you to understand that we heard you."

That was the saddest part, Marsha thought. They heard every-thing.

"We take it very seriously indeed I've set up an appointment for you with Glassman, for Monday." He glanced at her. "You may have heard us speak of him."

Marsha nodded. She'd heard them speak of him many times, in the next room over, or in the hall when she was in bed at night, their voices loud enough for her to hear. *If she keeps this up we'll have to send her to Glassman.* She was finally going to meet the Glass Man

"The point is, I can't help you with this. I'm your father. We're too close. Whatever you were doing down there, it was bound to have something to do with me. I'm the last person on earth who can help you with it. It's just not my proper job, Marsha. You can work it out with Glassman.

"What we *are* going to work on, you and I," he said, turning back to the window, "is our old nemesis. Our old, old friend."

"Empathy," said Marsha.

"Empathy," he said, "and respect for other minds, and you will, Marsha, believe me, you will learn to accept that other people are just like you. They have their own feelings and needs, just as you do. You are only one of many."

"And I am not the center of the universe," Marsha said.

"You don't bother me in the least, Marsha. You are going to learn that human beings are not dolls to be manipulated according to your whim. That not even a stupid person appreciates having his intelligence insulted, his integrity violated. That everyone is special, individual, unique, just like you. That people are not machines for you to wind up and point in any direction you want. You thought you could make that Lazenbee character do God knows what, you think you can make your mother and me run around like chickens. . . ."

Marsha watched her father as he talked on and on about what she thought and wanted and felt, as he always had, as though her head were made of glass and crammed with tiny lettered blocks constantly rearranging themselves for him to read. When she was little she had believed that this was true. But that was silly. He was just guessing. He didn't know anything.

As he talked he took his left hand out of his pocket and placed it flat against the window frame. He was wearing a light blue sweater over a shirt of darker blue, and the colors belonged together, the cuff and the rolled sleeve of the sweater, and his arm was bent just so at the elbow, and long and thin, but strong. This was the arm that had held her still, so grudgingly, so he could punish her, and it seemed to Marsha now that there was magic in it. Which was silly, because it was attached to her father, and people were not machines, to be taken apart and put together every which way. But the longing came back to her again, the longing to forgive, which was silly too, but so awfully strong that she had to look away, and even then, not looking, she couldn't bear it.

"You're crying now," he said, "because you feel sorry for yourself."

Marsha shook her ugly head no, and no.

"Yes," he said, coming near to stand over her, "and some day, not tomorrow, but some day you will learn to cry for other people."

She reached out blind with both hands and grabbed the arm. He let her do this. She pressed her face against it.

"But it's good that you're crying now," he said, with pity in his voice, measured, like milk in a glass cup.

She said, "Please don't say any more," but she didn't have the breath to make it plain.

"It's a good start," he said. "Go with your feelings now. This is how it begins."

Beyond sense and reason, Marsha was afraid he was right, and she tried again to make him just be still, but he wouldn't stop saying I know, I know, I know.

RÉSUMÉ

Here is the kind of person I am. You and I could be close friends for ten years, and then someone else could come along, and I would know the person for, say, one month, and he would say something derogatory about you, like you're a pompous jerk or a backstabber, and I'd say, Gee, I don't know, but I guess I can see what you mean I have no moral fiber. And I'd still go on being best friends with you. But if I were with this other person I'd pretend to agree that you were a jerk

Or I could be at a party, or waiting in line at the post office, and a total stranger standing next to me could say something totally out of line, like Niggers are the scum of the earth, and I'd just pretend not to hear him, or if I couldn't do that I'd say Excuse me in this superior voice and walk away. Only I wouldn't just stalk off and stand someplace else. I'd really act like I was looking for the bathroom, or I was late for a dentist appointment I'd make a big deal out of checking my watch and keep craning my neck looking for the next bus.

In fact, sometimes when I'm talking to a black person, and it doesn't matter if it's somebody I know or some guy painting my house, we'll have a normal conversation, only all the time I'm thinking, Hey, here I am talking to a black person, or when the conversation is over I'll think, That was a pleasant conversation.

203

It's like a nervous twitch. But I guess I don't think that's as bad as the other stuff, about being a coward.

I've done a couple of things that looked brave. I saved someone's life once. I grabbed a little kid's arm just as he was about to run out from between two parked cars. I'm pretty sure the bus was close enough and going fast enough so that the kid definitely would have been hurt. Although I could obviously be kidding myself about this. But (a) no one saw me do it, except the kid, who wasn't too impressed, because kids expect you to save them; and (b) all the time I was moving toward the kid, reaching out for his arm, I was seeing in my mind what my life would be like if I didn't do it, or if I didn't do it right: I would be the guy who didn't save the kid. So really I was brave because I was a coward. The other time I was in church, almost twenty years ago, and the pastor, this real mossback, was ranting about draft dodgers, but I didn't care because I had to go to the bathroom. Finally I stood up and walked down the middle aisle; and, as you probably know, half the congregation filed out behind me. Just before I got to the men's room one of the deacons caught up with me and started patting me on the back, and soon I was surrounded by well-wishers. Of course I had to put off going to the bathroom so that people wouldn't make the connection. I was quite a local hero.

I don't cheat on my income tax, but then my father never did, and that counts for a lot. You learn certain habits when you're young. Just because you have good habits, that doesn't make you a good person. Although, for what it's worth, I'd never cheat on a résumé.

I still vote Democrat.

I cheated on my wife once. I tried to weasel out of doing it, but then it turned out to be the best sex I ever had. I never did it again, but it wasn't a penance, oh no. I was doing myself a favor.

The only reason I didn't half-blind Billy Flanagan is that his mother called him just then and he turned his head and the arrow grazed the bridge of his nose, nicking it with the green feather on the way by. Lots of times I drive drunk, or half-drunk, which is worse. I could have killed a small army by now. I could have filled a hospital with quadriplegics. But I never killed anybody, oh no, and I never robbed, and I never told an important lie.

I even cried once on someone else's account. I saw Nixon's pets, those POWs, getting off that plane in Washington, or wherever the hell it was, those sad bastards, and this one guy says, with tears running down his face, "God bless the President! God bless the Commander in Chief!" I burst out sobbing in my own living room, in front of the wife and son. I was just getting over the flu, admittedly, but I really did have a moment there

Still. The fact is, I could easily have been a Good German.

Now at this point I could do two things. I could say, But look, I'm *not* a Good German. But that shouldn't cut any ice with you. It doesn't even impress me. Here's the other, more interesting, way I could go: I *know* I'm Good German material. That is, I may not amount to much, but I don't kid myself. So I should get points, etc.

But I'm not going to go that way. Not because you wouldn't fall for it, because, frankly, you're not too predictable. Meaning no disrespect, of course, but every once in a while you don't make perfect sense to me. For instance, every hour of every day of my life. Example: the wildebeest. The wildebeest population is kept down by every year wiping out most of them with crocodiles, thirst, starving to death, fire, drowning the babies, and finally this parasite that makes the weakest ones turn around and around until they drop, and then, still breathing, they get torn apart by hyenas. That one goes right by me, I have to admit. I'm sure there's a good reason for it, though. It would have to be a good reason, wouldn't it? Frankly, I can't wait to find out what the reason is.

But I'm not going to go that way because it isn't anything special to know you're Good German material. Even the real Good Germans knew what they were. Surprised? Do you think you can have a wormy soul and not know it? Just how stupid do you think we are?

What do you think it's like, living with a wormy soul? What would you know about it, you son of a bitch?

Well, enough about me. Let's talk about you. What are you going to do about me?

It's pretty obvious what you've got planned for my wife, you've tipped your hand there, and I must say it's pretty, well, extreme (I was going to say diabolical!), considering what a nice woman she is, even though, of course, she's a Good German too, though not as Good as me. I'm just guessing, but I'll bet it's going to be something fast for me, like heart or a brain hemorrhage, because I've seen how you like to mix it up.

Sometimes, I know, you like to go the other way, for variety, to stump the experts, like: car crash, car crash, dormitory fire, convenience store stickup, and last, but not least, for the remaining survivor, the Tragic Accident While Cleaning the Gun. But the odds are against this, so I'm betting it's the other thing.

Here's an idea, though: Don't do it. Let me live forever.

Now don't just say no. Think about it first. Ask yourself this: Why not? I'll wait. Take your time.

Now I'm betting you came up with an answer, and it satisfied you just fine. So what is it? You shouldn't mind letting me in on it; I mean, even if I don't get it, which I probably wouldn't, it's got to be so deep, so *wise*, that it would just blow me away. I mean, it's not as if I wouldn't be impressed. It's not as if you'd be risking any loss of face. You could only gain. Whatever the reason is, it's got to be so great, so colossal, that there's no chance at all that I would, say, laugh and laugh and point at you and laugh even harder and run around telling all my friends, my Good German friends, what a dangerous incompetent idiot you are. So what's stopping you?

Last try. Let's make a deal. You ready? Here it is. You let me live and here's what I'll do for you: You let me go on living, forever, in this body, on the earth, which is my kind of place. In other words, you, for your part, refrain from killing me, the Good German, the wormy little coward, and you know what I'll do for you?

Nothing. Not a god damn thing.

You've got to admit, it's a fresh approach.

JENNY

When Jenny was twelve she hosted a birthday party for her best friend. She had baked the cake herself and planned to bring it to the table when time came for the big ceremony. She rehearsed the lighting of the candles, the dimming of lamps, the solemn entrance and presentation. But when the moment came, when the cake was fully ablaze in the pantry, she dug in her heels and pushed out her jaw and refused to carry it in. Why on earth not? her mother asked, and Jenny knew there would be a reckoning; but paraffin was dripping onto the butter frosting, so her mother brought in the cake.

Then everybody sang "Happy Birthday" in the magical light of her cake, and again Jenny, who had had every intention of singing, couldn't bring herself to do it. This often happened when she sang hymns or recited the Pledge of Allegiance. Instead of really joining in, she did her trick of mouthing the words behind a face that felt, from the inside, pleasant, tolerant, faintly detached. She remarked the apparent ease of most of the others, especially her mother, whose voice was the loudest and most assured. Their good humor amounted to a natural humility before which Jenny felt both contempt and deep shame. She could sense in only a couple of the girls a squirming unease with the occasion. She wondered if they, too, were just pretending to sing. She thought it unlikely that anyone else would have hit on her trick.

When the door had closed behind the last guest her mother turned on her. "If you could only see your face," she said, and stretched her mouth into a flat, artificial smile and squinted in a dumb show of fellow feeling, producing the expression Laraine Day and Rhonda Fleming affected to avoid wrinkles around the mouth, only hideously exaggerated and grotesque. "You think everybody is looking at you," her mother said. "Nobody is looking at you."

Jenny knew that what her mother was saying was true, and that her mother's cruel imitation of her was accurate. She was horrified; and though not angry at her mother—who clearly had been driven to it—she immediately knew no one had the right to be quite this honest. "When you put on that act," her mother said, making the face again, with tears in her eyes, "you look like you have something the *matter* with you."

"Then it's a good thing," Jenny answered back, "that no one is looking." She was a heavy girl, tenderhearted and prone to sullenness, and too big for punishment.

"It makes you look feebleminded," said her grieving mother, who later apologized, and was forgiven. It had been the sort of scene, Jenny thought, that made you sorry for everybody.

▼ ▼ ▼ ▼ ▼ ▼ ▼

Jenny longed for that grace with which most people submitted to ceremony. That effortless surrender of the spotlight; that mysterious willingness to become part of a mob, and more: to be *seen* that way, reduced to the obscurity of a class photograph. The worst thing about ceremony was that your next move, the next word out of your mouth, was predictable. Whether singing, dancing, or reading Mother Goose rhymes to a child, she felt fixed, pinned, as though turning, in a dangerously predictable arc, upon a microscope slide; or encased for good within a cheap glass

212

paperweight. Jenny was, she knew, a prideful, self-centered girl, whom no one, not even the ones who loved her, would ever accuse of being a good sport.

This had to do with her relationship to God, whose existence she had taken for granted before her parents first mentioned him, at that time when she was still the center of the solar system and the sun had not yet muscled her out of the way. Even when she owned it, Jenny's universe was not particularly hospitable, and the God of her infancy was not her loving friend. Friends don't watch you in the bathroom or read your mind or kick over the magnificent towers you build with wooden blocks. God did these things to Jenny, not out of wise love, but simply because he had the power to do them. God was very much like Jenny, only bigger.

God and Jenny had an understanding. He did not always watch Jenny, and she could not know when he was watching and when he wasn't. The point about God was that he *could* be watching. He observed her hypothetically and from a great distance, and for reasons she never really wondered about. She assumed she was special in some way.

When her parents introduced her to the Bible and the church, Jenny believed without question, as most children do. She was a pious little girl and so for many years believed in a being who dandled children on his knee, answered prayers, and loved all sinners equally. She sang solos, gave Children's Day sermons, asked her Sunday School teachers questions that stumped and embarrassed them, so eager was she to grasp the entire setup and all its implications, for her.

By the time she was twelve and balked at submitting to her friend's ceremonial day, the church, in refusing to admit a Negro family or even circulate a Good Neighbor housing pledge, had proved itself worthless, and her Sunday School teacher, who knew he was wrong but "had a family to support," was revealed, under her merciless grilling in class, as a stupid and frightened man. Inevitably she lost her faith. The church she belonged to was liberal and Protestant; its minister and elders let her go without rancor, with kind wishes for a safe and interesting journey. Much later, when lapsed Roman Catholic and ex-fundamentalist friends told her about their struggles with guilt and community recrimination, she was to remember her own leave-taking as a wide-screen cinematic event, a comic take in which all the believers lined up at a riverbank, dressed like pioneer farmers, shading their plain square faces from the sun; waving to her as she pushed off into a current that, according to their professed belief, was sure to carry her over a roaring falls to annihilation. "Bye-bye, dear!" they cried. "Write when you get the chance!"

▼ ▼ ▼ ▼ ▼ ▼ ▼

The God of Jenny's infancy, that cryptic, hypothetical observer, did not evaporate along with her faith But since he was a given, a constant, the source of her perpetual embarrassment and pride, she thought she was agnostic, and when her mother said, "Nobody is looking at you," she did not dispute her. Jenny never had paid much attention to other people, so it seemed only sensible and fair, though sad, that she herself moved about in the world unnoticed.

On the night of the party, Jenny, truly sorry for her arrogance, longing for grace, resolved never again to do her trick; which didn't work anyway From that time on she sang Christmas carols, "Happy Birthday to You," the school fight song, "America the Beautiful," "Blowing in the Wind," and all other necessary songs, in full voice; when asked to join in on a chorus or clap hands to a beat, she joined in and clapped hands; she marched down aisles, recited the Girl Scout creed, saluted flags, said grace, wore name tags, repeated solemn oaths, and shook hands with the total stran-

214

ger to her right. And not once in thirty years did she fail to find such an occasion hateful and freshly humiliating.

▼ ▼ ▼ ▼ ▼ ▼ ▼

In adolescence Jenny fell down a lot, even for an adolescent. Her frequent tumbles, some of which were spectacular, punctuated and enlivened an otherwise dreary stretch of life, so that later she was grateful for them. They were just about all she could remember of this time. They provided proof that her youth had actually happened.

She wasn't exactly clumsy. According to her mother, the problem was inattention. "You walk around in a dream." Jenny tried even harder not to think about herself, to attend to what her mother called the real world, and with this increased effort the real world receded even further, to moon-size, and she became even less conscious than before of stairsteps and curbstones, of mud puddles and glare ice, of gravity itself. She fell downstairs and upstairs, and tripped on the satiny gymnasium floor; she butted into doorjambs and spilled out of school buses and crowded elevators, and, during those moments when silence really was essential, she brushed against light switches or dislodged large metallic things that landed with a long, sonorous clang; and once, while standing still to receive an award for excellence in conversational French, she just dropped, like a forsaken marionette.

She wondered sometimes if she were doing some kind of unconscious penance. She got so used to falling that she didn't much mind; if she fell alone she took no notice of it. When falling in public, though, she embarrassed herself by laughing, often beginning to laugh before she even hit the ground. No one, except her mother, ever laughed with her. Maybe she didn't look as hilarious to the world as she did in her mind's eye. She tried not to laugh. It would have been pleasant to hurt herself, to break an

ankle and have to be carried, to suffer concussion and lie motionless at the foot of the stairs, pale and alarming, the focus of
consternation. But she never achieved more damage than a scraped
knee or ripped stocking, and did not see, really, how others
managed it.

▼ ▼ ▼ ▼ ▼ ▼ ▼

For years she thought of herself as someone who fell a lot,
only slowly realizing that this was no longer true; that at some
point, in college or maybe shortly after, she had stopped. "I was
always off balance," she told her husband. "I flew through the air
with the greatest of ease." She amused him by pointing out in-
famous accident sites in her old neighborhood. He told her that
his adolescence, too, had been humiliating, though in a different
way. She thought he missed the point; or could not have guessed
that her old disequilibrium seemed in retrospect a kind of enchantment. That, even at the time, it was not really humiliating
at all.

Jenny loved and married the first man to love her and propose
marriage, a gray-haired young man, the youngest child and only
son in a family of ten. He had grown up in a jungle of fond
women. Most of his sisters were pretty, good-humored, friendly
girls, and he knew everything there was to know about them.
Though he loved them, he resented the loss of sexual mystery.
He was sick of women who made sense. He loved Jenny, and
married her, because she made no sense to him.

She seemed to him never to be fully *there*. She was a ponderous
girl, weighed down and distracted by the invisible baggage of
her own world. He would occupy her full attention only inter-
mittently, and when he did the blast of unrelated signals she sent
confused and delighted him. For instance, she was a wonderfully
bad dancer, with good rhythm and coordination and sexy hips

216

and a degree of self-consciousness that was almost morbid. When they danced close and she hid her face in his shoulder she seemed, rather than cuddling, to be abandoning to him the shell of her body, and often, as he put them through their paces, he got from her an absurd sense of danger, as though something terribly important rode on what they did, the pattern they made on the dance floor. She was sullen and sweet in unpredictable turns. In just the way that some people have presence, she had *absence*.

They produced a son who, every day of his new life, had to learn by trial and error some new technicality in the natural or moral law. Apparently *he* did not take this personally. This mystified Jenny. She wondered if men and women differed in this fundamental respect: if women got the Big Picture at a much earlier age. Her husband didn't know what she meant by "the Big Picture" (it was a phrase she remembered from Driver's Ed), although the idea amused him. They watched the boy on his new hobbyhorse, galloping faster and faster with increasing grimness on the garish, squeaking toy, discovering a new form of monotony. "I mean," she said, "that maybe little boys don't appreciate how powerless they really are. Maybe they're born into a fool's paradise." He said that a fool and his paradise are soon parted. He said, "When you're a kid, anything is possible. There's a whole great big world out there." She gave it up. This had been her point exactly.

She always spoke to her child in a normal voice, and with her full vocabulary. The ability to croon and talk baby talk had not, as she had hoped it might, emerged along with the baby himself, like the instincts to cradle and nurse. She adored her son but would not play the fool for him. When he got a little older and tried to put her down—climbing or hanging from her body as though it were a piece of furniture, trying with stubborn intrusive fingers to mold her face like a lump of clay—she withdrew from

217

him and showed him her cold displeasure. A few of her friends, glimpsing these occasional displays of power, assumed they were political acts, and approved, or thought they should. Her husband and those friends who knew her better understood, and liked her a little less for it.

One summer day, when she was almost thirty, she and her husband went to a wedding of close friends, an outdoor wedding in a Japanese garden in the city park, and she was the nearest she would ever come to beautiful, in soft gray silk and ruby-colored sandals. After the wedding she took her plate of little tea sandwiches and her glass of champagne and walked, sipping, in the sunshine, wearing the light proudly, like a sable coat, and sank down in the grass in the deep shade of a ginkgo, on top of an enormous dog turd.

In the car going home, and for some years to come, she was to describe the event variously as her "formal passage into a world beyond embarrassment" and the moment she first truly understood "the meaning of irony." "And it really wasn't all that bad," she said.

"You keep saying that," said her husband, at the wheel, leaning as far away from her as possible, his head halfway out the window.

"The worst possible thing happened," and she said, "and it wasn't that bad!"

Her husband didn't agree with either statement, but kept this to himself. That his wife could invest significance in such a non-event was just the sort of thing that continued to endear her to him. He made a drama of loosening his tie and gulping the outside air, while she laughed and laughed.

▼ ▼ ▼ ▼ ▼ ▼ ▼

She quickly lost her pretty young looks, which had mostly been a matter of high coloring. She simply faded, at a pace she

218

could follow in annual vacation photographs, and what emerged was her adult face, sharp-featured, intelligent. She took it well. "It's sad," she would say, "but interesting, too." She saw the slow decline of her body as a kind of progress, and took an admittedly absurd pride in it, as though aging were a show-biz turn. She regarded her middle-aged smoker's hands, rumpled and crepey where the childish dimples used to be, and smiled with deliberate, ironic pleasure.

She was becoming a better person. She was able to focus on matters outside herself for increasing stretches of time. In the company of friends, with whom she had always been generous with time, hospitality, and gifts, she was now generous with her full attention. She was able to read and think more intensely about difficult, abstract subjects. She could sometimes see, within herself and others, glimmerings of nobility. She thought she might some day become wise. She was very, very happy.

"The thing about getting older," she often said, "is that the good stuff gets better, and the bad gets worse. Life becomes terrifically *real*." She tried not to show off but could not contain her passion for the adventurous nature of human life. "Anything could happen," she said, and surrendered, with no loss of pride, to "all the possibilities." She smiled at how far she had come.

▼ ▼ ▼ ▼ ▼ ▼ ▼

Her mother died, yelling, in horrible pain, unable or unwilling to recognize her own husband, her own daughter. En route to the cemetery on the interstate highway the right front tire of the hearse blew, and the long cortege joined it in the breakdown lane. Mourners left their cars and milled around, arguing about what to do. "This is terribly dangerous," a man said "We're sitting ducks out here."

Her father sobbed without covering his face. She trotted, light-

219

headed, over to the hearse driver. "What happens now?" she asked, and the man said, "Let's put it this way, lady. The spare isn't all that easy to get at."

▼ ▼ ▼ ▼ ▼ ▼ ▼

Her best friend's daughter was run over and killed by a school bus, as it pulled gently away from the curbing in a heavy rainstorm. The driver, especially conscientious on that day, had counted the number of disembarking children, had not put the bus in gear until, through sheets of rain, he counted all ten safely across, had counted once more to make sure. Only then, waving, had he started to roll. One of the brightly slickered figures was a mother, a tiny woman from Laos. The tenth child knelt in front of the bus, adjusting the snap on her new pink boots

Her friend called on her at this time, and she had to go. The woman's grief was ice water into which she plunged daily, with increasing dread, and by the time her friend was sufficiently healed to be left alone Jenny had been cured, for good, of her boosterism for the Possibilities.

Jenny began to sleep poorly and she could not control her waking imagination. In vivid daydreams, perversely detailed, her son was crushed, and she drove the bus. She lost all control over the fantasies, which ran automatically, in a seamless loop. She quit her job, stopped driving, refused to leave the house, badly frightening her husband and son, who shouted at her and demanded normality. And when the craziness vanished (which it did, suddenly, like a patch of fog on the road) she was different.

She had accepted the news of her son's mortality, of the precariousness of his position; she had fought it the way any child fights bitter medicine, and yet when she got it down it wasn't so bad, and by itself it would have had no lasting effect upon her character besides its vague aftertaste of iron, a permanent but easily accommodated disability. But the news the bus driver brought stuck in her throat. She could not without great inner adjustment accept the fact of the bus driver, though he was as real to her as her own mirror image. His kindly foolish face became a fixture of her landscape, frozen at that moment when the little Laotian woman turned to wonder at two children screaming, crouching, pointing at the anonymous hooded tenth child submitting to the bumper like a penitent. On the comic verge of comprehension the bus driver waved, with that timeless, stylized manner of the perfect foil, and fate whizzed toward him like a custard pie.

She resumed normal life, did chores, loved her family, and was frequently happy, but she now had a permanent appetite for outrage. Her face in repose was never in repose at all, but tense and mulish, with the lowering brow and hard pursed mouth of her infancy. Her face in repose was intimidating but also slightly funny, in just the same way the naked face of a thwarted baby is funny. Because she was an adult her face set into this expression, leaving a permanent record, so that even when reflecting delight or gratitude it displayed, in its pattern of tiny lines around the mouth and between the eyes, the proof of self-contradiction. Sometimes, in public, she realized she was talking to herself out loud, usually in furious argument, and found that she did not particularly care, even when strangers caught her doing it.

She talked back to the figures on the Nightly News, and eventually stopped watching all televised news because, as she put it, "Why should I have to look at them, when they can't see me?" Often she threw the newspaper on the floor or whacked it against something, with an abrupt cracking sound that startled and annoyed her husband. He got so he could guess which story would set her off. "The little kid who fell through the ice," he would say, without looking up, or, "The silo fire," or "Beirut."

"*God*," she would hiss, "what a world."

221

He had learned not to look up at these moments because the sight of her, truculent and bellicose, aroused a sudden pity that broke his heart, and a dangerous impulse to laugh.

Once she actually shook her raised fist, with the crumpled newspaper attached, extended like a thunderbolt. "Seven thousand dead," she whispered, nodding her head, in the manner of an ancient, reminiscing survivor.

"Do you realize what you're doing?" he asked her, with a trace of his old delight. "You're taking an earthquake *personally.*"

She said, "Anyone who doesn't take earthquakes personally is an idiot."

▼ ▼ ▼ ▼ ▼ ▼ ▼

Then her husband's father, whom he strongly resembled, died in mid-sentence of a heart attack, one month after a reassuring checkup. Her own father, uncharacteristically drunk, fell in the bathtub and blinded his good eye, so that he had to give up driving, and retire early from his job, and could barely read large print. And her son developed what was ultimately diagnosed as a Fever of Unexplained Origin, which came and went for two months and then came and stayed and gradually climbed to a life-threatening level, so that he had to be hospitalized.

All this happened in one year. And at the end of the year, during the Christmas holidays, she herself came before a radiologist, a Hungarian with a Gypsy name and a permanent air of distraction, so that with every question she seemed to jolt him from reverie. At his polite request she slipped the straps of her jumper off her shoulders and let the dress puddle at her waist, while a nurse stood guard. He had her sit up straight and put one hand on top of her head, and then the other, and then both. He kept looking back and forth between her right breast and the X-ray on the screen behind his chair. He seemed to disapprove of the X-ray, as though it were a poor likeness. They faced each other across his desk piled high with folders and thick manila envelopes; there was an ashtray, with ashes in it; there was a square lucite paperweight from the MGM Grand Hotel, and trapped inside of it a pair of tumbling red dice. She said, "I've always thought a mammogram sounded like something you'd send someone for a joke."

He came around the desk, never taking his eyes off her breast, and petted the one spot, on the outside close by the nipple, with the smooth pad of his thumb. He arched over her, the other hand gripping the back of her chair; her face was inches from his chest; she could smell him through his shirt, foreign and tangy. "Roll your head forward," he said, and she did, with closed eyes. "Let it fall back." She let it fall against his wrist.

"Like a bellygram," she said, "or a candygram."

"I don't understand it," he said. He left her and went back over to the X-ray.

She said, to his broad back, "My son is terribly ill."

He told her to pull up her dress. He had to say it twice. "Is she dressed?" he asked, and the nurse said she was, and left. When he turned around his face showed nothing, even though he looked straight at her. He slumped into his chair, and after a moment, still deeply abstracted, beat out a sudden rhythmic tattoo on his desktop with the tips of his fingers, like a reveille. Instantly he focused on her and smiled in a comradely way. "These things are so . . . unpleasant," he said.

"Oh, yes," she said.

"Well, it's nothing to worry about," he said. He started to resubmerge, but caught sight of her face. "You can see," he said, with a casual wave at the X-ray, "that it's just fluid. I can't understand why your doctor couldn't tell. You're fine." He ushered her to the door. "You have nothing to worry about," he said. She kept nodding. She shook hands, and with her free hand grasped his upper arm by the shoulder, and gave it one strong, familiar, knowing squeeze. He laughed behind the closing door. "Bellygram," he said. "That's very funny."

▼ ▼ ▼ ▼ ▼ ▼ ▼

During Jenny's childhood there had been a family two houses down from theirs, the Leemings, who, by the time she became aware of them, were already beginning to achieve local fame through their calamitous luck. At one time, according to the older neighbors, the Leemings had been an ordinary, unremarkable family, and then one of the children had drowned, or fallen out of a tree, and after that, one by one, the rest of the Leemings sickened and died, and the father, who didn't die, became an alcoholic, and his mother, an eighty-year-old former school principal, took to wandering the street in her slip in the early evenings. People were horrified but solicitous. People recoiled in primitive, superstitious reflex, but steeled themselves and behaved decently. They stood by the Leemings. And behind drawn curtains they talked about "the luck of the Leemings", and sometimes they had to bite their lips to keep from laughing.

Now it seemed obvious to her, as she walked each morning through hospital corridors toward her unconscious son, that her little family had taken a pratfall off the edge of the civilized universe. Her husband would die without warning, her father after an inexorable decline. Her child was already beyond her reach. She would be the last to die. The radiologist had spoken to her in a kind of code, his immediate diagnosis utterly irrelevant.

She remembered riding home from church in the backseat of the Nash when she was eight years old, with both her parents in front, her mother's blue hat with the little black net veil, and how the car stalled just when they were almost at the driveway, and the car in back of them speeded up to pass, and the solid thud and then the Leemings' Irish Setter airborne, boneless, lofting

224

away like a baseball, and how, before the dog hit the pavement, her parents' ferocious laughter rocked the car.

She sat at the foot of her son's bed and cooled her palms on the metal rail. Her head was bowed, her face white and slack. She swayed very slightly, in a tidal rhythm, and gracefully, like sea grass. Jenny rocked, finally, to sleep, in distant, reliable laughter

▼ ▼ ▼ ▼ ▼ ▼ ▼

When her son woke up he watched her for a while, to get his bearings. She did not look much like his mother She slept, her face turned toward him, her right cheek squished against the rail. Her face was doughy, like the face of a plump baby, and just as placid. She looked in sleep as though she hadn't a hope or a care in the world. It frightened him to think she had lain like this with no one to watch over her. He called out to her and she opened her eyes without urgency and saw him.

His mother's eyes were as unguarded and clear as her sleeping face. He read great surprise and then, unmistakably, just before she cried out and embraced him, an awful impersonal dismay, something like resignation and something like disappointment.

Days later, when he got up his nerve, he asked her what she had been thinking, to make her look like that. She answered readily, without a hint of shock at his question. "I was just getting used to the idea that we had been singled out," she said, with a new kind of smile of her face, a half-smile of deep private amusement. "I thought I was special in at least that one way." She bent toward him and whispered, close to his face, grinning amiably, frightening him: "Your mother always was a fool," she said.

▼ ▼ ▼ ▼ ▼ ▼ ▼

His new mother often called herself "Silly Old Moms." Her appearance was always careless. She let herself get plump, and even when she dressed up her slip would show or she would forget to put on stockings, or her blouse, buttoned wrong, would gape at the bust or waist. She learned to present herself to him or to his father for inspection. "Am I okay?" she would ask, with her silly smile. She played the clown for him and his friends, and as he grew older this embarrassed him more and more, because, while she was sometimes funny, she was just as often cornball and obvious, and he cringed at his friends' indulgence.

"I like your mother," one of them said. "She looks right at you. She really *sees* you, you know? She doesn't hide a thing."

Yes, he thought, that's it exactly. She just doesn't bother anymore.

She went downtown with him one day to help him shop for college clothes. She tripped on the curb of a traffic island at the center of a busy rotary, fell hard, sprawled forward on her hands and knees. He knelt to help her up but she didn't want to move. She seemed willing to remain forever in this bovine, victimized position. "Wow," she kept saying, without rancor, "that really hurts." He hauled her upright, but with her hair half out of its bun and her stockings torn at the knee she looked even worse. She refused to turn around and go back home to change her clothes. "I'm fine, honey," she said. "Nobody's going to notice."

He lost patience. He had to shout to make himself heard above the din of the chaotic encircling traffic. He gestured with an angry sweep of his arm, pointing out to her the surrounding dangerous hubbub, their absurd position on the island, their awful exposure. "Somebody just *might* notice you, Mother," he said sarcastically, shaming himself. "Somebody *could* see you. Doesn't that matter to you at all?" She shrugged and smiled her weird private smile and said something he didn't catch. "Mother, I cannot *hear* you." He had never been so embarrassed in his life.

"I said, So What? Who Cares?" She regarded him with cold sympathy. "What are the odds?" said Jenny.

226

THE
JAWS
OF
LIFE

According to Hannah, real life just happens, whereas stories make sense. When you put real life in print, she says, you show it up for the pointless mess it really is.

I wouldn't be bothering with this now if Pillbeam hadn't turned his face to the wall. I don't blame the guy, but he could have saved me a lot of trouble. Although, I don't know. Lately there's this phenomenon that happens to me when I'm just about asleep: I'm actually *falling* asleep, drifting down nicely, and then there's a noise in my head that jerks me wide awake, and it's inside my brain, but deafening. It's a little bit like a high-voltage buzz, but much more, really, like the jagged shriek of grinding, twisting metal. I feel like a sardine, with the lid rolling back, and up above, in the blinding light, this huge devouring face.

The point being that everything really happened. The story I'm about to tell you is true.

▼ ▼ ▼ ▼ ▼ ▼ ▼

My name is David Swallow. (That's really my name. I haven't even changed the names.) My wife's name is Barbara. She's forty-five, two years older than me. She's a housewife. I'm a wine merchant (Swallow & Mamoorian, "Where Every Year is a Good Year"). I do the buying and my partner, Cosmo Mamoorian, does

229

the selling. His wife's name is Hannah, and she writes the Big Hannah children's books. These are the only people you have to keep straight. Barbara, Cosmo, Hannah & me.

So, Barbara and I were eating dinner one night and she said, "Linus Pauley." Obviously she said it in some context, but all you have to know is that she said it, "Linus Pauley." This is what starts the whole thing rolling.

Barbara is not stupid. She's a lot better read than me, for instance. She's a college grad, whereas I got drafted out and never went back. But she sometimes gets names wrong. That's no crime, but wait: when you tell her about it *she doesn't listen to you*. She says "Carlton Heston." She says "Johnson & Johnson" when she means "Masters & Johnson." I used to correct her, pleasantly, but she never took even ten seconds to tidy up the files. If this isn't the kind of thing that bothers you, you won't appreciate how, over twenty years, like the chirpy chirp chirp of the cuckoo in your clock, this adds up, if not to actual torture, then at least to malicious ignorance. I held my breath for the echo of an "ing," and even tried to convince myself that I *had* heard an "ing," or *could* have heard an "ing," in some better world than this one But no. And I must have been subtotaling ever since we got married, because this single tiny provocation did the trick. Tilt! Bingo! Major League marital atrocity! I, a passive, amiable guy with all the suppressed violence of Mister Rogers, suddenly got a righteous urge, so that my palms tingled, to slap her handsome, confident face, howl in her ear, pull on her hair like a bell ringer. I thought, Nuts to You, Lady. You want grounds for divorce? I'll give you grounds for divorce. Etc., though not, of course, in so many words. This is the best I can do to reconstruct the crucial moment. It's not perfect, but close enough.

Much later when I explained it to Barbara she laughed at me. To this day she doesn't know me at all, really. She called me an opportunist. "You were just looking for an excuse," she said. Which is ridiculous, because then I would have had someone in mind, which I didn't. I mean, what occurred to me, when she said "Pauley," was not the *desire* to cheat, but the possibility that I could if I wanted to. There's a world of difference. Of course, I'd always known it was literally *possible* to cheat, I'm not a moron, but now I knew it was *actually* possible. And besides, if I had been wanting to fool around, as Barbara pretends to believe, I wouldn't have been wanting to do it "in general," that doesn't make any sense; I'd have wanted to do it with some particular woman. That's like saying you've always wanted to fly, only not any special kind of plane; or, you've always wanted to travel, but you didn't know where. Nobody does that, or not many people, anyway.

▼ ▼ ▼ ▼ ▼ ▼ ▼

Coriander Menard. Coriander Menard was my first mistress, if one afternoon makes a mistress. She can stand in for the rest. She was a part-time counter girl at the store; she was a child of a child of the sixties; she was a flake. I took her to a motel, a fact that kept her in a constant state of wonder. She kept saying, "I can't believe this place." "A vibrating bed! I can't believe it." "I can't believe dirty movies on the TV! Can you believe that?" She was twenty years old, pretty in a big-eyed way, much too thin, brutally stupid, and creepy. When we were naked she said, "Let's pretend we're the last man and the last woman on earth."

I was hoping she meant something like "If I were the only girl in the world and you were the only boy." But no. "Let's pretend instead," I said, "that we're the *first* man and woman on earth." This was a new one on her. ("I can't believe you thought of this!") Of course, *I* didn't want to pretend anything. Barbara and I haven't pretended anything in twenty years, and we never have any trouble. Barbara's as regular as Big Ben. The whole thing was degrad-

231

ing. She latched onto the phrase "naked and unashamed" and repeated it and repeated it until I thought I would lose my mind. She never closed her eyes. She showed me my first multiple orgasm; it was not a pretty picture. By my count she came five times, and afterwards, hunting under the bed for her high-top sneaker, she patted my knee in an absent way and said, "Don't feel bad."

There was more to Coriander Menard than this; lots more; but I wasn't going to stick around to find out what it was.

Then there were, believe it or not, two Barbaras, and a nice woman named Kelly. And then, at last, came Hannah; and this is where it really gets going.

▼ ▼ ▼ ▼ ▼ ▼

Cosmo Mamoorian looks exactly like he sounds. Hannah does too (actually I think we all do) but I'd better describe her anyway. She's taller than me, lots taller than Cosmo; she must weigh as much as I do; her voice is almost as low as mine; she's older than Barbara; she's got long, black and gray hair, so coarse and wiry that when she undoes the braid it springs out around her head like the business end of a huge broom. Now that may not sound appetizing, but believe me, Hannah is a very, very sexy woman. She's got one of those larger-than-life deep-throated laughs that grabs you right between the legs. For years Barbara and I suspected she sometimes did exactly that to Cosmo when we went out to dinner: he would break off in mid-story, or mid-sentence, and look sort of dreamy and pop-eyed.

Actually we always liked Cosmo better than his wife. Barbara said Hannah was theatrical and self-important, and always "on stage": "the kind of woman with whom you can go just so far and no farther." (Boy, was she wrong!) Barbara especially disliked Hannah's books, all very expensive, and aimed at the 8–10 age

232

group, and all illustrated by Harry Kong, a sick cartoonist who hit paydirt when he switched to illustrating for Hannah Critics and psychiatrists loved his stuff, which turned all of Hannah's monsters, who were already pretty frightening, into slobbering, bug-eyed perverts Hannah never sold a manuscript until she teamed up with Kong. "My Evil Ones," Hannah said, "put the child directly in touch with his most crippling fears." Our sons were in their teens when Hannah made it big, which was lucky. Had they been younger, Hannah, childless herself, would have wanted to use them as guinea pigs. Like all bullies, Hannah had terrific staying power.

So the first move was hers, an under-the-table grope at Mamma Giso's, which I was so sure was an innocent mistake that I told Barbara about it later, and we both had a satisfying "suspicions confirmed" type of laugh. By this time I had pretty much given up on adultery and was feeling well off and pretty close to my wife. Barbara's quite a woman. As I may have mentioned, she's smarter than I am, but that's all right, because she's never taken advantage—certainly not in public, to show me up, and never even in private, although she must know it as well as I do. It's always there, but she'd never use it. That's how smart she is.

But of course it wasn't a mistake after all, as Hannah made clear on the next dinner date, and then she dropped in at the store, chatted with Cosmo, came into my office, closed the door, said "You're in heat, David Swallow," and smiled like a panther, if panthers could smile. She was sexy, and extremely alarming I said, which sounded stupid even to me, "Men don't go into heat, do they?" and she said, "Then I guess it must be me."

Considering this steamy beginning, we didn't do much for a long time. We met for lunch in a lot of Polynesian restaurants. We talked and talked about Barbara and Cosmo, how much I loved Cosmo, how "fond" she was of Barbara. Hannah did most of the talking. "We must content ourselves with fantasy, David Swallow." We drank a lot, especially me. It was the only way I could stand all the gassing, which was Hannah's idea. I'd reel back to the store at two or three in the afternoon, and there stood Cosmo, happily greeting old customers, who really were like friends to him—loyalty means everything to Cosmo; or handing some pretentious couple a line about how he'd never cook with a Bordeaux that wasn't a classified growth. There he stood, trusting and content, and no alcoholic blur could mask his martyr's halo.

We stopped being discreet, if getting blotto three times a week in public in a small city is your idea of discreet. We started, when the four of us were together, eyeing each other over the heads of the poor saps we were married to; we met in pantries and briefly in the bedrooms abandoned by my sons, and once in the Mamoorians' first-floor lavette; we clutched at each other like teenage rebels. Then one stormy night the three of us, minus Cosmo, who had a cold, went to see *Flower Drum Song* or some damn thing at the Community Players, and I dropped Barbara off and took Hannah home. And there, in her driveway, with crashing lightning, etc., we did this, and then we did that, and in no time we'd done so much that only the letter of the law remained to be broken, and then we broke it.

▼ ▼ ▼ ▼ ▼ ▼ ▼

Now, when you're a kid sometimes there's some other kid that your mother hates to have you play with, and so does his mother, because when the two of you get together you act like criminal lunatics. When you're with this kid it's suddenly a wonderful idea to play toreador with moving freight cars or pee all over your sister's new dollhouse. I think Hannah and I had something like this effect on each other. She called it a *"folie à deux,"* but really we just drove each other nuts, and the oddest thing is, I liked

234

her even less than before. I hated the arty things she said, I hated her great big bullying laugh, and I hated most of all the way she said "David Swallow" in this vampy voice, when she'd been calling me just "David" for fifteen years.

But she was the best. I never even thought in terms of good, better, best until Hannah. I'm a simple guy, and sex has never been a competitive event for me, or a perfectible skill. Now, Barbara and I are great—I never realized how great until I started fooling around. I had thought that maybe variety, youth, thighs so slender there's a space between them at the top (I always wondered what that was like) would spice it up. But for my money, there's no place like home. You don't bump into each other there, or say a lot of asinine things, and she smells just right, and if you're tired or frightened, or you feel like a jackass, here is the one place you can come where the story is always good, and always ends well.

Hannah was like this, only cubed. Suppose you're twelve and small for your age, and it's bedtime, and you go upstairs, and there, in your bed, is Your Mom. Who is so familiar that you can't even see her face, plus she's still bigger than you, and stronger, and she knows everything, and you can do, you must do, for her sake, *anything you want*. That's exactly what Hannah was like. We didn't have to pretend. We weren't even very noisy. We were quiet as mice.

If this sounds perverted to you, or comical, then you have my sympathy. Hannah was so good that I didn't even feel as sorry for Cosmo as I had before, when we were just talking about it. It's hard to pity the world's luckiest man. As to why Hannah, of all women—pushy, phony, foolish Hannah—had this gift, it's still a mystery to me. All I know is, it made me crazy for her. I alibied, soaped myself with Irish Spring, and never booked the same motel twice, but I was just going through the motions. The future of my marriage and hers and of my friendship with Cosmo was just as real to me and as important as a six A.M. wake-up call is to a happy drunk at midnight.

▼ ▼ ▼ ▼ ▼ ▼ ▼

So, three months of delirium. Then I ran home one morning because I'd forgotten to dress for a semiannual wine and cheese deal we throw for VIPs, and there sat Barbara in the middle of the living room rug, hugging her knees and crying. Barbara never cries. I almost threw up. She jumped up and wouldn't look at me; she was embarrassed and furious. I followed her around the house calling, "What's the matter, honey?" but she kept saying it was nothing, and then she said, "Get the hell out of here," and I got the hell out of there.

Hannah was pasty-faced when we first met that afternoon, in the Tiki Room, but her main concern seemed to be whether Barbara had told Cosmo, or was likely to tell him, and even then she didn't seem very worried about losing or hurting him. In fact, I could swear she was enjoying the soap opera. She sat in one of those enormous wicker thrones, filling it to groaning like the Queen of Honolulu, breathing smoke and rum fumes, issuing decrees. "Barbara's a survivor." "Cosmo will kill me, of course, or himself." She was majestic, embracing her fate with royal disdain (crushing the life out of it, in fact, mashing its little surprised face into her unavoidable bosom); but you could say the same thing about a sinking ship; and being what I am, I was scampering for the portholes.

In twenty years I had never seen Barbara cry like that. I felt guilty and afraid, and not just for myself. I feared something worse than retribution. Seeing her so lost, just that one shot of her face when she looked up at me from the floor, was like that morning in San Francisco when I leaned against the savings bank to tie

236

my shoe and the bank moved. If a building can nudge you, like some girl passing notes in civics class, then we're all in the soup.

So I slunk off, leaving Hannah heaving with dramatic lust, but no hurt feelings because she was so full of herself that she didn't even notice. On the way home I had to pull over to the breakdown lane and stop the car to puke, on just two drinks. When I found Barbara in the den she was reading the paper. I said, with my coat on, swaying on my feet in front of her, that if I were any kind of man I would abide by whatever decision she made, I would leave home, if that was what she wanted, and take her every blow without raising a finger in my own defense; but that I was a spineless worm, and would stay right where I was even if she pleaded or hired lawyers or called in the SWAT team, because here was where I belonged, and I couldn't face life without her.

She looked at me for a long time without expression. "You may have to," she finally said, but I didn't pay much attention to the weirdly impersonal way she said it because she hadn't said "you *will* have to," which meant I could take a breath.

"There's hope, then?" I asked.

She stared at me with what looked like scientific curiosity. "That depends on what you're hoping for," she said, then added, with a wide, tight-lipped smile, "you Egregious Ass."

So right then I knew what you've already figured out, that she hadn't been crying because of Hannah, that it was something serious that had nothing to do with me, and now it was much worse because I had spilled the beans all over her. *That depends on what you're hoping for.* There were shadows under her eyes and her hair looked wispy and fine, like baby hair. This is the woman I got pregnant with Davy in the upstairs bathroom of my first and only boss, Old Man Fenneman, during his annual Christmas party for the serfs, while in the parlor directly below us, the old poop

237

eked out carols on his Hammond organ and people tried to get drunk on Cold Duck punch, and someone knocked feebly on the bathroom door. We were stone sober, too.

Maybe she saw something in my face. Whatever, she wasn't angry anymore. She patted the cushion beside her, and I sat down, still in my coat, and we were quiet for a while. She told me, with my face against her neck and her wispy hair in my eyes, that she was going into the Lying In in two days to have a lump removed from her breast. She said there was every chance it was benign. She tactfully avoided mention of her mother's recent death from breast cancer. She apologized for having taken it so hard. She stroked my back and rocked me. "If all goes well," she said, "I may divorce you and I may not. At the very least, I'm going to make your life a living hell. But you can see that now is not the time for that." I said yes. "The only thing I can say now," she said, "is that it's the most tasteless thing you've ever done. Not the affair, which by the way if you ever tell me who or how I'll kill you, but blundering into my crisis this way with your ridiculous antics."

Later, when we lay in bed trying to sleep, she said, "You know what it's like? It's like making an obscene phone call to the gas chamber. They take that poor man—Chessman? Harold Chessman—they strap him down, they're about to drop the pellet, and ring! ring! It's the special telephone! And some giggling kid, dialing numbers at random, wants to know if they have Prince Albert in a can." She took my hand in the dark. "David? Your timing stinks."

Yeah, I said, but that's the one thing that isn't my fault. I'm not responsible for the sequence of things. I know, she said. I'm not blaming you for that.

▼ ▼ ▼ ▼ ▼ ▼

I became a different person then, the way anybody would. It was no big deal. I was up early the next morning with the runs,

238

and all day I was shaking and crampy with fright. So was she. But it shouldn't surprise anybody that when Davy called from college that night to ask for money and shoot the breeze, I joked with him in a normal voice and told him we were just fine and Mom says hi but she can't come to the phone because she's powdering her nose, and she was standing right beside me holding my hand and plopping tears on the kitchen counter.

The point being that sure, I'm an ass, but I can do what I have to do, the same as other people. It was the worst forty-eight hours I had ever spent in my life so far, but, as Barbara said, it was only a taste, and we had to save our strength.

The afternoon before the biopsy Hannah came to the store while Cosmo was at lunch, and found me in my office, trusting the care of our wealthiest customer to Coriander Menard, a fact she ignored. She shut the door and pressed her shoulder back against the glass; she was still enormous, but she didn't loom large. She was at the wrong end of the telescope, along with my own feet. And I still wanted her; but that was just sex. We're both silly people, but she is sillier than me. "Cosmo may know," she said.

I heard "cosmo méno," some kind of password in a false language, like Pig Latin, and didn't think anything of it. That's the state I was in. She sat down across from me, crossed her big legs, and arranged her face in a mask of tragedy. "You know what I'm going to say, don't you?"

"No." I was just wondering, idly, how she could sound so ridiculous, when her nylons, whispering at me like a prompter, still had something to say.

"Poor David," she said. "You look like I feel." She made a complicated business of extracting a cigarette from her purse, lighting it, expelling smoke. "I'm going to be brutal, David. It's over. *Finis.*"

I had a terrible moment of contempt for her, and I couldn't stand to look at her face. My eyes dropped to her tits, her unavoidable bosom, and I had an ugly thought then, and made a repulsive wish. I was ashamed right away, but my momentum in the other direction, toward blaming her for everything, was so great that I had already started to say "Barbara's got a breast" and had to finish it.

"A *lump*," Hannah gasped, hugging herself, and now she was two hundred percent real. "Oh no. What have we done?"

"We haven't done anything. Well, we did something all right, but we didn't give her cancer, which she may not even have. Probably doesn't have," I added, like the incantation it was. Neither Barbara nor I, in all our frightened exchanges, had once missed this cue.

"How *could* you?" Hannah said. And slowly shaking her head —she really was dramatic, even when she wasn't putting it on— she rose and walked out the door, "without a backward glance."

And burst in again five minutes later, with her face the color of cream of wheat and one hand clutching shut the front of her blouse, having not, as I had assumed, stalked out of the store, having instead gone to the bathroom. Without shutting the door she leaned across my desk, yanked the blouse open, scooped her right breast from its sling with a rough violence that hurt even me, and screamed, almost without sound, the way you do in nightmares, "Feel this, you son of a bitch! You murderer!"

▼ ▼ ▼ ▼ ▼ ▼ ▼

Isn't this sickening? I can feel it still, fantastic, like a single dried pea under an eiderdown mattress. I closed the door, on the off chance that discretion would some day matter to either of us, and let her flail away at me, literally and otherwise, until she wore herself out. Then I uncorked a bottle of Palmer '61 and poured us each a blast.

That afternoon Hannah didn't care about her image, and spoke, in a dull voice, only when she had a fresh thought. She was purified by fear. She still talked baloney, but it was sincere baloney. This was when she gave me all that stuff about God as the writer, the writer as God, the organizing intelligence behind a good story, the "pointless mess of real life." Just this once, in how she handled the pressure, she reminded me of Barbara. She called her breast lump "a terrible idea," rather than a "tasteless thing," but I think they were thinking along the same mysterious lines.

"I feel," she said, rubbing her eyes with the heels of her hands, "like one of Harry Kong's shaggy, shambling beasts." I told her she wasn't making sense. *"Au contraire,"* she said. "I'm making as much sense of this as I can. Think about it, David. First I was having good dirty fun with you, and then I accidentally killed your wife, or at least caused her unimaginable hurt, and now I've got comic tit disease. The worst of it is there's no goddamn dignity in it for me, and I'm so scared." Later she said that the worst part was "feeling so grotesque." When the wine was gone—we knocked it back like draft beer—she said the worst of it was "suffering and dying in a clown suit." She sobbed for a long time, in a rhythmic, hopeless way, and very quietly, as though she were alone. "It isn't *right,*" she said. "It isn't *funny.*"

I took her on my lap and held her big shuddering body in my arms, which couldn't encompass her. I was in a fair amount of pain. I felt like Atlas. "Hey, Guy, hold this a second," and the next thing you know you're all alone with the world in your hands. When she calmed down she was quite embarrassed, I think. As she left to tell Cosmo—about the lump, not about us—we hugged and patted each other on the back, like the two old friends we were. And that was the end of that.

It was funny how Barbara and Hannah, who couldn't have been more different, had this nutty idea in common, that everything that happened to them was one more piece in a big puzzle. I

241

never knew that anybody thought that way. I sure don't. It seemed pretty clear to me that the *worst* thing was that my wife and Hannah were in danger of mutilation and death. It was the only thing, really. And here they were worrying about bad taste, and how they looked. The point being that if somebody walked up and shot me point blank and I had one minute to live, I wouldn't spend it asking why. Would you? I'd either try to kill the guy, or just scream and cry like a baby.

▼ ▼ ▼ ▼ ▼ ▼ ▼

So next morning I drove Barbara to the hospital for outpatient surgery, and then, because she insisted, went to the store, where Cosmo, his whole face swollen shut, told me the news about Hannah's breast lump right in front of a customer, a well-dressed woman in her sixties, who picked up her Oloroso, placed a kind hand briefly on Cosmo's cheek, said "You *will* get through this," and left, with the two of us looking after her and staring rudely at her bust.

When I told him about Barbara he sobbed freely and wrung his hands, which was more than I could do. I told him what I had come to expect, after considering the odds: that everything was going to be all right. Of course I was scared, but I still figured it would be okay, for both of them. "Don't say that," he said, clutching my wrist. "Why not, for God's sake?" "You're really asking for it," he said. Everybody was nuts about this thing but me.

We settled in for a clammy, diarrhetic morning, me waiting for a call from Barbara's surgeon, Cosmo for a call from Hannah, who was at her gynecologist's. And I can tell you right now that nothing educational happened between this point and when we got the word. I'm no wiser now than I was then; and if you've ever waited for crucial news, you know what it's like. So I could come right out and give you the biopsy result now, except why shouldn't you suffer a little, and also, something did happen in the meantime, and even though it was beside the point, it's too big a thing to leave out. It's a great big stupid thing. If someone asked you, "What did you do today?" there's no way you could leave this out.

What happened was the phone rang. Cosmo picked it up and looked at it. I had to pry it from his fingers. It was a guy named Pillbeam, a salesman for Lamour Tropical Liqueurs, and a rear wheel had come off his car on the Industrial Park off-ramp, and he'd had to abandon it there, loaded with cases of syrupy booze. He was at a phone booth, waiting for a tow truck, and he'd used his other dime to call us. I asked him why. "Look," he said, "do you want this stuff or not?" His voice was shaking. I said, "Not particularly," and then he cracked up, whinnying, on the edge of hysteria, and said, "You must have excellent taste!"

"Where's the regular guy?" I asked him. "Where's Hal Glossop?" Glossop had always been the Lamour man, this guy was a nut. He said, "What?" I said, "Where's Glossop?" He said, "I'm sorry, there's a fire engine." "Skip it," I said, but he didn't hear that either, and I had to yell "Glossop" into the phone at least four times, which is annoying enough under normal circumstances and with a normal name. Cosmo was staring at me, dazed and fearful, every time I yelled this nonsense word he seemed to inch back closer to the brink. In the end I told Pillbeam I would come right over, collect the booze, and give him a ride to the nearest Rent-a-Car. He was only a mile away, and obviously incapable of looking after himself. Besides, it was something to do. It's always good to keep moving.

Cosmo was frantic. At first I thought he just didn't want to be alone, but it wasn't that simple, or that sane. He was terrified that he was going to get "my" phone call. "I couldn't stand being the one to tell you," he said. "Jesus," I said, "do you have to look at it that way? What if it's good news?" He said, "Don't *say* that."

"Cosmo, I'll only be fifteen minutes. Take the phone off the hook." He looked at me like *I* was crazy.

Finally he decided, believe it or not, that if he got "my" phone call and the news was bad, he would lower the shade on the front door. I left him standing behind the center checkout, looking stoically away from the telephone, with one hand square on top of it. Whether he was willing it to ring, or not to ring, who knows.

▼ ▼ ▼ ▼ ▼ ▼

You couldn't miss Pillbeam. He was sitting by the curb on a stack of Lamour cases, against which leaned a life-size cardboard woman who looked like Lena Horne and dressed like Carmen Miranda, except that the fruit on her head was disturbingly alien. She cradled a bottle of orange Lamour and said "Let's Mango, señor." We loaded the cases in the rear hatch and stuck the display in the backseat. "Did they really expect us to set this up in the store?" I asked, and Pillbeam said, "Apparently so." He was maybe late fifties, his suit was shiny and baggy, and you just knew he lived in some cheap hotel, there was an ex-wife dogging him for alimony, he drank a lot, and not Mango Nectar. When guys like this are intelligent, they're even more depressing. As I drove I tried not to look at him. *"Sauve qui peut,"* as Hannah would say.

But I had to ask him if he was all right. His skin was gray and his eyes bright, and he had that air of fever-pitch gaiety you'd associate with someone who's about to yell "Whoopee!" and dive out the window. "Pillbeam," I said again, "are you all right?" He still didn't answer, and I thought, swell, I'm going to have to cart this sad sack to the emergency room. I pictured poor old Cosmo manning the phone.

Pillbeam spoke. "Do you remember Victor Mature?"

"Yeah," I said. "Sure. I remember Victor Mature."

244

"I used to live next door to him," he said. "Good old Vic Mature."

This forced me to look at him, and I growled, "Snap out of it, Pillbeam I don't have time for you."

He regarded me with hurt, rational surprise. "I'm all right," he said. "This is my normal—" and then a pizza delivery van, running a light, smashed into Pillbeam's side of the car, turning us into the path of a gorgeous '56 Chevy, turquoise and cream, which bore down on my side of the Toyota like the Avenger of Detroit and punched us out with almost no damage to itself. When we came to rest my car had what felt like a wasp waist, and Pillbeam and I were pinched together inside it.

For a while I kept drifting in and out, and in dreams I grappled with Cosmo, trying to keep him from lowering the blind. I came awake to bruises and cracked ribs but otherwise okay, except that I was pinned between Pillbeam and the door and couldn't move anything but my head. Pillbeam looked bad. He was unconscious, soap-white and bleeding heavily from deep scalp cuts. The Mango girl, her sharp-edged hat crumpled by Pillbeam's head, splattered with Pillbeam's blood, grinned at him from the backseat. The upholstery, front and back, reeked of fermented tropical fruit.

I could see nothing distinct through the translucent, rock-candy fabric of the windshield, the whole surface of which pulsed a deep ice blue from the revolving light of a police car. State troopers knocked on the side windows, and pressed their sun-burned faces to the glass. I couldn't roll mine down and I couldn't reach Pillbeam's. The guy on my side shouted at me to try opening my door, but I didn't feel like it, and Pillbeam's guy, wrestling with the door handle and rocking the car, yelled, "This one's frozen, too." Soon it seemed like at least thirty troopers walked around and around the car, running their hands all over it. I felt like we were on display in some showroom of classic wrecks.

Finally my guy came back to the window and yelled, "Buddy?

245

How are ya, Buddy?" I said I was just fine "How's your friend?" I said he was just fine. "Listen, Buddy," he said, "we gotta get you out of there." Right. "We're waiting for the fire department now. We're gonna have to use the Jaws of Life. Get me?" Check

He shouted at me not to panic, and after some time he came back and told me again not to panic, this time with a new urgency in his voice. By now I could smell, above the nauseating jungle rot, the sharp, relatively pleasant tang of gasoline. "Nothing to worry about, Buddy" came through the glass as a muffled scream. He couldn't know, and I didn't have the energy to tell him, that worrying about your own life can be, under certain circumstances, mildly refreshing. I didn't want to die, and yet it felt so good just then, so clean and simple, to be hurt and immobilized.

Pillbeam moaned and stirred. He turned his head and looked at me "How are ya, Buddy?" I asked him He blinked once for "yes." He cleared his throat. "Smell?" he inquired. I told him it was his own stinking rotgut but he knew better "Let's leave," he said. I told him we would in a sec. He started to sink back into unconsciousness, from which, for all I knew, he might never return. "Pillbeam!" I said. "Tell me about Victor Mature!" He said that Victor Mature was a Hollywood actor in the 1950s, and then he asked if we were doomed.

"All I know," I said, "is that they're bringing the Jaws of Life."

He seemed to perk up at this His expression grew alert, intelligent. Then it kept on going, and turned loony. *"What did you say?"* he demanded, and I said, "We need the Jaws of Life." He began to laugh, dangerously, with fresh blood framing his eyes like sideburns and who knew what injuries to his guts.

"You know what I'm talking about, don't you?" I asked, and he said, "Yes, indeedy!" "It's a hydraulic rescue tool," I said, through sirens and flashing red lights. I raised my voice. "It's got cutting pincers and spreading jaws."

246

"Oh, yes," gasped Pillbeam.

And outside somebody said, "I don't know about you, but if this blows, screw them, I'm outta here," and somebody said, "Shut up, they're conscious."

"Hold on, Pillbeam," I said, as the car began to yawn and creak like the hinge on a big steel oyster, and Pillbeam just kept on laughing and bleeding.

▼ ▼ ▼ ▼ ▼ ▼ ▼

So that's about it. If you want the final score, it was three to one our side: that is, in favor of the human race. I was good as new in four weeks. Pillbeam was as good as ever in just under six months. Barbara was benign and fine. Hannah got it.

I've never been alone with her to talk, about it or anything else. Barbara spent a lot of time with her after the big operation, and visited her every month during her chemotherapy, because Cosmo couldn't stand it. Barbara never said much, except that Hannah was strong. Whenever I see Hannah, when the four of us get together, she still laughs her crotch-grabbing laugh and sometimes gives me a secret sentimental squeeze. Cosmo has brown circles under his eyes and has lost at least thirty pounds.

Barbara was so happy with her luck, and I was so banged up, that she didn't kick me out or subject me to a long frost. Instead, every now and then, when I'm not expecting it, something sets her off. Just last week when we were having a normal Sunday breakfast, reading the paper and so on, I made some remark about Pia Zadora and Barbara leaned over and whacked me in the mouth. Then she was okay again. It's unnerving, but I'd rather have it this way than talk about it a lot. I don't believe in talking things out.

Although about six months ago I really wanted to tell this to somebody—the whole mess, Coriander and Hannah, the lumps, and what they did to her beautiful breast, and the pizza van, and my good friend and partner defeated by a plain black telephone. The only person I could tell was Pillbeam.

He was still in the hospital and mildly sedated, but he seemed willing to listen. As I talked, certain events, like my stupid confession to Barbara, struck me as funny for the first time, and when I finished I was laughing at everything, the crash, the cancer, everything. Pillbeam smiled politely. "Sorry," I said, figuring maybe he was in pain. "But the point is, I can see it now, the funny side. It's a big joke, right?"

And Pillbeam, my laughing bleeder, said, "I don't get it," and turned his face toward the wall.

"Come on," I said, to the back of his bandaged skull, "you must have been laughing at something."

He said, "I was just being agreeable. I'm an agreeable fellow." Then sighing he asked me to please go away.

So here is where I am so far, and this is all I know: the world is a big sardine can, and some of us are too agreeable for words. Most of us, really.